THE **BLOODLIGHT**
CHRONICLES

RECONCILIATION

D1153567

STEVE STANTON

ECW PRESS

Published by ECW PRESS
2120 Queen Street East, Suite 200, Toronto, Ontario, Canada M4E 1E2
416.694.3348 / info@ecwpress.com

LIBRARY AND ARCHIVES OF CANADA CATALOGUING IN PUBLICATION

Stanton, Steve, 1956 –
Bloodlight chronicles : reconciliation / Steve Stanton.

ISBN 978-1-55022-954-7

I. Title.

PS8587.T3237B56 2010   C813'.54   C2010-901262-3

Design and artwork: Juliana Kolesova
Editor: Chris Szego
Development and typesetting: David Caron
Printed and bound in Canada

This book is set in Garamond 3, produced by Linotype in 1936, designed by
Morris Fuller Benton and Thomas Maitland Cleland in 1917, based on the work
of Jean Jannon in the 1600s and Claude Garamond in the 1500s. The chapter headings
and folios are in Bank Gothic, designed by Morris Fuller Benton in 1930. The book is
printed on Legacy Offset, from 100% post-consumer-waste recycled pulp.

The publication of *The Bloodlight Chronicles: Reconciliation* has been generously
supported by the Canada Council for the Arts which last year invested
$20.1 million in writing and publishing throughout Canada,
by the Ontario Arts Council, by the Government of Ontario through
the Ontario Media Development Corporation and the Ontario Book Publishing
Tax Credit, and the Government of Canada through the Canada Book Fund.

Canada

Canada Council   Conseil des Arts
for the Arts   du Canada

  First printing, 2010

Mixed Sources
Product group from well-managed
forests, controlled sources and
recycled wood or fiber
FSC   www.fsc.org Cert no. SW-COC-002358
© 1996 Forest Stewardship Council

ANCIENT FOREST ™
FRIENDLY

"Have you seen the gates of the shadow of death?
Have you comprehended the vast expanses of earth?
Tell me, if you know all this.
What is the way to the abode of light?"

Job 38:17–19

ONE

Zakariah Davis surveyed the V-net booth from across a darkened, deserted boulevard. The night was calm, but he felt a prickly unease like a static charge on the nape of his neck, a promise of adrenaline and strange neurotransmitters. A waft of air carried a faint odour of exhaust and mouldering refuse as a pregnant moon waxing gibbous laid a gossamer sheen on the suburban cityscape. The streetlights were long dead victims of power entropy, but the V-net terminal was still fully functional, an early public booth without the usual armaments, about a dozen years old school. A field technician had tested the electronics down to Sublevel Zero the previous day.

In a compulsive ritual of invocation, Zakariah caressed his scalp where the network cable entered his skull just above and behind his left ear, a permanently hairless semicircle on the side of his cranium. He combed his fingers through a wavy tangle of hair atop his head and set his teeth with determination, psyching himself up like an athlete before a big game. He'd been a field runner his entire adult life since receiving the Eternal virus at twenty-one, his only vacations spent underground when he was too hot to surface on the net, squirrelled away with his young wife and baby boy in dark basement apartments in downtown free-zones. He reached up to the V-net plug dangling from his left earlobe and tapped out a simple binary code with a pointed fingernail. The correct time flashed briefly in the upper right-hand corner of his field of vision. He had three more minutes until rendezvous.

Camouflaged in the dark green coveralls of a metro rep, Zakariah hurried across the street and keyed open the V-net booth with his new set of retinal prints. He surveyed the photo-electrics and deadbolts in search of tampering, then set up his doorstop and mirrors with care. Safe inside, he buckled himself into the launch seat and laid his wrist on the biometric monitor. His eyes strayed ritually over the ceiling in search of nerve gas ducts or any other modifications as he unclipped his plug and inserted it into the V-net console beside his head. A two-way flatscreen in front of him came to life with a menu of possible realities, but Zakariah was already diving to Main Street.

The City glowed with alien phosphorescence. The impossible architecture, unbounded by gravity, paid only passing homage to realtime mechanical conventions of depth and distance or light and shadow. Buildings that seemed about to topple never did. Pathways that seemed ready to disappear in the distance instead branched up into labyrinthine candelabras. Rooftop spires rose in spindly curlicues that sparked with energy like lightning rods. Pop-up billboards flashed the daily fads of fashion. Zakariah flew far above the twisted metropolis like a wary bird of prey as he rode the virtual datastream down. He tasted burning semiconductors—a keen electric choke in his throat that reminded him of home. Home again. Sound rose up in a blended hum of babbled incoherence and dissonant music from the digital underground, a chaos of raw communication.

Zakariah quickly located his target, a private conduit just inside the City perimeter, and glided to street level with slow precision. He was not interested in making a lot of ripples on Main Street. He preferred to remain unnoticed, a ghost without shadow, a cypher without substance. He landed to a full stop with clean grace and nary a vibration. He scanned the datastream without making eye contact with any pedestrian or sensory node. No trackers, no greysuits. He strode purposely to the conduit, stepped inside, and willed himself downlevel.

The fall to Sublevel Zero was much slower, experientially. He had time to peruse the steady string of advertisements scrolling on the walls, time to role play once again his scheduled meeting. His new avatar had made a flawlessly discreet entry to the net. His tech team had provided a stable linkup, his presence solid and virtually free of feedback interference. He held his hand up in front of his face and could see only vague outlines through it. Biomagnetic resonance detectors produced an exact duplicate in V-space, eliminating the need for webcams and bulky band-width, but Zakariah used illegal enhancements to disguise his avatar to suit the occasion. He was imaging an electric blue jumpsuit, a workman's outfit that wouldn't stand out in a crowd.

Sublevel Zero swarmed with bodies—pimps and tourists mostly, and hawkers pushing unlicensed nanotronic accessories. Zakariah brushed quickly past the colourful street chatter, being careful not to touch anyone or anything. Some of the escorts had dirty transparent holograms that betrayed cheap systems and promised nothing but trouble. A bad routine from one of them could fester in a system for weeks and ruin the best of implants. "Enhancement, turbo fantasy," one of them whispered, her face pockmarked with feedback. She reached out a ghostlike hand, offering a free tester in passing, but Zakariah ducked away from her shadow.

Probably a greysuit undercover, Zakariah thought to himself with gathering paranoia. Half the users Sublevel were on Main Street payroll, quietly stockpiling data for correlation and causality reports. His survival code did not allow for extraneous interests—no strings, no dancing, no delay to destiny. Zakariah found his appointed terminal and keyed in a private code known by only two users.

"You're fashionably late," said a large man sitting on a clear plastic floater as Zakariah entered the room.

"I don't like waiting in line," Zakariah answered with a social smile.

"I'm a busy man," he said. He shifted in his chair, his thighs bulky with fat. He wore an ill-fitting brown business jacket with matching pants, a poor attempt at legitimacy.

"I'm sure the markup is worth your while."

The broker still refused to smile, his face grainy with repressed emotion. He imaged a flat credit board in front of him and read, "Nine piggyback transports of fresh grain, Grade A Canadian wheat."

"Any trouble at the border?"

The man looked askance, artfully taken aback. "Really, Mr. Nelson. We run a professional outfit."

"I meant with the Eternal watch in such high gear these days."

A shiver of interference ran through the broker from top to bottom, and Zakariah knew instinctively that his new avatar was about to be sacrificed. He suppressed a surge of panic and kept his own signal clear as crystal by utilizing mnemonic techniques gained from decades of experience.

"Grain is on the list," the man said evenly, searching Zakariah's image with critical care.

Zakariah stood stolid for inspection, already planning his escape.

"We wondered what you had in mind," the broker continued, "for so much grain."

"We're making bread," Zakariah said as he imaged his debit voucher. "This is Sublevel Zero, after all."

"Of course." The large man smiled finally and offered his palm up, fingers pointed skyward.

Zakariah hesitated. "I expect at least sixty minutes."

Another shiver of interference passed through the avatar before him. So, not even sixty minutes. Zakariah wondered if they could possibly be on a greysuit monitor in realtime.

"Those damn Eternals have got the whole net in an uproar," the man whined. "Not that I blame them for living," he added hastily with obvious discomfort. "It's just getting so hard to do business these days."

"Do you expect me to make nine transports disappear in less than sixty minutes?"

"They're only twenty miles from the interstate," the man whispered, his face tight with panic.

"We had a specific agreement."

"We've still got it. Can't you see I'm giving you everything I have? Damn, it's your own hide you've got to worry about." The broker's image began to break up, his face a mask of tension, his overhead palm glistening with sweat, with promise.

Zakariah felt his body hum with energy as he raised sparking fingers to seal the deal. As their hands met, electronic assets were instantly transferred through a series of bank accounts in several countries, a tax-free cryptographic trail that was virtually indecipherable, a white market. Zakariah recoiled like a launching missile and quickly vaulted out of the room. A few hundred miles south of the Canadian border, nine green lights flashed on the dashboards of nine transport cabs, and nine nervous drivers gunned black smoke up dirty stacks.

Back on Sublevel Zero, Zakariah noted greysuits in both corners of his field of vision. He grabbed the nearest avatar and forcefully mixed energies to disguise himself. He ran down the street diving and rolling through every hawker on the boulevard in an orgy of digital intimacy. Fleeting tastes of mindprobe experiments and dysfunctional sexuality assaulted him as he spread his signal over a hundred parameters, traceable and yet untraceable, everywhere and yet nowhere at all, in a desperate gambit for freedom. A handful of weaker avatars got snagged in his resonance field and trailed behind him like rag dolls, squawking and complaining about their civil rights, as he tumbled into a public zoomtube and punched in a panic abort.

A rocketlike feeling of momentum thrust him upward, inward, burning his brain with fire. A coarse vibration pulsed through him, a black energy of demon overclocking. He felt that he would surely die, as time slowed, stopped, twisted, and stabbed a knife in his forehead.

Zakariah peered through red fog at an angry V-net flatscreen. A blinking message, "DO NOT ATTEMPT TO MOVE. HELP IS ON THE WAY," glared at him in three official languages. His smoking V-net plug had melted into the console beside his head. He reached into a pocket of his coveralls, pulled out a pair of red pliers, and clipped his cable clean behind his left ear.

Part of his brain seemed to shut down, his experience suddenly shallow, one dimensional. He struggled against a feeling of infinite loss as he pushed open a vaultlike door with deadbolts stuck eight inches out into the air. He carefully collected the doorstop and mirrors that had saved him from lockdown, quickly scanned the crime scene for evidence, and hurried away into the suburban evening, a burned runner again, a fugitive. Without a V-net plug he would eventually die of information drought, an addict without a fix. He was cut off from society, from his family, from all public and private systems of commerce. He was wired with the mark of the Beast and could not live long without that sustaining neurotransmission. An ambulance siren sounded in the distance, a keen wail like an animal in heat. Suburbia was a bad place to hide in a manhunt. Zakariah glanced up at the grey skyline, quickly got his bearings, and headed downtown.

Mia Davis stood with clenched fists at her side as she presented herself before the leader of her small Eternal community. She felt grubby and haggard, having thrown on black jeans and a blue belted tunic in haste. Buzzed out of a deep sleep by a terse and formal text message on her handheld, she'd skipped her morning workout routine, and her body felt dulled with a numbing fatigue as a result. She had guessed the worst and was blocking the possibility from her mind.

"Your husband's been burned again, Mia," Pastor Ed told her. "We think he got away unscathed, but there's no way to be certain at the moment. I'm sorry."

Mia glared at him. Pastor Ed sat behind a simulated wood-grain desk that seemed too small for his bulky frame. His shiny grey hair rolled like ocean waves above his perspiring brow. His small nose and square jaw gave his face a blockish appearance, grim and unmovable. Behind him, a single line of hardcover books stood on a shelf against a background of unfinished gypsum board. The community had just relocated after an infiltration and kidnapping, and the good pastor had little time for painting or decorating.

Mia closed her eyes in frustration. How can this be happening? She had seen Zak just a few hours ago. She carved her bristly hair with the tips of her fingers, her long nails scratching harshly along her scalp, trying to blunt her inner pain with tactile discomfort.

"It was his first run with this new wetware," she said finally, and levelled her gaze. "He should have been squeaky clean."

The harsh office light seemed sterile; the air smelled stale. Pastor Ed sighed but appeared comfortable in his role, a quiet man behind a desk, a man with responsibility on his shoulders and hard years etched on his forehead. "I know. Something went wrong. We're checking our sources. Did he say anything to you?"

Her eyes tightened with anger. "You think I'd burn my own husband, the father of my child?"

"Of course not, Mia. Try to calm down."

"Zak's run should have been routine. Any eight-bit hacker could have pulled it off without a hitch."

"We're just gathering information at this point, for damage control." Pastor Ed spread his arms in a plea for composure.

"Zak never talks, not even to me. He never flinches under

pressure. That's why he's the best."

"He'll be okay, Mia. We both know it in our hearts."

"He's not okay, Ed. He's injured and isolated on the street."

"We're working on it."

Mia turned away. "God," she said, not entirely in vain. She began pacing the tiny room, back and forth from wall to wall, spinning on her toes, feeling her chi building to a crescendo. "How long will he be exiled?"

"We think ninety days will be enough to lose all tracers. We can't risk the community for one man."

"He could be dead by then."

"Mia, we've been through this before. I know it's not an easy life. I've tried talking to Zak myself."

She waved his words away with a backhand swipe of her arm. "Sure," she spat. "What was it this time? More chips and trinkets for the brain wizards? We're no better than the world if we've got to have the same hardware."

"Bread, Mia. Just food, that's all."

Mia blew out a tantric sigh of resignation. A simple public service. Was that too much to ask? "Did it get through?"

"All of it. People are rejoicing in the camps tonight." A smile flickered briefly on the pastor's face and faded to granite. "Some people."

"I'd better go tell Rix before he hears it on the street."

"It won't be on the street, Mia. We're keeping this tightly wrapped."

"I understand. I'll be discreet."

"As soon as Zak gets to a safe enclave, we'll drop a wetware team to rewire him. Try not to worry. He's the best there is."

"Can you be straight with me in my time of trouble, Pastor?"

Pastor Ed rubbed his chin warily. "I can try."

"Has he been fitted with a mindwipe circuit?"

Pastor Ed dropped his hand to his lap and sat back in his chair, his face grim. "What do you know about mindwipe?"

Mia shrugged shoulders now aching from lack of exercise. She spread innocent palms. "The schematics were smuggled out of a government lab a few years ago," she said. "Any attempt at brain infiltration sets off a permanent memory erasure program. It's for our protection."

"I really couldn't say, Mia."

"I thought not. Will he remember me, Pastor?" She bit her lip until it hurt. She would not cry in front of this bureaucrat.

Pastor Ed sighed. "He may remember some things, memories with strong emotive content particularly. Love never dies, Mia."

"Am I allowed to go after him?"

"You?"

"He may need me."

"It really wouldn't be feasible. You don't have the experience for field operations. Any Eternal is at risk outside the compound."

"C'mon Ed, I'm a tai chi master with kick-box training. I can subdue a grown man without breaking a sweat. You can't expect me to sit around like a war bride making bandages. There must be something I can do. Rix is almost an adult now. I could drop out for awhile."

Pastor Ed picked up a pencil and tapped it on his desk a few times. The sound seemed amplified in the sterile little cubicle, a judge's gavel in a dusty courtroom. "I'll look into it," he said.

Rix scanned his flatscreen lazily, online but unplugged, just hanging out with his friends. Ostensibly, he was toying with today's homework module, but he found it difficult to concentrate on schoolwork before breakfast. A text message scrolled across the lower portion of his screen. It looked like a hostile pop-up that should have been blocked automatically. He pointed at it with a finger diode and tapped delete in his palm. It scrolled by again.

Your community has been compromised. Take evasive action.

Rix stared at it thoughtfully. This looked like fun. He highlighted the message and tapped the mike on his pinkie finger.

"Are you the doom and gloom girl?" he asked, translated to text only, no video.

What makes you think I'm a girl?

He chuckled. "The lack of profanity gives you away."

:-} Fair enough.

"You jumped my firewall, you hacker."

Plug up and meet me?

"I've already got a girlfriend."

Liar.

Rix's smile faded fractionally. He tapped for a tracer. "Who are you, anyway?"

A distant relative. I'm just trying to help.

"I don't have any relatives."

Is that what your parents told you?

"My parents told me never to trust anyone online."

Good. Then my message is complete. Bye for now.

His flatscreen returned to normal, a brewing maelstrom of information. He checked his chats but could find no references to the doom and gloom girl. He had been singled out for a private communication. His tracer came back with an IP address that turned out to be a vagabond. Typical hacker protocol. A breakfast icon chimed from the cafeteria.

His community had been compromised. Again. He wondered where his parents would drag him this time. They always seemed to be on the move, always running just one step away from trouble. He never seemed to catch up in realtime. How was he ever going to make friends or get a steady girl? He never knew what to say to people in person, how to act, what to wear. All he had was his online gang and he didn't even know where most of them lived. They used names like nightshade and bestboy and swapped source code like candy. Half of them were probably informants for the government gestapo. Oh well.

He snapped his fingers to exit his programs and began packing his duffel bag.

A wooden door creaked on rusty hinges as Zakariah pushed it open and stepped from a dirty back alley into an antique computer-repair shop. Fluorescent tubes overhead glimmered dimly with the last dregs of ballast energy. A couple of dead monitors stood on the scratched and chipped countertop before him, with coloured wires hanging out the back like ponytails. Coils of white fiberoptic cable hung from a pegboard wall on short metal poles.

The trip downtown had been uneventful. Zakariah had not risked public transit with a telltale burnt wire hanging behind his ear and had talked to no one. The streets were relatively quiet after the nighttime ban on combustible fuel, the pedestrian traffic minimal and the trolley-bikes sporadic. A promise of morning was on the horizon now, the sun beginning to glimmer through concrete canyons like an orange spotlight piercing the smog.

"Jimmy?" he asked the shadows down the hallway.

"Saints from the grave!" cried a familiar voice, and a bald gnome of a man shuffled into view, his smile wide on a plump, rounded face.

"Jimmy."

"Zakariah! You out slummin' again after all these years?"

"I've been down south."

"Travellin' without a plug, too," noted Jimmy with a mischievous smile. "You on a breakout?"

"I went straight years ago, Jimmy . . . sort of."

"Yeah, me too." He winked with a smirk. "You look older now, all grown up."

"You lost your hair. Why don't you get a transplant?"

"Hey, the little chickies love the dome, zero. All the young sliders are shavin' every day to keep up." He grinned playfully.

"You still chasing teenagers, Jimmy?" Zakariah replied in kind. "I thought you would've moved on to better things by now."

"Hah, that's about as funny as yesterday's strong crypto."

They chuckled together for the sake of old times. It was an archaic joke, but it bound them together across the years.

"Yeah, I heard you went gaming big time," Jimmy said. "Saw your shadow sublevel a coupla times. They finally burned ya?"

"Not the first time. Can you help me out?"

"You always were a cheeky slider. What, a dozen years go by and you come in out of the night dirty with tracers and 'spect me to bake you a birthday cake?" Jimmy hunkered low and stared up at Zakariah, daring him to answer. His grey coveralls were dirty and spotted with tiny burn holes from hot solder.

"Well, Jimmy," said Zakariah carefully. "I was in the area."

Jimmy looked in wonder at Zakariah, waiting for an explanation. When none came he burst out with a laugh. He held his gut and roared, shaking his head in disbelief. He stepped around from behind the counter, locked the old wooden door with a triple bolt, and walked away into the shadows, signalling for Zakariah to follow.

A custom implant was far beyond the expertise of a back-alley bootlegger, but bastard plugs floated regularly through the underground, some stolen from corpses, some completely unregistered. With an old terminal, one could get to Main Street at least but not to any Prime levels. Nothing hot, Zakariah instructed, nothing that could be traced back downtown.

Jimmy sat with a monocular lens on his right eye, reading serial numbers on components and checking them against an inhouse computer.

"You've got a goldmine here, Jimmy," Zakariah stated as he surveyed some of the plunder.

"This ain't the half of it. I got thirty-to-life in detox with what I got stashed," said Jimmy grimly. "You can't move this junk like in the old days. You should see some of the new quantum circuitry coming out of the black labs, piggyback architecture. Chips that speed each other up, that *learn* to go faster." He raised an index finger. "Now, that's the PH-phat future, my friend. If I could sell out I'd go clean and rest my weary backside in a Prime Three gameroom forever."

"I could dump the lot for you, Jimmy, for sure. How much do

you need?"

Jimmy stopped and whistled a slow exclamation. "You scare me, mister."

Zakariah caught his left eye with a solemn stare. "I've got connections. I've got resources. I need maybe three weeks to re-wire an avatar."

"If the greysuits don't crash me in the morning. I knew you were either heaven or hell when you walked in the door."

"You could have flushed me out the alley, Jimmy. It was your decision."

"Maybe I shoulda." He turned back to his work and picked up another trinket. "You were different than all the other sliders on the move back in the day. You played with fire but never turned on a buddy. We had a good thing going, you and me, before you zoomed uptown for fame and fortune."

"A lot has happened, Jimmy." Zakariah paused and swallowed a crack in his self-confidence. "I'm Eternal now," he declared softly to Jimmy's back.

The monocular lens hit the table and rolled noisily away. Jimmy's old face turned white except for angry red spots at his temples. "Holy ghost," he whispered. "You've brought the demons down on me."

"It's a fraud, Jimmy—everything you've heard."

Jimmy turned slowly, grimly, his eyes wide. "You've got the virus?"

"I've got it."

Jimmy licked dry lips. He closed his eyes briefly as though in prayer or meditation. "Sure," he said finally. "Sure. It had to happen." He chuckled at this new revelation. "You were heading right for the top, I could tell, reaching for the big ticket. Sure,

I'll sell out to the Eternals, if you can make it happen. I got no choice now."

"I'm sorry, Jimmy. I figured you should know, of all people."

"Yeah, I guess you don't blab it to every hussy in the night."

Zakariah held up his hands to ward off the thought. "No street stuff for me, Jimmy. I've got a wife now. And a son, Rix. He's already wired to hack the Beast, just like his dad."

"The glorious future, eh? You're all gonna live happily ever after." Jimmy smirked. "Kinda poetic, ain't it?"

Zakariah felt his throat constrict with emotion. Forever was a long time. Too long and too far away. "My boy isn't Eternal," he croaked. "Not yet."

"No?"

Zakariah shook his head as he struggled with his private devil. This was the reason he survived. This was the reason he fought day after day for a better world. "The virus is not transmitted by human contact. I can't give it to Rix. I can't buy it on the street. I'm still trying to track down the Source."

Jimmy frowned up at him with reflected agony in his eyes. "They make you watch your own kid die?" he asked quietly.

Zakariah stared at his oldest friend, the man who had taught him how to hack V-space long before the Beast had even attained self-consciousness, perhaps the only man he had ever trusted.

"I hope not, Jimmy."

TWO

Rix could make out but a bare phosphorescent shadow of the V-net horizon before him, a jagged silhouette glowing purplish and eerie in the darkness. He felt like a gangster in his hooded avatar, moving furtively in an unknown and dangerous cityscape. He'd had a vague tracer on his dad's lifeline, but the datatrail had evaporated like a wisp of fog in a blast of car exhaust, leaving him lost and uncertain. This section of Sublevel Zero was completely unregistered, the pavement patchy, the empty shops mere facades, the whole area under construction by the minds that used the V-net. The continuum grows with every use, his dad had told him, it is a function of need, of infinite accessibility. You can't be afraid of V-space; it doesn't exist. Only ideas exist, imaginations.

Rix shuddered. His dad's advice sounded so real, so near, drawing him onward into the ever-expanding digital frontier. Any sense of distance in V-space is only an illusion, his dad had told him. Information swirls around us at lightspeed, faster than meagre senses can register. The user is everywhere at once, the runner nowhere at all. Whatever you experience in V-space has already happened—the net is a glorified history book, a detailed account of human experience. Don't be fooled by mere sensorium. The future is inside your head.

"Dad?" Rix spoke out loud, breaking the haunting silence with a word.

"Well, what do we have here?" An elderly man, stooped and wizened, materialized a few feet in front of Rix and blocked his way.

"Who you lookin' for down below?" asked a woman's voice beside him where a shimmery figure failed to become completely tangible.

"You lost, kid?" asked the man, buzzing with bad vibration. "What kinda hardware ya usin'?"

Ghosts, Rix thought with alarm. Vagrants trying to pirate a stable system. He didn't dare let them touch him. He might never get them out of his brain.

"I'm using a school terminal," Rix lied. "I was on a class trip but got lost." He imaged an access code for his local school system and threw it at the man's feet.

"I can't use that trash," the man snarled, peering closer. "You look like a plughead to me—virgin wetware, I'd say."

A flash of red pain jumped up around Rix, and he stumbled backward in surprise.

"I think we got a good one, Shasta."

Rix searched behind the man for the shimmery pirate. He whirled in panic to see her only inches from his face. He felt an emptiness, a gut-wrenching silence. Her image was pockmarked with feedback sparks, her wetware diseased and failing. She reached for him.

Rix jumped and dove for the sky. There is no up or down in V-space, his dad's voice told him patiently. Main Street is merely a convenience, a backdrop reinforced by constant use.

Rix turned the world upside down. He stood on a cloud, on an imaginary ceiling. The pirate followed him quickly and reoriented to face him. The woman flickered above them and turned in a circle.

"Shasta, you old boot," the man called up to her.

Rix backvaulted away from the man, deeper into the sublevel corridor. Darkness grew thicker as he ran. Through holes in the pavement, Rix could see stars below, a vast freefall universe of negative data. He jumped over the abyss, walked a balance beam between eternity and forever. He wondered if the pirates would dare follow him out this far. How would he get back to base, back to realtime?

"Dad?" he whispered.

A sparkling brilliance lit up ahead of him, momentarily stunning him with blindness. Beside it stood another man, a tall shadow like a granite monument.

"This is a temporary conduit for you," spoke an unfamiliar voice. "Tell your mother to meet me at the north sanctuary. Tell no one else."

"Dad?"

"Don't touch me in this form, Rix. I've got some hybrid circuitry here that is very unstable. You know I love you."

Rix felt a terrible urge to cry, to just let loose his panic and fear in a burst of emotion. But that would never do, not here, not now, not ever.

"I'm sorry I had to bring you down this far, Rix. I can't trust anyone in the community right now. Things are not always what they seem."

Rix choked back his sobs. "Some hacker's been trying to spread doom and gloom," he whispered.

"We've got to keep moving before anyone gets a fix on us. You know I love you, Rix." The black figure bore no resemblance to his dad, a hulking shadow against a fiery backdrop of light. The voice sounded foreign, mechanical.

Rix nodded and dove for Main Street.

"I can't believe Zak would drag you into this, Rix. Are you absolutely sure it was him?" Mia rubbed her blond pelt of hair as she sat in her son's dorm room trying to piece her life back together. There were no pictures on the wall, no curios on display. His duffel bag was already packed in the corner.

"He programmed a conduit out of nowhere, Mom. Only an uplevel gamer can do that."

"Could it have been a phisher or a fake?"

"No, it was him. He said he couldn't trust anyone. I think we're all he's got left."

She stared at Rix reclining on the small cot in his room. Where was the little blond boy that used to play soccer with her on the playground? Where was the young teenager who had been sponsored for wetware surgery at such an early age in the hope of another gifted runner for the community? The little lost boy. The person before her seemed more like a man, a gangly adult, his bangs now long and scraggly and hanging down in a shock that covered one eye, his chin jutting forward with cynicism, his V-net plug blinking below his ear like a Christmas decoration.

"But why? It just doesn't scan. The community elders are desperate to track him down. A mobile wetware unit is on twenty-four hour alert!" Mia jumped up and paced the tiny

room, gaining tactile solace from the fluid grace of her movements, burning excess energy from her chi. Her boots caressed
the ground like tiger paws as she walked quickly back and forth,
chewing on a thumbnail.

"Do we have any family, mom?"

Mia stopped, temporarily frozen by this new thought. "Of
course we have family."

"Anyone living?"

Mia squinted, wondering where this was coming from. "My
mother died when I was young. My father was killed in a raid. He
was Eternal, but it didn't stop the bullet. You've heard the story."

"Yeah." Rix nodded. "What about Dad's side?"

"His parents split up when he was young. His mother died
soon after. He had a baby sister, who went to live with his father.
They disappeared."

"How old would she be?"

"What's going on, Rix?"

"Nothing. I was just wondering."

"Well, let's keep focused here. Try to remember the last conversation you had with your dad, before the run. What did you
talk about?"

A blush of hot blood crept into his cheeks. "Just guy stuff,"
he said.

"Like what? C'mon, Rix. It could be important."

"Just chicks and stuff."

"Anyone in particular?"

"It's nothing really. You remember Viki?"

"The young Madison girl? You're not thinking about a contract with her at your age?"

Rix shook his head and lowered his gaze. He rubbed his

knuckles with his thumb. "Mom, it's not like that," he mumbled. "She's not allowed to see me any more. She got the virus."

Mia felt her body slouch with defeat like a balloon deflating. "Oh, Rix, I'm so sorry. It's not fair." She sat down on the cot beside him to curl her arm around his neck in a brief hug. She felt immense distance spring up between them like a yawning chasm. Her own son was of a different human species, one still subject to death. It wasn't fair.

"What did Zak say?" she persisted. "Did he say anything out of the ordinary?"

"He was upset. You know how he raves when he gets excited."

Mia closed her eyes with resignation, nodding, thinking about Zak's silent temper, his stubborn will. She could easily imagine the scene. Her husband could be a menace when his hackles were up.

"He said he was going to do something about it. He said he'd waited long enough."

Mia hung her head and squeezed her bottom lip between her teeth in thought.

"You know I'd pass my blood on to you if I could, Rix."

"I know, Mom. It's okay."

"Your dad would, too. It's all he thinks about."

"Don't cry, Mom."

Mia stood up fiercely. "I'm not crying." She brushed her cheek and began stalking the room again. "He must have given Pastor Ed an ultimatum. He must have tried to cut a deal with the elders." She stopped and stared at her son in horror.

"They burned him," she whispered.

The deciduous trees up north spread a heavy canopy above the forest floor, trapping moisture for a fertile jungle below. The bush trail was overgrown with creeping vines and ferns, the path unrecognizable. Mia stopped again to check her compass and adjust the shoulder straps on her harness. The lush smell of pine sap and summer flowers tickled in the back of her throat and she coughed into her fist. She felt old and out of shape, easily winded and weak. It was one thing to run a treadmill for twenty minutes or grind through a short morning workout, but backpacking like a commando all day was a bitch for an old girl. She'd been a strong hiker in her youth, a traveller, a mountain climber—before she got the virus and needed a safe haven from the vampires, before her blood became a black-market staple. The community offered organizational security, safety in numbers, survival. Eventually the humans would all die off, she told herself in consolation, and Eternals could live in peace.

She reached the tiny cabin just before dusk. The clapboard siding was painted green for camouflage, the plain cedar shingles on the roof mottled grey and brown by the elements, invisible to satellite reconnaissance. She dug up the key where it was buried under an oak tree in a rusty tin can and unlocked the padlock on the door. The grey barnboard walls felt damp, and the bed smelled musty. Tattered curtains had rotted off their rods and lay like rags under the windows. The air smelled of mice and mould.

She risked a small fire in the cookstove to dry the place out. Under two floorboards she checked the cache of freeze-dried foodstuffs and first-aid supplies. Everything seemed in order. With fish from the lake, a person could live for months on this stash. Wild cranberries for vitamin C, spruce needles if necessary.

When the kettle boiled, she steeped a tea bag and poured out the first weak infusion. Darkness fell suddenly as she sipped tea and warmed her hands on the ceramic cup. She wondered if Zakariah would make it tonight.

She felt sure she hadn't been followed. She'd told friends she was going to visit an elderly aunt in New York City, wincing inwardly all the while at her deception. She was a terrible liar and would never make a good field agent.

Mia sighed and tipped her wooden chair back against the wall. She cocked a dirty hiking boot on a short birch stump that stood beside the cookstove for splitting kindling. The last time they'd been here, she'd been pregnant with Rix, newly Eternal and recently married. Life had been glorious and full of promise, each day the first morning of forever. The virus had been running rampant in her blood in those days, changing her physically and mentally in the first blush of contagion, regenerating neurological tissue and filling her with quiet ecstasy moment by moment.

She could feel that deep joy even now, sitting in the same chair again, staring at the small crackling fire. She sipped her tea and savoured the warmth in her chest. A stick cracked outside.

Her body stiffened, breathless.

"It's only me," said a familiar voice.

Mia tipped her chair up, placed her tea on the birch stump, and bounded for the door.

"Zak, I love you," she promised into his neck.

"I love you, too, Mia. I waited an hour to make sure you weren't followed."

"I could barely find the trail."

"The landscape has changed. You remembered the mnemonic."

"North-northwest to Coon Lake and hang a left. It's good to be back after all these years."

Zakariah smiled wearily. "Sorry I ruined your life, honey."

"I've still got you. That's all I care about."

"And Rix," he added.

"Is that really why they burned you, Zak? Did you pressure Pastor Ed for an ampoule?"

"No, I didn't pressure him. No more than usual."

"It makes me so angry. He's hiding something."

"How do you know?"

"He seemed shifty."

"Shifty? Pastor Ed?"

"Okay, why is it such a big deal? Why can't they just get an ampoule from the Source for Rix? Viki Madison got one."

"I don't know. Perhaps the Source is not easily persuaded. The community may have much less influence than we imagine. Let's not worry about it right now. We've got some catching up to do." Zakariah reached for his wife again and kissed her with a lingering embrace. "Did you bring any food?" he asked into her shoulder. "I haven't eaten all day."

"All your favourites," Mia said and began rummaging in her backpack. "But first down to the lake with you," she said as she handed him a bar of soap. "You stink."

Zakariah grinned. "It's cold."

"I'll stoke up the fire for when you get back." She ushered him gently toward the door. "I'll have hot soup ready in ten minutes."

She watched his back disappear into the foliage outside, the only man she had ever loved. Her chest ached at the thought of him in danger again, on the run without friends, without hope. They seemed to have spent their whole life together ducking and hiding, fugitives from the world. But no one could touch them here at the sanctuary. The cabin was off the grid, off the V-net, a temporary refuge from the tyranny of civilization. She emptied a pouch of freeze-dried soup into a metal pot and added boiling water. She threw a softwood log on the fire for a quick blast of heat.

For three glorious days they relived their honeymoon fantasies and planned an uncertain future as their existence was stripped back to basics by simple privation. Food and water and heat during the night became prime concerns. Sex became the highlight of the day. Why couldn't they live this way forever? Why go back to the community at all?

They spent hours by candlelight discussing strategies for life. Perhaps Zak's days as a field runner were over. There were other areas of service to the virus. Perhaps he could go into programming or training, perhaps assist in wetware surgery. There were lots of frontiers and an infinite playground of possibilities. First he had to get rewired himself and get a clean avatar with no echoes on the net. He could go legit. He could start from scratch. Everyone should be allowed one chance at rebirth.

The afternoon sun was hot, the sky cloudless, and Mia rubbed oily sunscreen on her husband's shoulders as they sat on rocks by the lake. The air smelled sweet with fertility, and light danced upon the waves.

"We have to trust someone, Mia. We can't hide forever."

"No one deserves our blind faith, Zak. Not the community, not the V-net controllers. Certainly not the brain wizards with their laser knives."

"I trust you, Mia."

"Well, that's a start."

"Maybe I just pushed too hard on this last run. Maybe a

simple error was made, a spelling mistake in some background code, a botched password. This stuff is so complex it borders on the metaphysical, the interface between man and machine, the mix of electrochemical neurotransmitters and raw digital energy."

Mia rubbed fruity sunscreen on her arms as she watched Zak dangle his bare feet in the water from a rock ledge. His body glistened with oil as the dazzling sun seared their skin. His naked back rippled with finely toned muscle.

"You just can't go back and offer your brain on a platter, Zak. It's too dangerous."

He nodded reluctant agreement. "We're at war with an invisible enemy. There's no doubt about it. We need to get to the high ground, the front line. I can't be a pawn in someone else's game; you know that. I've got to see the big paradigm. I've always pushed the limit. What I'd really like to do is get off-planet right to the Source."

"C'mon, Zak, don't be crazy. There's no advantage to being Eternal if you go and get yourself killed." The words left a taste of acid in her mouth, a sarcastic edge that she rarely used with her husband and regretted instantly.

But his face had already crinkled with disgust. "Yeah, right. We've got too much to lose now, so we just sit back and let life pass us by. We quarantine ourselves in little ghettos of experience, physically and mentally."

"You're scaring me, Zak. You've always scared me."

"Why'd you marry me then? Why waste your time?"

Mia forced a tight smile and placed a hand on her breastbone as though that simple support might help calm her raging blood. She dared not force the issue and risk alienating him. She decided to play it cute, to let it blow over. "Oh, nice buns, strong shoulders."

"Seriously."

Zakariah stayed solemn.

"Buns are important for a woman. What do you know?"

"C'mon."

"I fell in love with you, silly. I don't know how it works. I just try to maintain it, to build it up."

Zakariah stared at her for a few seconds, his face a stoic mask. Then he frowned and hung his head with a sigh, a burned runner again, a failure. "I guess it's a lot of work sometimes."

Mia draped a long arm in comfort around his shoulders. "I've never been attracted to anyone but you, Zak. If I lose you, I'm afraid I'll lose most of myself also."

"I'm a gamer, Mia. You wouldn't like me if I became something else." Zakariah turned again toward her, searching her eyes with his own, probing her soul.

What did he want from her? All she had was the bare truth, nothing more. Wasn't that enough? She pulled away, feeling self-conscious. "Don't be afraid to try me, Zak. People grow. People change. You're not hustling on Main Street for access time up Prime. The stakes are higher."

"You know I love you, Mia."

"You could turn yourself in at the Eternal Research Institute."

"What?" Zakariah jumped to his feet in surprise. He took a step back. "Sell out to the ERI? You've got to be kidding."

"At least it's safe. Better than getting caught by vampires or government greysuits."

"They'd make me a guinea pig. They'd fill me full of needles." Zakariah began to pace back and forth on the rock ledge behind her.

She turned awkwardly to face him. "They'd give you clean wetware and constitutional protection as a research volunteer. I've heard it's not so bad. What choice do you have, Zak?"

"What about us? Would you follow me into prison?"

Mia looked off in the distance, pained by the thought of separation. "If that's what it takes," she said finally. "I could say goodbye to Rix for a few months."

"A few months?" Zakariah shook his head. "We might *never* get out of the ERI once they get their hooks in us, Mia. We'd be on death row in there."

A bird twittered happily in a poplar tree above them, a high and resonant tremolo. They both looked up in response and watched the grosbeak sing from the very tip of the tree. Oh, how happy are the birds, Mia thought with envy, their innocence unmarred by consciousness. Free will was the greatest of all sins and the most precious gift from God. She longed for a pathway through this darkened maze of life. She needed help. Just one simple signpost to show her the way.

Jimmy Kay looked up from the latest batch of nanocrystals in his cultivation lab. His ranch house in the Nevada desert was miles from the city, and he was unaccustomed to visitors. A red warning light glowed above the door, indicating that a perimeter alarm had been triggered. He secured his equipment and changed the access codes. Cops? Tax accountants? His mind wandered through a long list of vulnerabilities as he locked up the lab. There was no reason for anyone to bother him this many years into his retirement. No reason at all.

He ambled to his office and checked his webcam surveillance. A single man was walking up the long driveway. A single car was parked near the front gate, blocking the entrance. It looked like a civilian electric vehicle with upscale aerodynamics, not government issue. The slow approach was an obvious invitation for a full scan, a token of peace. Fair enough. Jimmy triggered for electromagnetics and whistled. Heavy tech.

A wirehead with lots of alloy in the brain. Coaxial cable down the medulla and into the left shoulder, down the arm to a small briefcase of V-net candy. No weapons, unless the briefcase itself was a weapon. A metal belt buckle, an archaic defiance of spaceport protocol. Nice touch. The man's stance was confident, his pace unhurried, a tourist just out for an afternoon stroll.

Jimmy made his way past potted yucca and ferns to his front entrance. He swung open both doors and stood watching the man approach. An insect buzzed at his ear and he brushed it away.

"Nice day for a walk," he said when the man was in range.

The visitor stopped at the sound. He raised his hands up as though for a wand search, his briefcase dangling. He had a full head of hair brushed up high from his forehead, greying at the temples. Crow's feet radiated from wide, placid eyes.

"It's okay. I've logged a full scan."

"You know why I'm here," the man said, no trace of inflection in his voice.

A tickle danced in Jimmy's spine. One of Zak's demons had tracked him down.

"He's not here."

The mystery man nodded once in recognition. His expression indicated that he already knew that and much more. Too much. "I sent the message to meet him downtown."

Jimmy grimaced with distaste. "He was there all right, but he left."

"I figured he might return to his old haunts in time of trouble. I'm glad it worked out."

"You burned him?"

"A nudge perhaps. I can't control everything."

"I did what I could for him." Jimmy shrugged. "We used to work together."

"I know. I've watched you both for many years."

A kaleidoscope shifted in Jimmy's mind. Was that a veiled threat? Blackmail? He wondered what evidence the stranger might have to implicate him. A lot of critical data had gone through his hands over the years. A lot of borrowed passwords, technical illegalities. What difference could any of it mean now?

"You might as well come in, then." Jimmy made his way to the mini-bar and pulled a beer from the fridge. "Want a drink?"

"Do you have an antioxidant?"

Jimmy nodded with recognition—a health nut, probably older than he looked, a rejuve user. He read some labels. "Peachfix, Betablock . . ."

"A Bee would be good."

"You want a glass?"

"Please." The man's smile was genteel, a bit snobbish, as though to drink from the carton would be *très gauche.*

Jimmy opened his beer and took a long slug from the bottle. He found a chilled wine glass in the back of the fridge and filled it with antioxidant. It smelled of carrots and lemons and looked like sludge. He threw in a casino stir stick and handed it to his guest.

They made themselves comfortable on cushioned divans and inspected each other. Jimmy sipped his beer, content to let the moment linger on home turf. He noticed that the man's briefcase computer was wired directly into his arm in place of a hand, some sort of experimental V-net jackbox. The man seemed poised and aloof.

"What does Zak want, Jimmy?"

"Who needs to know?"

"I'm his father, Phillip Davis."

"Really? He never mentioned a father."

"That's not surprising. We were estranged after a messy divorce. I haven't talked to him in twenty-five years."

"That's a long time."

"Blood ties never die."

"So you put him in play again after all those years?"

Phillip's smile went steely, and Jimmy sensed a fracture in his composure. "I want what's best for him. I made some mistakes. Perhaps I can make amends in some small way. He must have said something to you."

"He's looking for the virus, if you must know. He wants to inoculate Rix. He cares a lot more for his son than you ever cared for him." Jimmy eyed his guest carefully, looking for a flinch of conscience, a semblance of humanity.

Phillip pursed his lips in thought, his eyes still tranquil. "Good," he said.

Jimmy winced inwardly. What a cold piece of work. He wondered if Phillip had access to the virus. Perhaps he was Eternal himself. He looked too young to be a grandfather.

"Do you want to help us out, Jimmy? There's a good margin of profit for you."

"I'm retired."

Phillip looked around with a critical air. "You could do better."

"How much better?"

"An exponential increase. It's a simple smuggling operation, just like old times."

"Is the product legal?"

"The product doesn't even exist."

"But it will?"

Phillip bowed his head with the grace of a sage. "New nanochip architecture."

Jimmy smiled, feeling familiarity like an old lover. "I like chips."

"I'll leave the creative details of transport completely to your expertise."

"No strings?"

"Only the purse strings, Jimmy. Just the way you like it."

With a lump of pain in her throat, Mia stuffed her backpack with dirty clothes. "Rix is fine on his own," she said. "He doesn't need a babysitter."

"We can't just leave him there all alone."

"I know that."

"Well, one of us should at least check on him."

"I'd rather be with you."

"C'mon, Mia, I just want to chase some numbers with an old

friend while you get Rix ready for another relocation. He's not going to like the idea."

"How will I contact you? What if something comes up at the community? What if there's a purge?"

"I'll pick you up in a week, Mia. I promise. I'll scout out a safe home and we'll make a clean break." Zakariah peered out the window at dark thunderheads gathering beyond the hills. "You should try to get out before the storm hits, hon."

"Yeah. We're not very good at saying goodbye."

Zakariah turned with a comforting grin. "Oh? I thought we did pretty good."

Mia smiled, but her face quickly relaxed into a stern and worried mask. "I wish we had a plan."

"Just be careful. Assume the elders are compromised. Play the secret agent. Use your chi magic and keep Rix out of trouble for one more week."

"Rix can look after himself. You know he's the smartest kid on the planet."

"Well, he still needs a mother. He's got to be clean if he's going to get an ampoule."

"Do you really think it makes any difference? The moral imperative?"

"I don't know. I guess so."

"Why is it all so secretive?"

Zakariah shrugged. "Everybody wants to live forever."

"Then why can't we just give everyone an ampoule? Mass-produce the virus?"

"Too expensive, maybe." Zakariah shook his head. "I wish I knew."

"Neither one of us paid a penny for Eternal life."

Zakariah met her eyes. "The chosen few." He turned and looked back out the window. "Don't worry. Everything's going to be okay."

Mia stepped up behind him and kissed the side of his neck. "Goodbye, lover," she whispered.

Zakariah reached back and pulled her hips against him, but he didn't turn around. "See you soon," he lied.

Fifteen minutes after Mia disappeared into the forest, a knock sounded on the cabin door.

Zakariah carefully placed the last floorboard over his cache of food and stood up. "I am unarmed," he said.

Two men entered with humming stunrods in their hands. They both wore mottled camouflage outfits and black combat boots. The man in the front had short, bristly red hair atop a grey-whiskered face. Rivulets of sweat had drawn lines down his dirty cheeks. "We thought it best to wait for the woman to leave," he offered.

"Yes, that was good of you."

"You've been expecting us?"

"I saw you in the hills. Two camps, perhaps six men."

"Seven." The man brushed a spider from his hair.

"Are you free to tell me who you represent?"

"The Director of the ERI said to tell you to remain calm."

"That's it?"

"We have been instructed to drug you for transport," the man said and snapped his fingers at his partner. "I know you people dislike hypodermics," he said conversationally, "so I will offer you a caplet first." His partner, shorter and darker, with a mosquito net tangled on top of his head like a misshapen fedora, handed forward a plastic case. He had a police-issue firearm holstered on his belt.

The red-haired man advanced with a blue capsule in his fingers and stunrod raised in his left hand.

Zakariah held out his palm.

"On the tongue, sir," the man instructed.

"Are you going to carry me out?"

"This is a psychoactive sedative. You'll be able to walk. No cuffs. No ropes."

Zakariah took a deep breath and stuck out his tongue.

The men visibly relaxed as he closed his mouth. They silenced their weapons and smiled at each other. The caplet dissolved instantly. Strange neuro-inhibitors fled for his brain.

"Your reputation precedes you, sir," the red-haired man offered, patently pleased at the success of his mission.

Zakariah nodded once upward in recognition of the compliment. "Spare me the gallows humour, boys. Let's get on the road before the storm hits." As the words left his mouth he marvelled at the false nature of language, the poor semblance of meaning the sounds contained, the crude movements of his tongue twisting vibrations in the air to communicate. His thoughts were pure, powerful, his body a mechanical contraption that could never contain or express his true essence. His feet seemed to be miles away, his legs thin stilts reaching to touch impossible depths. His sense of balance cartwheeled as he struggled to stay erect.

A strong arm grabbed his elbow as he pitched forward.

THREE

*Y*our time is up. Destroy your hard drive.

Rix stared at the pop-up message with numb surprise. Some viral adware had jumped his borders. He checked his active downloads for infiltration. It was late in the afternoon in his timezone, and the locals were hanging out in an after-school chat module.

I'm not kidding. Go.

He pointed to the message and tapped his pinkie mike.

"Get lost," he said, voice only. Why give some digital parasite the courtesy of video? He tapped delete in his palm, but the pop-up persisted.

I spoke with you earlier. I know about your dad. Your mom went to meet him up north.

Rix felt a sudden surge of hormones sweep through him like a caffeine rush. The doom and gloom girl!

The goons are at the door.

An alarm began to wail and his monitor went bluescreen. Thank God he still had electricity. He stood up and reached behind his computer, found the toggle switch he had rigged on the power supply, and flipped it to overclock. The sound of sparks and a curl of white acridity told him the brain had fried. All of his contacts on the net, all his family connections, digital photos, and documents. Gone forever. No traces, no ripples.

He grabbed his grey duffel bag and lurched out of his room into a narrow hallway beyond, conscious of duty only. His job during a raid was to block the advance while the Eternals made for the tunnels. He was expendable in that regard, a rook on the chessboard.

He met a man with a combat rifle just outside the cafeteria, pointing it casually in his direction. He wasn't wearing a police helmet or an army greysuit, so that meant only one thing. Private enterprise.

"Don't move, kid," he said.

"I'm not armed."

"Well, I sure as hell am. They're just tranks, but they hurt like fire."

Rix dropped his gear and put his arms in the air.

"I'm a citizen," he said.

"Save it for the blood test, kid." The goon stepped forward and frisked him quickly. He stepped back satisfied. "We're going for a little walk. Anyone down that hall?" He pointed with his gun, lowered now but available.

"Yeah. Three apartments. Families. They may have been rounded up already."

"Let's just check, shall we?"

They poked methodically in every room and found the clutter of everyday life. Dirty dishes. Laundry. Rix recognized the smell of burnt hard drives. The Eternals were gone. The goon seemed unconcerned, not tremulous with his weapon. Rix knew the type. Mercenary. Flat emotional response.

They arrived outside to find a grimy transport truck with the back doors wide open. The goon motioned with his gun.

"Is this the truck to Auschwitz?" Rix asked.

"It'll be the Holiday Inn in comparison, kid."

Rix peered up into the truck, surprised to see such a crowd inside. His friends, some of them Eternal. The transport had been fitted with bus benches and seatbelts for such precious cargo.

"I'm a citizen," Rix said again. "I've got ID in my pack."

"You look like an activist to me. We have authority to detain you under the Evolutionary Terrorist Omnibus."

"The ETO is under appeal in every civilized state."

"Oh, so now you're a lawyer?'

"I'm a citizen, I tell you. I haven't got the virus."

"Then you've got nothing to worry about, do you? You'll be free in a couple hours." He smiled with undisguised malevolence. "Though I don't know where you'll go. This place will be razed. Get in the truck."

Rix held his palms up in a gesture of peace. "Just let me show you my ID," he said, stalling for as much time as possible, hoping for witnesses on the street, for rudimentary webcam surveillance—performing this simple public duty for his parents.

A rifle butt hit him hard just below the breastbone.

He doubled over reflexively, gasping for air. He fell forward as gravity claimed him and twisted his chin to avoid serious damage. His face landed just inches from the goon's shiny black boots. His cheek burst into agony and tears squeezed out of his eyes. He could not purchase a single breath of air.

"I tried to warn you, kid. Just get in the damn truck."

A mercenary always polishes his boots before a big job, Rix noted. He takes pride in his work.

A gargoyle lurked behind every tree. Lithe and noiseless they bounded from trunk to trunk, their scales green and slimy in the gentle mist of rain. They hunted Zakariah like a weakened deer, a slow and crippled stag that stumbled through the underbrush with the strong ones, his protectors. But even the strong ones could not hold the gargoyles at bay.

In time his mind was infiltrated, his thoughts contaminated. Eventually he was given up as a sacrifice to pagan gargoyle gods and carried aloft by screaming dragons up above the trees to the great black anvils where the dragons danced and threw forks of lightning at their foes. His body rocked and trembled with the sounds of warfare.

His stomach heaved and emptied itself, and gargoyles rushed to bring him water and red medicine, bickering and bantering with shrill whoops of malice. They touched him with scaly fingers and iced his temples. A ceasefire held for many days and whispered voices promised life and death, alternately, and each seemed attractive in its turn. Finally Zakariah found refuge in the music, a pleasant hum of music, white music, changeless, still.

In gargoyle heaven they ministered with sheets of white music and cotton towels, their white wings beating time like a pendulum behind his eyes. They forced gargoyle ichors down his gullet and flashed sparks from their eyes into his brain. A silver snake crawled up from the floor and stabbed his arm with pain, drank dry his rich red blood and left him parched and withered like an Egyptian mummy entombed in still white music.

He slept fitfully and woke again to white gargoyles with kind faces and red medicine. They led him from eyrie cave to eyrie cave and washed his body and shaved his face and dried him and dressed him. They laid him down in ashes and dust and asked senseless questions about life before death, about day before dawn. He slept again and woke to a world darker and more ominous. He asked for red medicine and was denied. His viscera contracted at the thought. Two white gargoyles shaved his skull. He prepared to die. Perhaps it would be easier this time.

He remembered his mother dying in this place. He remembered the same white sheets and antiseptic smell, the same clatter of hard heels on hard floors and rolling carts carrying poison. She had died of a heart broken and a soul crushed by life—by foul circumstance and bad karma.

His father and mother had owned an international import-export business in the far east. They were commodity traders, gamblers in expensive suits, a team unmatched in the annals of Chinese corporate finance. In days of renown they built empires of paper currency and lost them again with a bad roll of the dice, a bad technical trade, a change in the weather. Zakariah remembered the strange language of risk and reward—futures and warrants, call options and arbitrage, hedging caps and butterfly spreads; he remembered both the high-flying parties of celebration and the long dark nights of drunken solace. He remembered both victory and defeat through a young child's eyes.

In the end, weary and desperate and confused by alcohol, his father lost a forearm to an American conglomerate that he couldn't satisfy, and, fearing for his life, took his baby daughter from her cradle and disappeared into the night. The import-export company collapsed like crumpled origami and blew away in a cruel wind, leaving behind a single mother and her young son bankrupt and helpless. Zakariah never forgave his father, as he watched his mother slip into psychosis and the careless abuse of prescription drugs. Her personality caved in on itself. Emaciated and bewildered, she starved to death convinced that she was overweight and undesirable, convinced that her baby had been sold into slavery to pay for her mistakes, convinced that life itself was not worth the effort.

In gargoyle heaven she had her reward. In gargoyle heaven all sins were revealed.

Zakariah woke up on Main Street as if from dream to dream, without warning and without standard preparation. He tensed with alarm as V-space suddenly teemed around him, a million minds in motion. He wondered if he should try to move, if he should dash for escape while he had the chance, if he should jump downlevel and disappear like a rabbit in a hole. Out of habit he made no ripple.

The street before him pulsed with colour and mad digital rhythm. Human vitality sparked like a kaleidoscope, a random dance of pure thought. V-space was a place where no gargoyle could lay claim. He drank in the freedom. He was home again.

Are you getting a signal?

Yes, he's here. Be quiet!

I don't have it. I can't scan a thing.

He's the best, doctor. He's invisible. Now finish your job and get out of my brain!

Zakariah waited with uncommon patience. He tested the pulse of greysuits going by and measured his trajectory to the nearest conduit. He knew he could give the gargoyles the slip Sublevel, but once he flinched he would be committed to the full program. He had no idea how tight the gargoyle beam might be. He might have but nanoseconds to escape their tracers. Once free and stable, he would flip the chessboard and put a feedback trace on them, try to locate their base system and schematics. It was a simple gaming routine, now played for bigger stakes than ever. Somewhere his body was being held hostage.

"No delay to destiny," he murmured and dove for safety. In a blur of speed he locked onto the conduit and slid downlevel like an electric eel in oil. His first priority was a private system check to scrutinize his new wetware; he needed referent dates and copyright tags for basic equilibrium. He realized as soon as he began his dive that he had been completely rewired. The response time was impeccable, flexibility optimum, electronics cool and stable—hard, solid, his use of energy a mere drop in a vast ocean of potentiality, uplevel hardware for sure, incredibly expensive. Not a good first sign.

Safe in the conduit and down several levels without a single tracer online, Zakariah took a moment to inspect his new avatar. Feminine hands with long, silver nails, breasts hanging loose like softballs in front of him, hips flaring out like a lampshade. Holy ghost, he was a woman!

At Sublevel Zero he kicked off into the market square to test his new persona, revelling in the sheer beauty of his system logistics. Interference, drag, and feedback were all immeasurable. Background harmonics were squeaky clean, like ice, like solid superconductors. Mental awareness seemed vast and powerful, superhuman. He wondered if he was legal.

Zakariah approached a coterie of hawkers on the boulevard. One of them noticed him with a wide eye and whispered, "Regent," to the gang. They scuttled away in different directions.

"Out slummin', ma'am?" said a portly hawker off to his right, wearing a leather cap and a velvet leisure jacket. "For a hundred

I'll escort you down the lane," he offered with an elbow out graciously. "For five I'll take you to the moon," he whispered as he got closer.

"Is this fellow bothering you, ma'am?" said one of two grey-suits that appeared out of nowhere.

"No," Zakariah said.

The hawker backrolled it to the curb.

"Do you need any aid finding a conduit?" asked the other greysuit, checking his wrist monitor. "You know we must lock on all regents sublevel," he added apologetically.

"Of course," Zakariah stammered, feeling a strange sultry voice slip through his lips. "I'll take this conduit here. Sorry to trouble you." He stepped into a zoomtube and keyed a slow and stately climb upward.

Back on Main Street, Zakariah activated the nearest subterminal. His feed was locked, classified uplevel Prime, so he checked the background harmonics all the way down to the core until he found the crack. His situation seemed utterly ridiculous, impossible. If he was clean, if he was a regent, then the world was his oyster.

There had to be a catch, a glitch in the screenplay. He tossed in the crack code and found his pearl. Helena Sharp, Caucasian, employed by the Eternal Research Institute, unmarried, five-ten, 140 pounds. Eighty-seven years old.

Zakariah shuddered with disbelief and magnified the holovid. Blue eyes, bouncy brown hair, slender nose, taut cheeks—she looked perhaps fifty, tops.

He grabbed his virtual body. He checked muscle tone in his arms and legs, squeezed his buttocks. Only an Eternal could be so well kept. He was in too deep, he had gone too far. Somehow, he had entered a political and ethical minefield by impersonating a public figure. He cringed at the dawning realization. He had been set up for a fall.

He squeezed his breasts and held them up to view. "Who are they trying to kid with this babe?" he asked himself out loud.

He felt the echo of a system monitor sucking his background code, a watcher, a gargoyle, almost subliminal. He lost it immediately, but he knew he was running out of time.

He checked some financial information on Regent Sharp and came up with a bonus. She controlled assets that rivalled the gross national product of a whole directorate—a corporate shadowland of property and investments, a complicated snarl of leveraged financing and venture capital. She had power, influence—her time was chiselled out to underlings at great expense. What an act, what a life! Was Zakariah now required to hold it all together, to save the ivory palace from crashing down? He wondered how far he could get without a physical appearance.

"Is this some sort of psycho-cerebral stim game?" he asked the approaching watcher, and the transmission ended abruptly.

Mia returned home to find the Eternal compound quiet, the windows black like blind eyes, a haze of smoke stratified in the air. Vampires, she thought, and her gut wrenched.

She still wore her hiking boots and blue denim and carried a packsack of dirty clothes. As her bus dwindled away in the distance, she scanned the empty street for danger. It was a commercial district, and the compound had once been a warehouse for an auto parts manufacturer. There was always a guard on the flat-top roof, a watcher on the tower. Always, but not today.

She carried no weapon but had been trained for close combat. She could grab a knife from the kitchen and investigate her quarters, see what might be left of her life. Rix might have scrawled a note or a map or some other clue. The plate glass door was unlocked. No sound. No movement. She edged inside.

There was normally a token presence in the reception area, and kids playing in a daycare area nearby, but not today. She could hear a tap dripping in the darkness, and she smelled marijuana. Drawers had been pulled out of a desk and books lay strewn on the floor. She crept further into the building and checked the cafeteria, where a grey light filtered in from a row of windows along the high ceiling to show nothing but scattered papers and refuse.

"Drop the pack, lady, and step away."

Mia froze at the voice behind her. She unslung her burden and let it drop.

"Now step back," the voice insisted. "Keep your hands up where I can see 'em." The young voice carried a street-level surety that she dared not ignore. Some punk. She took three steps forward as she slowly raised her hands and turned on her toes.

"What happened?" she asked as she eyed her captor, just a kid with a knife, just a white-trash punk with garish tattoos. She could drop him in a blink.

"Dunno. Place was vacant when we got here. Anything nice in the bag?"

"Nothing."

He stepped forward and tapped it with his foot. He kept his knife, a hunting blade serrated at the base, trained on her.

Mia balanced her chi carefully, waiting for an opening. She began an incremental rhythm of preparation, an inner swaying dance. Her muscles began to tingle with anticipation.

"Who are you guys?" she asked conversationally.

"Lords of Death. This is our turf." He took another step closer.

"I've heard the name," she lied. "You're big."

He relaxed a fraction, just enough. She focused her chi and caught him square in the testicles with the toe of her boot.

He cried out and coughed once as he fell in a fetal position, and she knocked his lights out with a quick kick to the temple. She picked up his knife and hefted her pack. She held her breath and listened for noise, for any warning in the gloom. She smelled excrement as the young punk fouled himself. She checked his neck and found a steady pulse.

Mia hurried into the kitchen and found an orgy of waste and a stench of decay like a thick blanket. She gathered a few cans of vegetables and a bag of pasta from the mess and stuffed her pack. There would be little else left of value in the compound. White-trash druggies.

Moving down dark hallways with the meagre glow of her handheld, she walked quickly and quietly to her quarters, found it empty, ransacked. She checked Rix's room. No note, no explanation. His launch computer was gone, probably in a pawn shop by now. She let her chi sing as she pumped her adrenaline up a notch and prowled warily from room to room, looking for clues. A crow of voices warned her of gang members hooting it up in a commons room, but she didn't bother to investigate. The Lords of Death were not her enemy. She was at war with a nebulous foe, a legitimate evil.

She found her stash in the basement behind a loose concrete block in the wall. Some fake ID, enough cash for a free-zone hovel. She could handle herself. She cursed her bad luck, the incredible cloud of dark karma that seemed to follow her everywhere. Her community was in shambles, sold for the market price of eternity, her son gone without a trace. There was nothing left for Zak to return to now. She would have to find her husband, back at the north sanctuary or somewhere else. She needed him now more than ever.

A negative blood test landed Rix quickly out on the street. He plodded down concrete steps with his duffel bag over his shoulder and looked back at the low-slung building. An abandoned cigarette factory had been converted into a vampire den, an unregistered blood donor clinic. A sham. Sickness roiled inside him.

He felt powerless and weak standing on the curb looking back in disgust. What if his parents were in there? What could he possibly do to save them? The ETO prevented any serious inquiries from public agencies. A smokescreen of money protected the vampires. They were worse than the drug lords of lore, the infamous chemical cartels of South America. Now there was life on the market. Life and death.

Rix noticed a motorcycle just down the road. A young woman sat on it, holding a red helmet in her arm, gazing at him with obvious intent. She was stunningly beautiful and seemed to recognize him. Could this be the doom and gloom girl? He sidled up to her.

"You must be Rix," she said.

Rix smiled. She looked like a dream with limp brown hair hanging just to her shoulder and pert lips like pillows. She was dressed in motorcycle leathers and racing boots. He nodded.

"I'm Niko," she said and held a slim forearm out for a hand-shake.

"Nice," Rix said, still nodding, trying desperately to get his groove on as he shook her hand.

"Want to go for a ride?" she asked and lurched her shoulder forward with invitation.

"Where to?"

"My place?"

"Wow."

She smiled her platonic intentions with a roll of her eyes. "I've got a launch couch. You look like you could use a hit. Clear the head, you know."

Rix finally noticed her V-net plug dangling like an earring, but it didn't make him feel any better. This was moving way too fast. "You're taking a big chance," he said. "This place is awash in webcams. They're taking your mug shot down pixel by pixel."

She made an impish face at him, admiring his quick recon-naissance but unconcerned. "I'm not Eternal. Neither are you. These jokers have a one-track mind. They're simpletons with guns." She motioned again with her shoulder to get on.

There was no second helmet and scant inches behind her, but Rix climbed aboard with gathering paranoia. Niko hovered above him as she kicked the bike to life, a motocross racer with knobby tires and skeletal frame, a jumping bike grimy with dust. Rix admired the view despite deep misgivings.

"Hang on, cousin," she yelled back at him as she gunned the

revs, and Rix slipped his arms around her waist as she kicked the clutch out from under him. The front tire popped up with his extra weight in back, but Niko stood on the pegs and forced the handlebars back down. She accelerated quickly, clipping through the gears with smooth precision. She weaved through the traffic and leaned into every corner, cutting the inside track close to the curb to trim the microseconds just for the fun of it.

Niko took him to a street-level condo in the inner suburbs, two-bedroom, one-bath, half-garage. The street seemed quiet, windows intact, the grass combed of debris. Niko had plants in her living room, healthy green plants that had grown in one place for a considerable time. Rix gazed at them in wonder as Niko pointed out basic amenities. He had never stayed in one place long enough to own a thing that lived.

"Look, I've got to grab a shower," she told him. "There's food in the fridge, maybe a beer if you're old enough. Don't plug up till I show you my protocols."

Rix nodded. "Cool."

She looked at him as though there might be something else to say, then decided against it and turned. In a few moments Rix heard a blast of hot water coming from down the hall.

Rix made a sandwich of cheese and mustard and pretended it was meat. He found a can of beer and popped the tab. He sipped it and grimaced. It tasted like crap, but he decided to make a show of it in order to impress his hostess. She couldn't be much older than him, maybe two or three years. He might have a chance with her. He sipped at his beer while he scoped out the condo.

A young nurse presented a plate of food to Zakariah on an antiseptic white tray. Her blond bangs were cut in a razor sharp line
along her eyebrows. She seemed vaguely familiar.

"Any more red medicine?" he asked hopefully.

"Are you in pain, sir?"

She surveyed his head closely.

Zakariah fingered the bandages wrapped above his ears. "No.
Do you know who I am?"

"You're the new runner," the nurse stated by rote. "You're
supposed to be the best," she added doubtfully.

"Is this the ERI?"

The nurse eyed him askance. She shook her head and sighed.

Zakariah tested dry, broken lips with his tongue. "Okay," he
drawled. "How long since my surgery?"

"Six days," she answered coolly, ". . . sir."

Zakariah winced. Such a long recovery to beta state indicated
deep modifications and a corporate price tag he could not possibly afford.

"Have I done anything to offend you?" he asked.

"You called me a gargoyle," she said with false petulance.

"I'm sorry." Zakariah quirked his lips in apology. "You're an
angel of mercy and lovely to behold. I'm sane now, okay?"

The nurse grinned at his performance. "If you say so."

"Is this all I get to eat?" A glass of orange juice, a plastic cup
of red jam, and two pieces of toast stared up at him.

"I can make you something else." Her smile seemed hopeful,
a painted pink crescent on a pale background.

"Great. Pancakes and sausage?"

"Really?"

"Sure. And let the Director know the new runner's ready

for action."

The nurse's eyes widened with interest.

Zakariah flashed a candid smile. "So tell me," he added, "before you go, do they keep the Eternals locked up, or are they free to roam the facility?"

The nurse stiffened. "We're free to roam the facility, sir."

Zakariah stared, momentarily nonplussed. "You're Eternal?"

"We all help out as best we can. It's a research institute, not a jail."

"Great," he said quickly, considering the obvious. He tried another smile to calm troubled waters. "Never mind. You can call me Zak. I'm not really a sir."

"You can call me Marjy, sir. I'll be back shortly with your breakfast."

It took two more days to get an appointment with the Director. In the meantime the medics wouldn't let him anywhere near V-space. He was all wired up with no place to play, and he ached for Main Street like a bandit.

His diet improved considerably, and he resumed his daily exercise regimen. His strength returned. Marjy took the bandages off his head and hung a brand new V-net plug on his earring like a trophy. It itched there waiting for a chance to run.

An armed escort of three men took Zakariah from the medical building by electric car through a parkland of grass and trees and winding causeways. He saw a few people strolling leisurely and noticed a schoolyard full of kids at play. The guided tour through Shangri-La. He shivered with anxiety.

Outside the ERI office tower, a group of protestors marched along the sidewalk with colourful flags and posters—a young crowd, *nouveau riche*, representing a burgeoning and verbal middle class. One banner read: "Blood for Everyone!" Another small placard said: "No Blood for Guns." His escort took him past the disturbance to a quiet side door. Zakariah carefully noted the entry protocol, a simple card scanner, a weak and outdated system.

They took an elevator up to the penthouse level. The guard at the top, a monolith in a blue security uniform, pointed down the hall with casual ease. "Only door on the right, sir. I'll be here when you return."

Zakariah sauntered away, instinctively checking for escape routes, air ducts, skylights. He knocked on the door and wiped his palms on his thighs.

"Come in, Mr. Davis."

Zakariah stepped inside and closed the door behind him.

A woman looked up from the reception desk and stared at him appraisingly.

Zakariah gaped in alarm. Helena Sharp, unmarried white Caucasian, five-ten, 140 pounds. Years of training prevented a panic reaction. His heartbeat remained steady, but he knew he had crossed over into another realm. "I'm here to see the Director," he said calmly.

"Hips flared out like a lampshade, huh?" Helena Sharp stood up and walked from behind her desk. She was wearing a black business skirtsuit with white ruffled blouse, skin-tone hose, and black pumps. She sat on her desk and crossed her legs, and Zakariah noted a glinting V-net plug at her ear.

He grimaced. His very thoughts had been monitored. Some new tech infiltration. Go with the flow. Store all data. "I may have exaggerated somewhat," he offered. "I was under a bit of pressure at the time."

Helena nodded. "You performed wonderfully under the circumstances. You eluded all tracers, cracked my encryption in seconds, accessed all my private financial files and bank records. I think you could have cleared me out in a matter of minutes if I hadn't pulled the plug."

"I was being very cautious," Zakariah said, unsure of his footing.

"Indeed?"

"I didn't know it was a game."

"It wasn't."

Zakariah surveyed her carefully. He could see age around her eyes, but her sandy brown hair was youthful and lustrous, parted at the side and wavy across her brow. Her lips were robust, laugh lines muted.

"I'm sorry. I know this is a bit difficult for you—"

"I'm here to see the Director," Zakariah interrupted.

"Mr. Davis, please sit down." Helena gestured with her palm to an easy chair beside her desk. "I *am* the Director."

She took his arm and pointed him toward the chair. She poured him a glass of nutrient water from a carafe on her desk and handed it to him. Her hands were slender, fingers long and tapered. No rings.

"I know you're already considering the ramifications of all this. You're very fast," she said. When he didn't respond she walked behind her desk and poured herself a glass of water. She took a sip and stared at Zakariah over the rim, licking her upper lip with a pink tip of tongue. She took another sip and returned the glass to a silver serving tray.

She leaned forward with both palms flat on the desktop, safe behind her barrier of polished teak. "I'm not Eternal," she said.

"I wish I was. Soon I will be, if all goes well."

Zakariah sat quietly recording data, piecing it all together.

"I undergo chemical rejuve regularly. I take Eternal blood once a week. I really am eighty-seven years old." She paused and seemed disconcerted, and Zakariah took strength from this small show of vulnerability.

"When you squeezed my breasts, I felt it," she said finally.

Zakariah nodded. "Weird quantum science."

"Synchronous wetware. Two minds in a single avatar."

"It had to happen."

"Do you want it all at once, Mr. Davis?"

Zakariah focused his eyes on her pretty face, the inquisitive arch of her eyebrows, and playful tilt of her head. He smiled. "Call me Zak."

"Thank you. Call me Helena."

Zakariah took a long drink of nutrient water to put her at ease. He had enough information now to recognize a cloud of responsibility condensing around him, a game plan coming into focus.

"You kidnapped me, Helena."

"Better me than the local bloodlord."

"You screwed with my synapses."

"You're vastly improved."

"It's the principle of the thing."

"You would never have agreed in advance."

"You don't have the right to jump into my brain."

"I take what I want, Mr. Davis. I pay for what I need."

"What is the ERI to you? Some strategic corporate alliance? Do you think you can buy Eternal life?"

She straightened, her face suddenly austere. She pulled up an office chair and sat behind her desk. "Our interests coincide. Surely you can see that."

"I see a rich old woman who wants to live forever."

"I see a cowboy plughead who wants the virus for his only son."

"We're incompatible."

"We're complementary. Don't you at least want to hear my proposal?"

"Okay, fine."

"We're going offplanet to the Source. You and I. Together."

His body galvanized at the possibility, his quest come true. "Well, then, you got yourself a runner, ma'am." He raised his glass as though in ceremonial toast.

Helena pursed her lips at his quick change, then pressed her advantage. "I'm giving you a position as a field operative here at the Institute. You work for me. You will follow each detail with precision. Doctor Mundazo is the Head of Operations."

"Do I get paid?"

"Room and board just like everyone else. All the money goes into the lab."

"For what?"

"We're planning a public inoculation program."

"Is that right? What's the price tag on immortality?"

"That will depend on supply and demand. You're in charge of supply."

"So I work for free, while you get rich?"

"I'm not taking a salary from the Institute. I'm funding operations until the money runs out."

"You're a dangerous woman."

"Why, thank you."

Zakariah paused for a quick survey of his options. The woman had already hijacked his brain. He would be a fool to trust her, but he felt exhilarated by this new challenge. "I assume you have some guidance on the target?"

"Not a lot. The communications interface may be foreign, perhaps alien. Your special talents will be instrumental."

"So you want me to hack heaven and bring you the treasure on a pillow?"

Helena smiled. "That would be nice, if it's not too much to ask."

Rix decided it was time to confront his hostess, whom he now suspected was little more than a prison guard. She had a comfy launch couch with Prime One access, to be sure, and gave him food and lodging fit for a prince, but it felt like a gilded cage. Niko had spurned his every intimate advance. She ignored him completely most of the time and never volunteered even casual small talk, let alone secret strategies. On the rare occasions when she deigned to address him, her manner was abrupt and businesslike.

"I've got to find my parents," he told her over their usual evening meal of steamed vegetables and orange juice. "I can't just hang out here playing in V-space all day."

"You won't see your parents for a long time, Rix."

Rix slammed his palm on the table. "How do you know that? You leave every morning on your motorcycle. You never tell me anything. What do you do for a living? How do you pay for this fancy condo?"

Niko shrugged. "I'm a smuggler. Bio-chips, upgrades." She smiled with insouciance. "Nothing legal, I assure you. Not that it's any of your business."

"You work for a black lab?"

"It's a family venture."

"You said I was family. Is that why I'm here?"

Niko laid her fork down. She folded her arms under her breasts. She was wearing a pink tank top and showing a hint of cleavage. "Yes. It was my idea. I didn't want to see you on the street."

"Where are my parents?"

"Your mother is in hiding. She's staying off the grid, just like you. Your father is in play."

Rix gaped at her. *Your father is in play*. What the hell did that mean? "Tell me."

"I don't know the details."

"Liar."

Niko eyes shaded like a cloud passing. She turned her face away and looked out a window at gloomy sky beyond. "I like you, Rix," she said softly. "I would never lie to you."

"My father had a sister named Niko. You can't possibly be her."

"No. Your aunt is dead." She pressed her mouth into a thin line and turned back to face him. "I'm her clone. Just a poor photocopy lacking in hybrid vigour, I'm afraid."

"Cloning is illegal."

"Lots of things are illegal," she said. Her eyes dared him with stony defiance, but her trembling lips betrayed an inner wound. Rix recognized his faux pas like a blow.

"No. I didn't—"

"Oh, never mind." She waved him away. "I can't expect understanding from you."

"What's that supposed to mean?"

"You've lived your entire life on the run like a rat."

"So what?"

"So nothing. I'm just saying." She pushed her chair back and stood up. "I've lost my appetite."

Rix followed her into the living room. She reached for a magazine and fumbled through it as though trying to signal some distance between them.

"How did she die?"

Niko held her chin up and sighed through her nose, but kept her back to him, rigid. She tossed the magazine on the coffee table like a flapping bird. "She died during experimental surgery, back in the early days of brain implants."

"That's harsh."

Niko turned, arms akimbo, her face tilted up proud and defiant. "It was before my time. I don't know all the details. She wasn't my mother and she's gone now, okay? At least they kept a backup."

"Jesus, Niko."

Her face slanted into a delicate sneer. "Do you believe in Jesus, Rix? Is there room in heaven for illegal clones? Was I born without a soul, do you think?"

She seemed so vulnerable to him, so frail of spirit, that he could only open his arms for her and bite his lower lip. She stepped into his embrace.

"I'm sorry," he whispered.

"Never mind."

"I wasn't trying to be mean."

"It's okay, Rix. I'm a big girl."

They continued to embrace, and Rix felt his body respond with a weird mix of lust and protective responsibility. God, she felt good.

"I just want to help," he said. "I want to be part of the family."

"Be careful what you ask for," Niko murmured. She rubbed his back and sighed into his ear, barely a whisper.

"Well, you seem quite healthy, Helena," Dr. Silus Mundazo said from behind his clipboard. His head was shaved, his hands in latex gloves, his white lab coat clean and pressed. "Some indications of chronic stress, some weight gain in the upper body— nothing to write home about. However, you do seem to be exhibiting an unusual pattern of brainwave activity in the frontal and temporal lobes, no doubt from the extensive rewiring you've recently undergone."

"Could this be debilitating in any way?" She felt uncomfortable in her clothes again after being probed and measured by cold instruments. She preferred to dress slowly in front of a full-length mirror and check each layer for proper fit, not throw her clothes on hastily while leaning against a chair in a drafty cubicle.

He shrugged. "Heaven only knows, Helena. We didn't have this case study in medical school. For what it's worth, your partner exhibits much the same symptoms, along with elevated electrical activity throughout the cerebellum. His corpus callosum looks like a six-lane freeway."

"He's a special case. Flying with Zak is like riding a roller coaster. One is filled with dread and promise at the same time." Her button-up collar felt uncomfortable at her neck and her bra strap pressed awkwardly into her back. She wondered if she had twisted it while dressing.

"Any feelings of nausea, weightlessness, or stomach trouble after you unplug?"

"No."

"Any dissociative thoughts? Any voices?"

"No."

"And how do you feel about him emotionally?"

"Emotionally?"

"Sharing your thoughts, sharing your intimate secrets, that sort of thing." Silus Mundazo held his pen poised over his clipboard. His eyes stayed downcast.

Helena felt a wave of embarrassment and bristled in defence. "Zak and I have a business relationship, Silus. We're not sharing secrets. We're working."

Dr. Mundazo looked up, tilted his head slightly to the right. "The young hacker and the wealthy heiress?"

"Oh, spare me the innuendo."

"Are you having sex with him?"

"Certainly not. Good heavens, I can't believe that question is even relevant."

He pointed his pen at his clipboard, holding it up for her view. "It's under psychiatric profile."

"Are you studying to be a shrink at night school, Doctor?"

"Let me remind you of your history in the area."

"Of course I have a history, Silus. I've been having sex for seventy years."

"With younger men, I mean."

"They perform better."

"What?"

"You heard me."

"Fine. Duly noted." He dropped his clipboard to his side. "I have grave concerns about your situation, Helena."

"That's your job."

"I must caution you professionally, as a physician and friend."

"Go ahead, but I need Zak to get to the Source. I can't do it on my own."

Silus Mundazo sighed with a show of exasperation. "The side effects of this new synchronous wetware could be significant. You should be under close observation, not heading off into hyperspace with a known criminal. As you know, I am on record as being against the whole procedure. Well, the surgeons have come and done their white magic, and now gone back to their dolphins and baboons. I am left to shoulder the responsibility for a human guinea pig, and I don't like it."

"I'm sorry you feel that way, Silus, because I'm leaving you in charge while I'm gone."

"That scares me even more."

"This mission is important for the people of Earth, not just me. You've been Eternal for so long you've forgotten the fear of death."

"I can see that your motivation remains quite strong. Motivation has never been your weak suit in the card game of life."

"Do you think I am in danger of losing my identity? Sacrificing my cerebrum?"

"Is that what you worry about?"

"In the darkness of the night anything seems possible."

Dr. Mundazo squinted at her in study. He took a long moment to compose his thoughts. "I would think a shared personality could infiltrate your brain to the degree necessary to alter behaviour patterns. You could be controlled without your knowledge or approval. To some extent, of course, we are all influenced by various external media and environmental stimuli around us. But inside us, we like to think we have a tabernacle of consciousness, a private place where no one but God can intervene. Modern technology has taken that away from us now. I'm not sure how we as a race will react when every thought and every sin is exposed to public view."

Silus's blue eyes shone with resolve like hard diamonds, and Helena felt her composure weaken under his scrutiny. She puffed up her chest with a quick and resolute breath. She had gone too far to turn back now. "Unfortunately, we can't turn technology around, Silus. If we delay, we are run over and flattened underfoot. If we resist, we are branded heretics and burned at the metaphorical stake. If we surf the wave, if we ride the crest, at least we're still in the game."

FOUR

Prime Level Three was bright and clean, guarded vigilantly for the upper crust of society, V-net patrons who paid a monthly surcharge for privileged access. Colours seemed more radiant here than on lower levels, props and adornments animated with higher definition and detail, visitors more respectable and cultured. The entire level operated under Class B encryption, which was a mere formality to any serious hacker but served as a psychological deterrent to most users.

Robot browsers patrolled the streets, sniffing for stray data and gobbling up digital corruption. They looked like dogs to passing users, bulky guard dogs on wheels. The cybertrackers picked up loose files and fragmented data that might otherwise litter the streets and slow down access times. They kept the main thoroughfares antiseptic and comfortable, though they occasionally tagged on to unsuspecting tourists in their thirst for data and had to be dislodged by licensed quarantine control officers. It was a criminal offense to destroy cybertrackers or attempt to manipulate their programs, which made them a target of choice among empowered teenagers on the V-net, who systematically reprogrammed them for recreational warcraft.

Apart from bandit browsers and the occasional ghost avatar, problems and pitfalls were few on Prime Level Three. International traders and diplomats preferred to work uplevel where transmission speeds were optimum and signals unscathed over long distances. Currency experts and commodity speculators, for whom money was often measured in microseconds, thought nothing of the extra expense of working uplevel. The elite were continually driven higher by new and faster technology as they vied to escape the huddled crowds clogging the V-net levels below.

High-profile advertisers targeted the upper levels with billboards, icons, and animated hyperlinks of all shapes and sizes. Cartoon poster boys, sexy teddy bears, and other corporate animatrons offered free exotic vacations and offplanet eccentricities to passersby. Financial consultants, nutritional managers, and spiritual gurus vied together for the latest spark of innovation to capture the fleeting interest of jaded and often cynical users who had already seen the whole world before breakfast. The sophistication of an exploding marketplace demanded outstanding leaps in software development and engineering, and the early programmers who pioneered the Prime-level architecture now held the status of idols in a false religion, exaggerated beyond simple belief, glitzy facades that made mockery of their quest and true accomplishments. Knowledge was power, but business was business.

Helena Sharp had a personal login meter on Prime Level Three and an attractive escalating discount program with free bonus points for air and space travel. She coalesced precisely on schedule to give her quarterly report to the World Council, an unofficial, unpublicized quorum of twelve international power brokers who jokingly referred to themselves as the dirty disciples. Eight males and four females sat around a long, translucent table that looked like a thick slab of smoke-filled glass.

Helena nodded in recognition to the four corners and sat down at the end of the table directly opposite Chairman Tao, a broad-shouldered, stony-faced avatar with flowing white hair and the impeccable image of expensive electronics. He was rumoured to be representing a biosystems conglomerate, but his various allegiances were shrouded in secrecy. He was a biochemist and had been a brilliant scholar in his youth.

Other major financial interests had their places around the table—telecommunications, petroleum multinationals, desalination moguls. Everyone had everything to gain and nothing to lose but money—which was itself merely an illusion, an electronic aberration for which lesser people lived and died. *What will you pay to live forever, my friends?*

"Are we under Triple-A encryption?" Helena asked.

"Not yet. We're accessing the Beast now that you're here," the Chairman replied smoothly. He waited a few seconds, grinning like an emoticon. "Fine, we have confirmation now. We may begin, gentlemen and ladies."

Problems, Zak piped up in Helena's inner ear.

What? she probed.

A massive program has kicked in to crash your party, third from the left. Can't you feel the harmonics?

She eyed the image sharply, a small Japanese woman with black bangs cropped high above her eyes, wearing a black satin suit over a plain pink blouse. She could sense nothing amiss.

How can they crack a Triple-A code from the Beast? It would keep a bank of supercomputers crunching for weeks.

That they even try suggests resources far beyond imagining, Zak responded. *Perhaps they access the Beast themselves. In any case we will have a few minutes of grace at least.*

"Director Sharp, I'm sure you don't need an introduction. I believe you know everyone here intimately. Ostensibly this is a refinancing hearing, but frankly we want a full report on the Eternals. Your mandate has dragged on somewhat."

The air bristled with a new severity as all eyes turned to face her. Helena pasted on a politician's smile. She took a moment to collect her thoughts. "The Eternal communities continue to grow at a slow but steady rate. They live in segregated, some-what frightened enclaves throughout the civilized world. We monitor several in continental America and have infiltrated a handful. They lack stable organization and have virtually no communication with far-flung outposts. They seem to have little enthusiasm, ambition, or political sophistication. In many areas they are hunted by black-market bloodlords and in less devel-oped countries have been harvested like livestock. As you know, at the Eternal Research Institute we take blood only from willing volunteers, and then only according to established guidelines from the World Health Agency."

"Oh, spare us the public relations," said one balding young man to Helena's right, Carruthers, a petroleum magnate. "Any breakthroughs in the transfusion program?"

Jerk, Helena thought.

Careful, Zakariah replied.

"No," she replied evenly. "The transfusions temporarily halt aging, but do not actively regenerate body tissue, even after months of regular treatments. When combined with chemical rejuve, cellular breakdown can be reversed up to a point, as we all know from personal experience, but the permanent catalyst continues to elude us."

"Why?" asked the Chairman bluntly. "We've all poured a lot of money into this project. Your Institute, your salary."

Helena continued unperturbed, smiling with practised charm. "The virus infiltrates every living cell in the human body, but not by any known biomechanism. On the subatomic level, we have recorded a series of unexplainable events centred around or within the mitochondria of individual cells."

"Events, you say?" asked Chairman Tao, tilting forward in his chair.

"Subatomic exchanges of energy, Chairman, producing light-waves up near the top of the visible spectrum."

"Impossible," he countered definitively.

"Even the black market is using spectral analysis to target Eternal blood. Hand-held units are being manufactured in the underground economy."

"A simple refractory phenomenon," the Chairman insisted.

Helena raised an eyebrow at him speculatively.

"Most of us don't have the technical expertise to understand this line of questioning," interposed the Japanese woman, representing a major corporate consortium that controlled three percent of the world's wealth. "What we are looking for is results, the black bottom line. Are we to understand that both are lacking in this report, Director?"

"Our progress has been slow, yes, and in fact we have reached an impasse of sorts. All hope of duplicating, modifying, or artificially transmitting the virus has now evaporated. I am not prepared to download the experimental data at this time, but it is available for burst transmission to appropriate terminals. Suffice it to say that we have exhausted every avenue known to medical science and have stymied some of the best subatomic theoreticians in the world. The financial reports, of course, are at your fingertips. All current activities are adequately funded."

"Are we giving up then?" demanded the Japanese women, Madame Shakura, her red lips a mere knife slit in her face. "Are you admitting personal defeat?"

Helena looked coolly at the Chairman for some exercise of his authority.

He remained silent, grim as a watchdog.

"Not at all," she continued unruffled. "The virus can only be transmitted in what we term its activated state. We have not been able to secure an activated sample, but have traced the source of several contagions. We conclude that the virus is being produced offplanet and shipped to Earth in single dosages. We suspect it is being cultured by a small but influential group who plan to use their superior technology to take complete control of this planet."

Several avatars glistened with white static.

Severe emotional trauma in all listeners, Zakariah whispered.

No kidding.

"Naturally, to shift our primary focus offplanet will require a considerable financial commitment from all those present," Helena said. "I have a full report ready for transmittal to authorized terminals, and I trust you will continue to support the Eternal Research Institute in all its varied research and development interests." *How much time do I have?*

Perhaps forty seconds realtime. I'm shutting down all our windows and back alleys.

"The first stage of our new program will require an envoy to the Source, which we know to be one of the planets in the Cromeus colonies. I have already booked passage for myself and my bodyguard through the Macpherson Doorway. I need an immediate commitment of funds to cover the trip."

"We cannot allow it," the Chairman croaked, "not you personally."

"We need time to digest this information," the Japanese woman stated.

Helena stood up from her chair and stepped behind it. "Madame Shakura," she answered icily, "I'm sure you can appreciate the importance of these events. All the world is clamouring for the virus. Whoever reaches the Source first will ultimately control the Earth. There are countless groups and governments vying for the information I just shared with you. My obligations are fulfilled. While this informal collusion may have had the luxury of working in the shadows at one time, we are now under the spotlight's glare. We lose ground every second we delay."

She walked up behind Madame Shakura, who twisted to face her. "In fact, your own security system is about to be breached any moment, and our precious Triple-A conference will be forced to an untimely end. I suggest this committee get its own house in order and leave me to my work."

Three members at the table stood instantly and stepped backward through transparent doorways that swallowed them like zippered envelopes.

The Chairman looked pained. "How could you possibly know this?"

"Have you confirmed already?" she asked.

"I have confirmed," Madame Shakura said, her image fuzzy with emotion. "I offer my deepest apologies." She prostrated her face low to the table.

That's it, Zakariah said. *We're being piped into Prime Level Five.*

Very clean. Expensive. Do you want to risk a trace?

Never mind. There's nothing left for us on this planet. We've burned our last bridge.

Helena bowed with respect to Madame Shakura, winked to the Chairman, and turned to leave.

"Get off here. Wait in the shadows. I'll be back in four minutes."

Rix jumped off the bike and surveyed the storefronts on the street—a pharmax, a public laundry, a cosmetox clinic offering surgery while-u-wait. They were in a decrepit suburban area that didn't look like much, but all the better for daylight subterfuge. He was on a mission at last.

Niko kicked back into the traffic and disappeared up the road. She was headed for a private heliport two blocks over, but he was not supposed to know the details. Plausible deniability, she called it, and he was cool with that.

They had taken a circuitous route to get here, constantly moving, turning, meandering. *Always assume you are being followed until you can prove otherwise*, Niko insisted. She seemed to be professionally paranoid, a chronic case, but Rix was glad to be along for the ride. He paced on the street as he waited. Everyone seemed to be staring at him. Was he acting too suspicious? Probably. He leaned against a lamp post and tried to look non-descript. He scowled and put on a sardonic mask, hoping to blend with the crowd.

Niko pulled up precisely on schedule with a black satchel between her knees. She handed the package to him and moved toward the gas tank to make room on the seat. He hopped behind her and felt the heat of the exhaust between his legs. They swung back onto the roadway and headed uptown toward purple foothills in the distance. He loved to feel the pressure of wind on his body, the thrill of speed. Niko was an aggressive driver; she obeyed the superficial rules of the road but wasted no time accelerating back to the speed limit after each corner.

They turned into a public parking garage after fifteen minutes and headed underground. Rix flipped up his visor as his eyes tried to adjust to the twilight. Niko pulled the bike to the side and stopped. She kicked down the peg and tipped the weight on the kickstand.

"Take the horns, cousin. I'll wait here for you."

Rix jumped off the bike, startled. He clutched the satchel to his chest.

"What, I'm making the drop?"

Niko stood to face him. She took off her helmet and fluffed her hair.

"The client asked for you. His name is Jimmy. Up three levels, you'll see an area marked with repair pylons, roped off with yellow tape. He'll be there waiting. Think you can handle that?"

"He asked for me?"

Niko checked her wristband. "We're right on the button. Just stick to the basic rules we established." She beamed reassurance at him. "You'll be fine. The package is prepaid, so you don't have to worry about money or anything."

Rix nodded, feeling hot and sweaty with anxiety. What was in the satchel? Drugs? Illegal biochips? What if he got shot? What if he went to jail?

He climbed on the idling bike and set the package between

his knees. So this was it, the life of a smuggler. *Be careful what you ask for.*

He stepped into gear and headed up the ramp. He quickly spiralled up to the third level, saw the caution tape, and parked beside an orange pylon. A man stood there, an older man, bald and slightly stooped, wearing dirty grey coveralls and holding a push broom.

"Are you Jimmy?"

The man leaned his broom against a support post and stepped forward.

"You must be Rix. Take off your helmet so I can get a look at you."

Rix hung his helmet on the handlebars and met the man's appraising eyes. He kept the bike idling but offered the package forward with a trembling right hand. Jimmy took it and peered inside. He pulled out a brushed-silver canister that looked like a housing for binoculars and slid it into a pocket inside his coveralls. "Thanks." He handed back the empty satchel.

"No problem. Do I get a receipt?"

Jimmy chuckled at that. "I saw you hack *Killer Warz* a few years ago. That was some twisted crack."

"Totally. But they kicked me off the game."

Jimmy held a forefinger in the air. "Not before you logged your rep. The technical term for that move is watermark feedback attack."

"I know. I read about it afterward."

"So you've studied the classics?"

"A little. Mostly I just feel the crack. I know it's there, like music. I don't do algorithms."

Jimmy nodded with recognition. "I know what you mean. I

can barely do multiplication without an app."

"So you wanted to see me?"

"Yeah, I just wanted to remind you not to waste your best tricks when the stakes are low. Watch for the breakout move, you know?"

"I've got lots of tricks left."

"I'll bet you do."

"You still play *Killer Warz*?"

"Not any more. I followed a few top players for a while."

"Some kind of talent scout?"

"I guess maybe I am. Look me up. We'll do a quick tour up-Prime someday."

"That would be awesome, but I'm using a friend's launch couch at the moment. She doesn't want me screwing up her schematics."

"Aaah. A ladies man. I'm impressed."

Rix felt a blush of blood but didn't let it faze him. Let the stranger think what he might. "You must have known my dad when he was young."

"I did indeed. How does that old folk song go?

'A legend in suburbia, a marvel of his time,
He was a rich kid on the hustle, but the lawyers
called it cri-i-ime.'"

Jimmy crooned out the last note and spread his hand for the final showman's ta-da.

"That's pretty good. Are you an ex-rockstar?"

"No, hardly even a digital guitar hero. I was a twenty-first century schizoid kid, not the brightest light, but I did okay over the years. I guess I was lucky to meet some talented people along the way."

"So what's in the package? I know I'm not supposed to ask."

Jimmy eyebrows popped at this break in protocol, but he smiled after a few seconds. "Rotaxane in a ground-breaking architecture."

"And that's good, right?"

Jimmy chuckled at the blatant admission of naïveté. "The competitive edge in nanotech, at the moment. By this time next year it will be duck soup. We're climbing high asymptotes." He shrugged as though to apologize for the manic progress of science.

"Well, it's nice to meet you, sir."

"The pleasure is all mine. It does my heart good to see the next generation taking the world by storm. Don't let anyone steal your gift, Rix. The future is your heritage."

"You sound like a V-space greeting card."

"I know. Funny how reality imitates virtuality."

Rix revved the throttle to warm the bike out of powersaver mode. "Will I see you again in the flesh?"

Jimmy's lips pressed into a thin line as he considered the thought. "I doubt it."

Rix slid on his helmet and gave the old man a thumbs up for good measure. Now that the deal was done he felt a pulse of elation in his abdomen. He was a smuggler now, a freakin' secret agent. He kicked into gear and wheeled a tight circle to head back down the ramp.

Niko waited for him downstairs, looking pissed and beautiful, pointing at her wristband monitor. "You had me worried," she said. "We're not supposed to chitchat with customers."

"I was gaining rapport with the client," he replied, regurgitating her own training jargon back at her. "Everything okay down here?"

"Nothing unusual. Let's wrap up."

"Hop on. I'll drive." The future looked so bright Rix had to flip down his visor.

The Macpherson Doorway had a diameter of just under one metre and required an orbiting antimatter facility to keep it open that wide. A steady trade of commerce used the tunnel, and humans could be sent one at a time in sealed capsules designed to withstand a microsecond of hypothesized nonspace, but the exorbitant expense kept tourist traffic to a minimum.

Colin Macpherson, the long-dead physicist after whom the transport system was named, had harnessed the power of wormholes, sub-atomic wrinkles in the fabric of space-time, by manipulating gravitational forces in tight parameters. He discovered the first blue planet beyond Earth, a lifeless sphere that was quickly terraformed to provide a breathable atmosphere and opened to colonization. His work brought humanity out of its cradle and spawned the rapid growth of the Cromeus outposts a century before the birth of Zakariah Davis. His ashes had been sprinkled on extraterrestrial soil, and his soul was rumoured to have been uploaded into the primitive communications network of the time, a legendary status he held to this day as the architect of a new world.

Zakariah had studied quantum field theory along with every other schoolboy, of course, and liked to think he had a layman's grasp of the anthropic universe—the exquisitely crafted mathematical constants necessary for the firestorm factories that built the carbon molecule, the precursor of life. Macpherson's equations had proved reliable in widening and stabilizing one of the natural wormholes of the convoluted cosmos, but the thought of actually becoming a part of the ongoing experiment still gave Zakariah a chill. Even after all these years, the fact of the matter remained that no one had yet located the alien sun, Cromeus Signa, on any stellar map. It was so far away in space, or perhaps time, that it shared no galactic landmarks with the universe visible from Earth.

"The Doorway works; that's all we need to know," Helena said on the shuttle trip up.

"If it closes down, we'll be stranded," Zakariah reminded her, unease like a sickness welling up inside him. "We'll be at the mercy of a repair crew and their financiers. The colonists must resent that dependence on old Earth."

"I understand they're almost self-sufficient now. It could be that they're pulling a lot more strings down here than we imagine. If they go to market with the virus, they'll control everything. We'll be puppets. Don't worry about the Doorway; think of it as a glorified elevator."

"Right," Zakariah agreed, but his stomach continued to roil. He pulled another antacid tablet out of a pocket and placed it on his tongue. He chewed noisily. "So the latest specs from the Cromeus colonies indicate a hardline V-net system with satellite repeaters. Crypto looks pretty basic but has probably been updated. Does that jibe with your own research?"

Helena nodded. "The satellite hardware is several years out of date, the V-space relatively undeveloped. All the elements are there for a full system. You'll probably be a god when you get online."

Zakariah squinted self-effacement at her and puffed a reply.

"I'm being half serious. Your intuitive grasp of V-net mechanics borders on the supernatural. These deep harmonics you mention—no one else has any clue what you're talking about. Your arcade-style approach to computing would be cerebral suicide to any normal person. I've seen it inside my own brain and I still don't believe it." The Director smiled, showing no offense. "Just like the Doorway—I don't believe it either."

"Attention, travellers," the intercom resounded in a deep male baritone, "we will begin deceleration in sixty seconds. Gravitational experience will approach 1.7 g for several minutes. Please buckle into your flight seats and secure all loose items."

"Yeah, well, I think you're pretty special too," Zakariah shot back to Helena with a grin.

She tilted her face with a sly twist on her lips as though considering a flirtation, then shook her head. "You just might survive after all," she replied. She had her long hair tied in a bun and tucked under a hairnet for travel, and she wore a fashionable grey flying suit with heat-reflective coating and a plain white turtleneck. The effect was austere, businesslike.

Zakariah wore an archaic white-leather NASA jacket that Jimmy had dredged up from a museum for good luck, the seams cracked and the elbows rough and crusty, and a pair of baggy silver flight pants, his shaggy hair fringed with the green highlights his nurse, Marjy, had installed during his recuperation from surgery. His jacket had set off a barrage of detectors at Richmond Station Earthside, and Helena had pulled rank on the Base Commander to get Zakariah on board. The special metallic lining had been designed to minimize cosmic radiation exposure above the atmosphere, and there would be bloody hell to pay when they hit the NFTA pre-launch scanners.

"Magnetic treadways on Macpherson Station are marked in bright yellow paint," the intercom resounded, this time in a higher tone, female, pleasantly efficient. "New Freedom Transit Authority requests that all passengers orient themselves to the public treadway in order to be quickly processed past inspection and launch points. Please have palm verification ready for the attendant on duty. For your security and safety, passengers are not allowed any carry-on bags or accessories. All registered luggage must be packed in appropriate launch tubes. Have a safe and pleasant journey."

A chime sounded. "Attention, travellers," the male baritone boomed again, "we will begin deceleration in thirty seconds. Gravitational experience will approach 1.7 g for several minutes. Please buckle into your flight seats and secure all loose items."

Zakariah thought of Mia waiting at home for his return. What would she think of him leaving the planet and jumping through the Doorway without telling her? She probably thought he was still kicking back at the cabin, and all the better for her. A thick patchwork of deception separated them now, a labyrinth of intrigue. All outside contact had been cut off by the Director since the experimental wetware operation, and he could not get on the V-net without her tagging presence. Helena lived inside his head and he would never get used to it.

In his heart he knew Mia would understand his motivation. It was all for Rix. Everything was for Rix, their shared masterpiece of creation. He remembered his first meeting with Mia years ago, when he had just received the Eternal virus and had found refuge in the nearest protective enclave. He arrived on the doorstep a blind novitiate, confused and wary, yet eager to learn.

An induction session followed and a welcoming celebration, a pageantry rooted in tradition, a mystery beyond understanding.

On a wooden bench in a back corner he noticed a fellow newcomer, a thin, blond-haired beauty with impossibly long legs, sitting in her own quiet confusion, her eyes moving from face to face, her vibrant smile flashing with each introduction. Zakariah sat beside her and joined in the rituals of community fellowship, and they shared that first evening together as blood siblings, adopted into a new extended family that neither of them might ever fully comprehend. Zakariah felt kinship with her from before the beginning. He felt that he shared her essence just by sitting close to her, that a higher authority had united their souls.

"Are you leaving anyone behind, Helena? Family and friends? A lover?"

"No, not really." Helena activated the touchscreen monitor on the seat in front of her. She made a point of checking obvious data. "Over time my friendships became business, and my business became friendship."

Zakariah nodded as he activated his own monitor. He checked the schedule carefully.

"I'm not really a monster, Zak. I'm not doing this just for money."

"Everyone's got a tangled web, Helena."

"The world needs the virus. It's the way of the future, our only hope for global peace. I don't believe the protectionist pap of the Evolutionary Terrorist Omnibus. The ETO arose from a misguided, knee-jerk panic by frightened politicians."

"It was a declaration of war. I live it every day."

"Eternals are not the enemy. They should be elevated, not downtrodden.

"Scientists say we're a vanguard of alien biology."

"Everything unknown is magic until we understand it."

"So what do you think, Helena? Is it science or magic?"

She looked down her nose at him, her eyes hooded. "I'm a scientist first. I'll proceed with clinical assumptions for now. What about you? You're the one with alien blood in your veins. Do you believe in magic?"

Zakariah matched her veracious gaze. He wondered if Director Sharp had a thread of compassion after all. "I expect the ineffable in the morning and a miracle by mid-afternoon, but I wouldn't call it magic."

She blinked at him, puzzled at his poetry. A deceleration burn took their breath away as it pushed them back into their seats.

"It took me a long time to find you," Mia said and watched Jimmy's head rise up from a cluttered holodesk bright with bar graphs and hyperlinks. She could see no hint of surprise on his stony features. The front door had been unlocked, and her calls of entry unanswered.

"That's good," he said.

"My name is Mia."

"Did Phillip send you?"

"No."

A shadow of consternation passed quickly across Jimmy's face. The top of his skull was shiny and smooth, his chin blockish and strong and showing a wisp of a goatee. He smiled. "Ahhh, private enterprise."

Mia took a few steps closer, into the male personal sphere. "So how have you been?"

"Good. Business is good. Still smuggling the same old shit."
He waved his hands at the bright confusion of data on his
holodesk. He winked out a few lights with a pointing diode.

Mia pressed her hands down on her long, knitted tunic. She
summoned her chi. "Zak mentioned your name with fondness
many times."

"That so?"

"Yes."

"So what can I do for you?" He smirked playfully. "For old
time's sake."

"I'm just checking back through his contact list. Hoping to
get lucky. Was he here?"

Jimmy grinned broadly. "He sure was, honey."

Mia felt muscles tighten involuntarily in her upper body. She
wished she could exercise more control. Zak would never have
flinched. "Where is he now?"

Jimmy checked his wristband, a gaudy designer model, probably fake judging by his reputation. "He should be dropping
through the Macpherson Doorway any minute now."

"You're kidding."

"He's heading for the Source of the virus. It wasn't my idea."

"That's impossible."

"Perhaps it is. Who am I to say? Zak seems to think he knows
what he's doing, poor sod. You're even more radiant than he
described, by the way. I was expecting some sort of karate kid
with a bandana round her forehead."

"You'll help me, then?" Mia watched his face carefully. She
didn't trust him. She didn't believe in urban legends about smug-
glers or the freeworld hacker ideology. But she was desperate. She

had fallen in love with a dangerous man and wanted him back.

Jimmy looked like he was stifling a laugh for the sake of social modesty, that he really wanted to belt out a howl at her audacity.

"You got any money?" he asked.

The gaping maw of the Macpherson Doorway lay on the other side of a gauntlet of laser scanners and detection systems. The large chamber echoed with the hum of heaters and oxygen generators. The launch tubes lay lined end to end in front of the Doorway like an assembly line of silver coffins in front of a powerful vortex. Seventeen capsules had been reserved for human occupants.

Zakariah studied the Doorway intently, feeling philosophical and trying to psych himself to readiness. In the dark centre of the orifice lay a foreign universe, an enchanted creation where humans had no natural home. He imagined the Doorway a telescope, and himself a speck of sand peering out into heaven, looking for a Source akin to deity, looking for his fate and his son's eternal destiny. While he watched, an incoming series of capsules materialized in the core and floated noiselessly down a conveyor belt with no apparent energy exchange—no sparks, no drama, nothing to indicate the mysterious forces in action. A magnetic friction system slowed them down, and a hydraulic restraining harness brought them to a complete halt. A team in bright orange staff regalia then manoeuvred the weightless containers toward the shuttlecraft cargo hold.

Out of habit and good training, Zakariah kept his field of vision in constant motion, his eyes like quick searchlights and his brain absorbing data like a sponge. He studied the launch personnel, the passengers in line with him, the domelike architecture of the chamber, the emergency exits above and below. He located computer terminals and ran quick schematics of the electronics layout. He located main power cables and traced them up to the ceiling.

He was the first to notice the assassin drifting down from above.

By the time Zakariah decided to move it was almost too late. He correctly determined the Director to be the target of the assassin's trajectory and rushed to protect her. He vaulted himself over her, pushing her down and shielding her from the assassin's gunsight, and he was suitably rewarded for his effort. A metal projectile entered his upper back, passed through his body at an upward angle, and exited his left shoulder just under his collarbone, taking with it a spurting gout of blood and bodily fluids. The projectile itself spun harmlessly away, and the recoil from the weapon powered the assassin's quick escape up into a tangle of air pumps and ductwork near the ceiling. The lights went out.

The gunshot echoed directionless in the chamber in a staccato cluster. Emergency bulbs blinked on like Christmas lights in the darkness. A bleating alarm began to sound, and airlocks automatically powered down for vacuum protection. Green lights switched to flashing yellow as computerized safety systems began a rigid program of security containment. People screamed.

Most of the onlookers had never seen a firearm in use, on Earth or anywhere else. None had any experience with gunshot wounds on the human body. A few panicked outright and launched themselves, flailing, in various directions.

Helena immediately stanched Zakariah's wound with a hand on either side of his shoulder. A female flight attendant knelt beside them within seconds and stared in horror at the wound.

"Signal ahead for a medical crew," Helena ordered. "We'll get him in a capsule right away."

The attendant nodded and rushed to get events in motion. Another attendant, a red-haired boy barely out of Academy, appeared with a first-aid kit. He pulled out a small bottle that looked like a fire extinguisher.

"We'll immobilize for transport," he told her with hesitant authority.

She obediently withdrew her crimson hands from Zakariah's greasy red NASA jacket. "Oh, Zak," she whispered as small globules of blood began to erupt from his wound and float skyward. A spray of white foam quickly stopped the flow and solidified instantly on his shoulder. In seconds his upper body was encased in pink protective armour. Several more attendants congregated on the scene amid a cacophony of wailing alarms.

"Keep these people back. A man's been shot," a supervisor shouted. "Let's move," he directed, "one . . . two . . . up," and four men hoisted Zakariah with quick but fluid grace.

Helena was shouldered aside.

"Stand back. Remain calm," the supervisor told her. "We're shutting the Door down after this capsule." They drifted Zakariah aloft past screaming metal detectors and flashing red lights and settled him gently in a silver sarcophagus.

Helena tagged after. "You can't shut it down. I've got to go along with him."

"No one gets in or out. Standard procedures. We're locked down for emergency measures."

"For how long?"

"Could be days, for all I know. Stand back, please, ma'am."

"But we're travelling together."

"Stand back, please, ma'am."

The lid closed over Zakariah with a hiss of pneumatic pressure, shutting the circus of noise outside. In the darkness of his tomb, he clamped his teeth against incoming pain as shock began to subside. "Goodbye, Mia," he murmured, and he felt his capsule begin sliding toward infinity.

It was the same dream he always had—the tunnel, the long, serpentine tunnel that led him toward the superlight in the distance. He didn't want to see the light; he knew he couldn't bear it. He felt fear, an icy terror that paralyzed his lungs. It wasn't fair, he wasn't ready, and he had too much work to do back home where he had been safe and secure. He wanted to go back, he wanted to see his family and friends, but the dream was relentless, his speed accelerating, the pure white resplendence coming closer and closer. At this fiery throne all his mistakes would be tallied and final judgment pronounced. White lies and black lies, immoral thoughts and actions, a dollar sign, a decimal here and there—*not one jot or tittle of the law shall be overlooked*, a voice told him, and a chorus of heckling laughter echoed around him.

Sometimes he screamed and woke up, sweaty and twisted in his blankets; sometimes he clenched his spine and closed his eyes and felt the white light consume him like a dust mote travelling too close to the sun, a wisp of galactic vapour in the abyss, a passing shadow in a cosmic void. *And if I die before I wake*, he recited, a childhood mantra, *I pray the Lord my soul to take.*

FIVE

By the time Helena arrived on the other side of space and time, Zakariah's trail had grown cold. She stood fuming at the desk of a local NFTA administrator in a shuttle station just outside New Jerusalem, the largest and most populated city in the Cromeus colonies. The air was dry and searing, close to one hundred degrees Fahrenheit, and she felt sweaty and flushed in her thick flight suit.

"What do you mean there's no record? The man came through just a few days ago. He'd been shot. He was bleeding all over the place." She offered her bloodstained arms as evidence.

The administrator, a young man with fair hair and a breezy tunic, looked up at her but showed no concern in his eyes. "Well, there's also a small timewarp variance to account for," he said as he tapped his computer screen.

"What timewarp variance?"

"I'm told it's about three percent. I think it has something to do with the variable expansion of space, but I wouldn't want to overstep my bounds. I'm not a scientist."

"Time moves at a different rate? Are you kidding me?" Helena felt reality bend around her like rubber.

The young man leaned forward to scrutinize his computer screen. "Here it is. There was a medical emergency on the log three days ago. The data's locked out due to a security investigation." The administrator shuttered his eyes a few times, his demeanour at rest.

"Well, where is he now?"

The fair-haired man smiled vacantly and shook his head. "I don't know. The data's locked out."

"Do you have medical facilities here?"

"Not really."

"Are there hospitals in New Jerusalem?"

"Three."

"Any idea which one might have been used?"

He shook his head again. "I wouldn't want to overstep my bounds. I'm not a doctor."

Helena curled and uncurled her fingers as she suppressed an urge to throttle this pansy-ass bureaucrat. "Can you direct me to an information centre?"

The administrator hesitated for a moment, his lips grim.

"Perhaps I can be of some aid," said a man behind her in bright falsetto.

Helena whirled to face him, a tall man, thin, with a gracious smile. Wrinkle lines radiated out from his eyes toward a brush of silver at his temples and brown hair tucked behind his ears.

"My name is Ian Miller. I'm from the Overlords. We missed you at the spaceport. There seems to have been some mix-up at the Doorway. Conflicting reports." He offered an arm outstretched in greeting with a flowing genteel mannerism.

Helena took his hand and shook it firmly in a signal of strength, remembering her early days as a hungry businesswoman. "My travelling companion was shot. Zakariah Davis. He seems to have disappeared."

"Good heavens. So it's true. That is most distressing."

"I'm still trying to put the pieces together."

"Perhaps I can help. I have transportation passes for both of us. We could check the hospitals." His friendly smile showed large teeth evenly spaced. His face seemed relaxed with the mature confidence of his years, but his stance betrayed some caution, his arms rigid at his side and spine tilted away from her. She must look a sight, and probably smelled like a vagrant after three days stuck in orbit.

"Thank you." Helena allowed herself to be led away. Her flight suit now felt like a suit of armour in the stifling heat of New Jerusalem. She cast a scowl backward at the young administrator at his desk. She could not seem to get her bearings among these strange people. They appeared not to use the simple social signals that she took for granted among humans. Apart from Ian Miller, she had yet to see any evidence of empathy or basic commonality, as though natural instincts were held in check by some higher power.

"You must be from Earth," she said.

He smiled and nodded. "Forty-seven years ago. Is it still that obvious?"

"I'm just feeling a bit of culture shock. And this heat is unbearable."

"We'll stop at an outfitter and get you properly attired. You may want to trim your hair. It's the beginning of first summer in this hemisphere. I must apologize for the horrid local cosmos."

Helena smiled at that. The man was a delight.

They stepped through plate glass doors into a fresh blast of hot air on a transit stand high above the city surface. An electric tram waited on a monorail as passengers queued for entry. Ian Miller handed her a plastic laminate on a loop of cord.

"This is a diplomatic transit pass for use during your stay, courtesy of the Overlords."

"Thank you," she said but realized that her every movement would now be subject to scrutiny. She swallowed back a wave of paranoia. They climbed aboard and sat on padded bench seats. No seatbelts, no hand grips. The tram eased slowly forward and accelerated gently.

"There's no evidence of fossil fuels on any of the Cromeus planets," Ian Miller told her conversationally, "so no ground transportation. Lots of geothermal power and volcanic metals."

"I see." Helena looked down from their lofty perch, feeling vertiginous. The crowds on the street below looked like frothy silver bubbles under their glinting parasols.

"You don't want to be out in the sun unprotected," he added, noting her interest. "The umbrellas serve as power-cell generators and communications array. Our technology is unrivalled."

"Efficient."

Ian Miller nodded, his smile pleasant. "We do our best."

They made a short trip to a local outfitter, where Helena had her hair cut short and coiffed up from her forehead like a crown. Ian checked through hospital databases on his handheld until he found Zakariah's admission data. Helena purchased a silver tunic fitted at the neck, tight at the waist, with puffy sleeves to the elbow and an air-cooling system built into large epaulettes and vented at the back. With a sigh of relief, she pulled on silver dress pants, belted with elastic and tight at the ankle to trap in precious moisture.

They ate a quick meal of protein paste in a cafeteria that was little more than a vestibule outside New Jerusalem Central West Hospital. The spicy grey food was provided freely to all inhabitants from ubiquitous vending machines at the touch of a button. No one ever went hungry in the Cromeus colonies, and no animal ever suffered, thanks to a single factory producing cloned cattle musculature. Baseline nourishment had become a human right, rather than a privilege, although finer delicacies were certainly available for a price. The guided tour, Helena thought to herself as she listened to Ian Miller's reasoned discourse. She might have preferred a chicken salad but was grateful for the education.

They confirmed appointments and said polite goodbyes, and Ian ducked down a flight of stairs to a subway underneath the building. Helena made her way to an elevator and, after several false starts and little assistance from hospital staff, managed to locate the appropriate wing and ward. She found Zakariah wearing blue hospital pyjamas with his left arm in a sling, busy dismantling a portable computer system in his room.

"Helena," he said in greeting, barely glancing up. "Come and hold this for me."

She looked back over her shoulder and rushed to close the door behind her. She stepped forward and held a pair of needlenose forceps as directed.

"What are you doing?" she whispered.

"This is what they use for a V-net link up here. It's a simple jackbox." He tapped the plug outlet on the face of the machine. "We had these when we were kids. This one's been modified."

"Modified?"

"It's bugged."

"Oh."

"I charged it to your account. I signed for it with your scribble."

Helena nodded, feeling uneasy. "You saved my life," she said.

"Yeah, the guy must've been an amateur. Here, hold this." Zakariah handed up a small black hard drive on a ponytail of brightly coloured wires.

"What happened to your hair?" Zakariah finally noticed her makeover. "You look like a queen from the Emerald City."

"Oh, thanks. You look pretty cute yourself."

Zakariah nodded and rubbed his unshaven face. He looked more like an prison escapee than a professional field runner.

"Are you taking the bugs out?" Helena asked.

"No, we should go with what they give us for now, rather than show our hand early. I'll let them see what they want to see. No harm done." He beamed with sly confidence. "That way I can put a trace on the tracers. It's an old user corollary: where data goes in, data comes out. The first rule of gaming is to know the limitations of your hardware," Zakariah said. He sounded like a lecturer in front of eager-faced students. "Okay, slide that drive back between these two brackets here," he instructed. "You ready to jack in?"

"Already? I thought you'd be convalescing."

"What do you mean? Resting?"

"Oh, excuse me. I had a weak thought."

Zakariah smile seemed devilish. "C'mon, Helena, the Source is waiting for us. I've flashed the BIOS to allow for our peculiar logistics. We can use twin avatars or share, but not both at the same time. Just like back home. This wall console taps directly into the hospital's fiberoptic mainline." He pointed to slots for audio, video, feelie, or game interfaces.

"What's the second rule?" Helena asked hesitantly, fingering her V-net plug on its pendant earring.

"The second rule is that there are no rules." Zakariah offered forward a thin extension cable that looked like a spider web.

"I've already arranged for a meeting with the Overlords," Helena said. "Face to face."

The silver cable drooped between them.

"How archaic," Zakariah replied humourlessly. "Who are the Overlords?"

"They're the Eternal power brokers up here. They contacted me upon arrival. We're already on the fast track."

"I see," Zakariah said. "So I'm flying solo now."

"I'm in charge of the mission. You work for me."

"What's the problem with a little tactical reconnaissance?"

"All I'm saying is to take it slow until after my meeting. This may be a sensitive political negotiation."

"I've outlived my usefulness already?"

"I didn't say that, Zak."

Something was wrong. Helena could feel it. Their relationship had altered dramatically. "You saved my life," she said, wondering if that was the key.

Zakariah waved his wrist backhand. "Don't fixate on it. You would have done the same for me."

Helena stared at him thoughtfully. Would she have jumped in front of an assassin to save him? She doubted it. "Taking a bullet for someone is a big thing to ask. I can't believe you're so blasé about this. What sort of medication are they giving you?"

Zakariah stood up, his stance confrontational, bristling with energy. "I'm ready for action, Helena. We're still a team. We're hotwired together like Siamese twins. Go by land, if you want—that's fine. I'll go by sea and fish the deep waters. When we meet again we'll both be enriched."

Helena took two steps back at his outburst, studying his every move. He seemed haggard and desperate, like an addict looking for a quick fix. He was a V-net junkie, but it wasn't just the sustaining neurotransmission that he craved so badly. Not after only three days. This was something more, some dangerous, driving need.

"I want you to rest, Zak. I don't want you under any pressure. And I don't want any action taken in my name on the V-net or anywhere else. Do I make myself clear?"

"Crystal," he replied, his face a stern mask.

They eyed each other intimately, comrades in arms now suddenly unsure of the shifting sands under their feet. Helena imagined a young and crazy cowboy ready to jockey for power on a strange new electronic landscape, a chronic gamer looking for new thrills and bigger deals. She shook her head. They were both tired, both stretched out taut like piano strings tuned near the breaking point.

"Thank you," Helena said. Too much was at stake to gamble at this critical juncture, to risk losing control.

"You're welcome," Zakariah replied, but there was little assurance in his voice.

Niko loved the smell of Prime Five, the playground of the rich and famous. She visited only rarely, when her mentor, Phillip, deigned to summon her, but the fragrance of the place always

overwhelmed her. Some artsy animator had programmed Prime
Level Five with a perpetual wind of freshness. The air was not
flowery with blossoms, nor saturated with cologne like some
feelie queen on Main Street. The smell was much more subtle
than that but unmistakable, a pleasant breeze with a hint of
moisture and a whiff of negative ions.

She wondered why anyone would bother trying to mimic
these olfactory sensations in her brain, this delicate incongruity.
Why spend time and money on the trappings of nature in a digital wonderland? The higher levels of Prime were the domain of
the Beast, and Prime Five was under Class A encryption every
microsecond, the source code scrubbed and filtered, antiseptic
and precise. The Beast did not tolerate mistakes or shirk on capital budgets. Out of this expensive ether, her benefactor coalesced
in a Buddha pose, palms on splayed knees in a lotus position,
completely at ease and confident. "Hello, Phillip."

"Niko, good to see you as always. You're looking well."

"I've been working out, keeping the temple in good shape."

"I know. You're amazing."

"Something you need done on the ground?"

"No, just a pep talk today. How's the boy?"

"He's hardly a boy. He's got all the hormones of a grown
man."

"Is that presenting a problem?"

"Nothing I can't handle."

"Of course. So he's progressing?"

"He's learning fast. He's a bit impetuous."

"Good."

"If you say so."

Phillip paused as though considering another conversation.

Niko wondered if he was multitasking, splitting his avatar on some other Prime level. Even in person he kept his inner feelings hidden away, and his online presence was dispassionate at best, but he was her father, one petri dish removed. She trusted him without reserve.

Phillip blinked back to focus. "Any sign of the Davis gift?"

"He's bright, but he's no savant."

"I suppose it takes a war to bring out the big guns."

"You want me to push him?"

"No, just keep him happy for now. After a few more days off, we will begin preparations for our return package. You do good work, as always."

"What's our upside on this deal, Phillip?"

"Do I detect a note of dissatisfaction?"

"No, I'm happy to serve. I was just wondering how anything of value might arise from colonial backwaters. What could they possibly have that we can't make for ourselves?"

"They have freedom from legislation in the Cromeus colonies. They have sovereignty to work unrestricted by fear and have developed a microcosm of experimental innovation. Our terrestrial governments continue to strangle the future, to mire important technologies in legal quicksand. You will be well paid, Niko. You shall inherit the Earth."

"Great, just what I always wanted."

Phillip chuckled at her sarcasm, but Niko could tell his heart was not in it. He had an acute sense of wit but rarely showed any joy.

"At night we dream of System Intelligence. By day we fight."

Zakariah rode the datastream like a Viking, a man of heritage and brazen courage. The sense of movement was visceral, the vibration coarse and palpable, like driving a motorcycle on a gravel roadway at night, each speed bump a spy subprogram tracking his progress. Digital parasites. One by one Zakariah located the tracer codes and mirrored the intruders until he became completely invisible to their roving scrutiny. The alien tunnel was dark, confining, far removed from the wide open space on Main Street back home. This V-net substructure was cold and linear, perfectly ordered, completely artificial—to Zakariah, it was an outright sham. Without the expensive password in his pocket, he would surely have turned back long ago. He had been promised his heart's desire and more, and he had nothing left to lose.

Each tunnel segment could only be accessed at one end and exited at the other into a candelabra selection of new portals. There were no common hubs or free creative zones—just stale architecture and predictable patterns. Movement was slow and halting in this dark virtual world, a place where logic defied reason. Zakariah began to install programs of his own to widen his access—trapdoors and zoomtubes at critical junctures—but this work was tedious and time consuming and he had bigger games to play.

"So you finally got the bandits off your tail, slumlord." A leprechaun-like image suddenly appeared in front of him, smiling with mischievous confidence, young, bright-eyed, with a long nose and pointed chin. He wore a red toque with white trim and a skin-tight red jumpsuit.

Zakariah could feel the hum of quiet power from this strange avatar, the expensive aura of deep, stable harmonics.

"Who are you?" he asked, spreading a gossamer shield over his work in progress and throwing false access codes in the ether around him.

The red leprechaun smiled at his efforts. "I'm your fairy god-mother, slumlord. I'm the best thing that ever happened to you."

"Are you with the Overlords?" Zakariah replied, probing for any traces of the surveillance programs that had plagued him.

"Nope. I'm with you. The female get-up is great by the way. Very convincing."

Zakariah looked down at his feminine hands, Helena's hands. He became conscious of the weight of her breasts in front of him, and her regal stance. He felt at home in this avatar now, his second skin. The stranger could not have discerned the truth of his heritage without prior knowledge.

He decided to play it straight for a few moments to glean whatever data might be available. His only other choice was to close the connection before he lost all his own secrets. "Then you know I've been having some trouble with this new architecture."

"Yep. I had the same trouble getting acclimated Earthside. I'm going to upload my own configuration for you as part of our business agreement. Don't worry too much about scaling the ivory towers on your own strength. You're already in play. The Architect will contact you when he needs you. For now, I can only warn you not to trust him."

"Right," Zakariah said, nodding, understanding nothing. "What's in it for you?"

The red leprechaun shrugged. "I have my duty of course and will fulfill it with token heart. We are all pawns of convenience on some level, slumlord, and as a fellow slave to circumstance I can only warn you: a blessing never comes as you expect it, and the source of a curse can be difficult to pinpoint. Your delivery has already upset the balance of power. The Architect's getting ready to crack the walls of heaven weeks ahead of schedule."

A pipeline conduit coalesced beside the little man, and he offered it forward with slender fingernails sharpened to dagger points. Only programmers who used the new laserboard systems needed fingernails that sharp. Zakariah braced himself.

"The most vital decisions are yours to make, of course. You'll need everything here." The young man clamped the conduit to a sturdy table that materialized beside him. "Secure your domain. The upload will take several seconds."

Zakariah took a moment to shut down his feelers and close all the back doors he had painstakingly tunnelled in the crude alien landscape. He felt like a young slider again, gambling with destiny for the chance of a bigger gig uplevel. All hope of retreat had vanished a long time ago. "Okay, dump it," he said and opened his mind.

The torrent came like a horizontal waterfall, like liquid electricity under great pressure. At first he could barely hold steady against the onslaught, let alone breathe or attempt to make some sense out of the screaming patterns of raw data. Red lights of pain and green of comfort alternated with a crazy blue laser body wash that seemed to penetrate right through his trembling frame like an x-ray strobe light. Groping like a blind man, he struggled to feel the vibration, the deep core code on which he might begin to build compatibility. He began to panic when he noticed his shortness of breath, his elevated, giddy state of consciousness. He felt weak and desperate, fighting for survival in a cruel universe. He was vulnerable, too vulnerable. He clenched every synapse against the rushing flow of energy.

The hyperpulse hit him deep in the abdomen like a lifeline, a manic hum undergirding everything. He focused on it, isolated it, and shunted it to his program core, gasping for oxygen like a drowning man. The source code fit like a missing puzzle piece in his heart. He sighed with pleasure as the torrent slowed and transformed into a recognizable datastream, smooth as a lazy summer river. It felt like Prime Level Five back home, like true love.

When he opened his eyes, the leprechaun was gone.

Director Helena Sharp pushed open double doors to make her appearance before the Overlords. The meeting room was opulent by New Jerusalem standards. The floor covering of beige nylon fabric approached the texture of Earthside broadloom, a far cry from the grey synthetic panels that covered most floors in New Jerusalem. Sparse functionality gave place here to soft cushioned sofa chairs in a circle around an oval coffee table that framed a clear carafe of drinking water and white ceramic cups. Overlords occupied three of the four chairs. Ian Miller stood in respect as Helena entered the room.

"Let me be the first to offer my greetings for the digital transcript," he said grandly. "We greet you in peace on behalf of all Eternals across the galaxy."

"Thank you," Helena replied, ducking her head in polite deference as she approached. The walls were hung with textured tapestries that vaguely depicted deciduous leaves in rose and grey neutral tones. Two cameras pointed down from corner braces on the wall.

"This is Prelate Markord." Director Miller pointed to the

seated elder. "And Director Smith-Beauchamp," he said with an open palm to the third man already on his feet and bowing graciously. He looked up to a series of display monitors on the back wall where faces looked on via webcam. "I introduce Director Sharp from Earth."

"Your beauty is rivalled only by your reputation," said Smith-Beauchamp. He was a bulky man with bags of flesh at his cheeks and neck. His smile effused an aura of gentle trust.

As she shook his mammoth paw and exchanged pleasantries, Helena noticed a downcast glare from Prelate Markord at such undue civility. She felt tension in the room, an uneasy, artificial calm.

The elder Prelate cleared his throat and got right to the point. "As the Overlord Cooperative has expressed to you fully, Director Sharp, we are happy to share resources with the Eternal Research Institute of Earth and extend our hospitality to you personally." His voice was steady and measured, his spine ramrod straight in the soft chair. He appeared frail and impossibly old for an Eternal, completely bald, his skin wrinkled and folded. His nose was hawkish and pitted, his eyebrows mere wisps of white cotton. "However, it appears that you or some members of your party have used our good graces for evil intent by smuggling computer enhancements through diplomatic channels to our rivals." His blue eyes locked onto her own like daggers.

Helena froze in complete astonishment before the Prelate. A crowd of silent witnesses on the back wall glared down with stern faces and furrowed brows.

"I'm afraid I don't understand," she said.

The Prelate studied her carefully. "Three-dimensional rotaxane molecular chips in cylindrical arrays, something theorists on this side of the Doorway have only dreamt about."

As a surge of shock passed through her, Helena remembered appearing before a boarding-school principal as a young teenager on a planet far away. A group of classmates had taken lipstick from her purse and drawn crude slogans on the washroom mirrors. A tutorial assistant had discovered her holding the bent and bruised evidence and staring in disbelief at red-painted obscenities. Helena remembered standing in the hall outside the principal's office, waiting in anguish to be punished for crimes never committed. She remembered the hot sting of a rubber strap on her open palms, her tears of pain burning with holy injustice. She would not gladly pay for the sins of someone else again, in this world or the next.

"I assure you I have no knowledge of any wrongdoing," Helena stammered. "Are you absolutely certain?" she asked, her voice breaking with anxiety, her pulse throbbing.

Prelate Markord spread his hands. "We have traced the shipment precisely to your arrival. We still don't know how something so valuable could have passed through extensive security systems unnoticed. We have reports of a terrorist attack . . ." He left unspoken possibilities hanging.

Helena could not believe it. She thought of Zakariah. Had he tricked her somehow? Had he used her? Had he ruined everything? Here she was with hat in hand before the most powerful figure on the planet—before one of the apostolic Eternals, perhaps the first human to carry the virus—and all he wanted was to clap her in irons and send her away.

She hung her head in dismay. "May I sit down?"

"Certainly, certainly," said Ian Miller beside her, taking her arm and steering her toward the sofa seat nearest him and farthest away from Prelate Markord. "This whole situation has been very upsetting for all of us," he added, glancing quickly to the Prelate and back again. "The damage has been done, unfortunately. Blame will fall where blame is due."

Prelate Markord remained stolid and grim. He scrutinized Helena with icy, buttonhole eyes, looking for any weakness, for a sign. The two others sat and fidgeted while Helena collected her thoughts. Her skin felt clammy with perspiration and her fancy new tunic itched against her flesh. "These rivals you speak of . . ." she began, trying to imagine such a question.

Director Smith-Beauchamp was appointed spokesman by a twitch of the Prelate's eye. "A corporation in New Jerusalem has developed the technology to upload human intelligence to drive, thereby creating an immortal community of cyber-entities with questionable legal status," he said.

"Fantasists," Ian Miller interjected.

"This movement has been gathering resources and power for some time, and now with the illicit advancement recently gained, they could conceivably wrest control of the whole stellar system from the Overlords and our colony allies. Although the New World is a pure and free constitutional democracy, much of the true political power in the Cromeus colonies is informal, and the current question of balloting eligibility of the cyber-entities is perhaps immaterial." Smith-Beauchamp poured himself a cup of water and took a sip as a show of civility.

Helena had difficulty following the native politics, but the question of human evolution intrigued her. Uploaded human consciousness? Artificial intelligence? The dividing line between man and machine was becoming increasingly blurred. "But surely the Eternal virus is of infinitely more value than human technology, no matter how advanced."

"Of course," Director Smith-Beauchamp agreed. "We have no doubt whatsoever. The so-called life they offer is cheap and frivolous, an empty, bodiless experience. We are certain it is just a fad and will die out in due time."

"But in the short term," Prelate Markord interrupted, "we cannot allow the interests of the Overlords to be compromised in any way."

"Do you have media resources at your disposal? Spin doctors to market the Eternal virus more aggressively in response? What countermeasures have you taken to make the virus more accessible?"

"That is not within our bounds," Prelate Markord replied coldly.

Helena stared at him in surprise, feeling quiet panic growing in her abdomen. "Is the virus produced here in New Jerusalem?"

"No."

"Where, then?"

"We don't know."

"Impossible."

"No one knows the true Source of the virus. It is distributed by emissaries, most of whom know little or nothing beyond their own strict mission. The ampoules appear to the chosen at the times appointed. It is the Overlord policy not to interfere in any way. We provide all our resources as needed only upon request, as is our legitimate duty. We are servants, not masters. We are grateful for the grace of the universe, not scheming to manipulate powers that lay beyond us."

Helena shut her eyes against a massive wave of nausea as realization settled in her bones. Her long journey had come to an abrupt dead end. The Source was not in the Cromeus colonies. The Source was somewhere further out in the void of space, beyond her reach. She could feel death hovering near her like a bony spectre. Her body longed to cry out in pain, to release pent-up tension in a tide of cleansing remorse.

"You cannot trace the Source?" she persisted. "Triangulate and map intercept points over time?"

"We would consider such efforts to be blasphemous, Director," Prelate Markord stated angrily. "Whatever influence we might have exerted on your personal behalf, we have frankly withdrawn since your arrival. We know why you have come, Helena, and we cannot offer you what is not ours to give."

She jumped to her feet in response, trembling with rage. "I have come for Mother Earth," she said. "I have come for all Eternals. The virus must be made free and accessible to everyone, or Earth will continue to fester in violence and misery. You cannot sit up here wallowing in opulent self-righteousness while mankind destroys itself. The virus can bring brotherhood and peace in place of genocide and disease. The virus can bring renewal and rebirth instead of pollution and decay. The virus offers us infinity, and you cannot hoard it to yourself any longer!" Clutching her fists, Helena glanced quickly at the other two directors, swept a haughty glare across the row of watching monitors on the back wall, and stalked away.

She turned at the door and looked back to test the surety of this strange nightmare one last time. Ian Miller stood with a sad and resolute nod as the monitors blinked off one by one. Director Smith-Beauchamp bent to confer quietly with the Prelate.

Ian Miller caught up with Helena in the main foyer of the building as she took a protein pouch from a wall dispenser with palsied hands.

"You are absolutely right, Helena," he said.

She straightened her shoulders and brushed hair from her forehead in a pretense of dignity, but could find no voice.

"A cup of tea perhaps? There's a sitting room behind the reception desk. Perhaps we could have some further discussion." He offered an outstretched elbow.

Helena accepted and was led to a quiet chamber, an austere lunchroom with black plexiglass tables and vinyl chairs. A small kitchen in the corner offered coffee, tea, condiments, and a microwave oven. Ian Miller busied himself boiling two cups of water while Helena squeezed grey paste onto her tongue. She needed nutrients to steady her nerves. She needed strength.

"I must apologize," she said from across the table and began to dab her eyes with a paper napkin.

"Not at all, my dear." Ian Miller reached inside the breast pocket of his tunic and took a tiny bag of tea from a small purse. He dropped it in his steaming cup. "Earth tea," he said with a smile. "It cannot be replicated this side of the Doorway." He held up another bag with a query in his eyes.

"Sounds wonderful."

He dropped it in and stirred it with a spoon, letting the leaves steep in the heat. When the drink reached an appropriate shade, he removed the tea bag and handed her the cup. "What I tell you now, I will deny if pressed. I have sufficient resources to maintain my position despite your efforts," he said.

Helena brought her cup to her nose and hid behind it. "I understand," she replied. She breathed deep the gathering aroma.

"Your little speech leads me to confide in you, Helena. I agree with every word. The Overlords are too narrow-minded to survive the future. I am Eternal, you understand, but I could die at any time. An accident, an uncommon disease . . ." He took a sip of tea. "The Soul Savers offer true immortality that can never be taken away. I've been uploaded," he said. "In fact, I backup daily so that no new experiences are ever lost in either realm. I live in two worlds now, though waking life pales in significance to the wonders of augmentation. I can afford the best domain, the best of everything. I have a mansion prepared in digital space, a safe secure home with every human comfort. It costs much less than you might expect."

Helena made no response. She felt weary, bone weary and drained by her emotional meltdown.

"I know you will appreciate enhanced life once you've tried it, Helena. Please come with me to experience some of the common areas where visitors are allowed. We have developed technology beyond flesh and blood. The sights, the sounds, the smells—it's all there and more than you can imagine. We have artists who live inside their fantastic creations; we have poets who pursue their craft in expressions far beyond human language; we have lovers who entwine their passions unhindered by the crude limitations of biology. All aspects of human evolution find their grandest design in the worlds created by Soul Savers. We are the future of consciousness, and eternity is but a step away."

Helena stared into a face flushed with veracity, an inner spirit brimming with confidence. Uploaded immortality? Was this her future? Was this her only open door? "It sounds too good to be true," she said.

Ian Miller took her right hand between his cup-warmed palms. "You can live forever, Helena. Your quest has not been in vain."

As Zakariah watched in wonder, the black walls around him shimmered and twinkled and became pure transparent glass. Layer upon layer above and below were revealed, a perfect compartmentalized cube, a planned community. Zakariah could see everything in V-space, every figure, every action, every transient program code and macrofile. Invisible zoomtubes popped into place at precise intervals like elevators in an office complex. A musical symphony overwhelmed him, the sound of a thousand watchful eyes recording, correlating, and sending data downstream to a central nexus, a harmony of balanced order, an opera choreographed by one master.

On Earth the V-net had an organic functionality—it had holes, loopholes, empty places that no one bothered to code because they weren't needed yet. No programmer ever coded in a vacuum for the sheer joy of working, and why create a city in such precise cubist proportions?

The entire network was a chimera, a fraud. This V-space was an artificial construct, a trap. Worse yet, it was a means to an end, completely manipulated from above for some ultimate purpose, one order of magnitude removed, one leap of faith higher. He should have guessed. The perfect symmetry of the architecture. The difficulties he encountered programming alterations. The system was never designed to be free. It was a prison of the imagination. It resisted change by its very nature, and Zakariah knew he could never cooperate with the architect of such a system. He wanted risk and reward. He wanted piracy and punishment. He needed hope.

The Source. What about the Source?

Remembering his true mission, Zakariah roused himself to action. All the extant data lay before him, and the promised master key had been dropped into his lap. This was the smuggler's buried treasure, the chance of his lifetime. A new exhilaration gripped him as he dove for the nearest zoomtube and dropped to the data hub like an eel in oil. He quickly programmed search routines and rolled them out like fighter planes into the ether. They travelled east and west across an alien V-space, back and forth, inside and out, mapping the breadth and height of the Cromeus colonies in search of the Source—every reference, every nuance, every possible target.

They came up empty.

No cultivation labs. No power hungry marketers. No alien miracles.

Zakariah shivered.

There was no Source, not anywhere in this blighted solar system.

All the data hits led to the Overlords, an administrative collective of elder Eternals, but on close study it became apparent that they wielded no control, no critical initiative. They were hapless servants at best, pawns in a game they could barely imagine. Zakariah blanked out his subroutines in anger. Had he come this far to be turned back empty handed? Where was the Source? Does a virus appear out of thin air, out of the vacuum of space? Impossible.

Spent of all energy, Zakariah drifted back toward the home pathway to exit V-space at his appointed terminal, thinking about eternity, thinking about his family and the fabric of life. His crusade was over. He had risked everything and lost.

He met himself coming back. A five-foot-ten female Caucasian.

"You betrayed me, you disgusting bag of filth!"

"Helena, nice to see you, too. Don't come any closer. We can't operate twin avatars in the same place without feedback problems. You'll crash the system."

"Don't get technical with me, you traitor. We had an agreement."

Quickly Zakariah threw up an encryption screen like red velvet draperies around them, but he wasn't sure how long it might hold inside this glass menagerie.

"Don't worry. No one can trace anything directly to us," he said.

"How could you be so self-centred and careless? You've caused political, economic, and social chaos on this planet, and you've ruined whatever chance we had to negotiate with the Overlords and ultimately obtain an activated sample of the virus. You've compromised the whole mission!" Helena's image was stroboscopic with emotion, flashing with rainbow hues of colour and interspersed with static interference—a pulsating discharge of psychic energy. "We've come a long way together, but I am not going to take the blame for your treachery."

"No one can trace anything directly to us," Zakariah repeated, edging away from a gathering buzz of dissonance. Helena was getting dangerously close.

"How did you do it? The Macpherson Doorway is so small and so carefully guarded. How did you manage to drive a truckload of hardware through in broad daylight?"

"Your image is breaking up. Are you sure you're in a secure booth?"

"Don't play coy with me, you traitor. I'll wring it out of you in person if I have to."

Zakariah sighed. "I had a few trinkets sewn in the lining of my jacket. That's all." He spread his hands theatrically in a faint hope of peace.

"But how could you have known about the assassination attempt? How could you have known the medics would send you through without a standard security scan?"

"Everything was under control."

Helena stood frozen for a moment like a marionette with hanging jaw and bulging white eyes, her arms akimbo. "You hired someone to assassinate me!"

"No, no, Helena. Calm down." Zakariah threw another encryption screen around them, a deep purple, fluffy blanket of silence.

"Calm down? I could have been killed!"

"Helena, a professional assassin never misses his mark," Zakariah said, feeling an echo of pain in his shoulder as he spoke the words. "I was the target all along."

Helena's image blinked out and returned more solid, darker, her face an ugly mask of outrage. "You poor, misguided, devious soul," she said. "I want you out of my brain the moment we get back to Earth. You're fired, and you are going to jail forever!"

"No one can trace anything directly to us, Helena. I keep trying to tell you."

"I don't care!" she screamed. She reached up behind her left ear and yanked her V-net cable from its socket.

Zakariah could feel the agony of her system crash inside his own head, a toxic flash of pain as his twin avatar severed the connection. They were wired as one, and he had betrayed her.

"I'm sorry," he said to the deep purple darkness as his quest for the Source finally crumbled around him. He had failed his only son.

The baby, little Rix, lay balanced in the palm of his hand, so small, so helpless, insignificant to the universe, but more precious to him than all the chips on Main Street. Born five weeks premature and struggling for every breath, little Rix had broken every heartstring in a tired and desperate field runner. Zakariah had sworn to God that he would not watch his own son die, nor would he abandon his flesh and blood as his own father had done. On the altar of his soul, he had promised Rix the best medical care, the finest education, and the virus that would give him eternal life, the virus that Zakariah carried but could not transmit to his own dear son. Not by blood, not by tears, not with money or influence or power. How often had this promise come back to haunt Zakariah over the long years? How often had the cry of a baby called him back to the altar that now defined his existence? If a man makes a pledge and does not keep it, what is there left of a man inside him?

Back in realtime, back in the hospital ward beside his jury-rigged jackbox, Zakariah stared at a blank wall and tasted absolute defeat for the first time in his life. But in the core of manifold bitterness he found a scent of honey, a cathartic epiphany of cleansing, to let his purpose go, to finally let fate have its bumbling way.

He showered leisurely and shaved off his beard and checked himself out of New Jerusalem Central West on a temporary pass. At the nearest restaurant he was able to obtain credit in the Director's name. He ordered the most expensive item on the menu, a prime rib garnished with orange vegetables that seemed to be a hybrid cross between carrots and potatoes. His left arm was still in a sling, but the young waitress was kind enough to cut his meat for him and speak at some length. She explained in detail the foodstuffs and spices that had been used to prepare his meal and told him the roast was beef, from a genuine cow grown in a sealed terrarium, but it tasted gamey to Zakariah, with an acrid, lingering tang.

The sun had already set under twin moons, but the city remained torrid and grimy from the day's heat and dust. The air seemed thick and difficult to breathe, even in the restaurant where air conditioning equipment roared continually in a vain attempt to create a comfort zone. The young waitress, Jasmine, promised a midnight rain that washed the streets daily, but Zakariah could not stay awake long enough to see it. His food had been drugged, and Jasmine cradled his head gently as he fell forward onto the table.

SIX

Niko threw up the garage door with the aplomb of a magician. She was wearing her biker leathers, so Rix knew they were going for a ride. She spread her arms with a flourish to point at two motocross racers with grimy rims and knobby tires. Beside Niko's familiar red bike stood a blue twin, looking like an animal ready to pounce, the front fender high up above long shock-absorbing forks. A jumping bike. A dirt screamer.

"It's not new, exactly, but it's not stolen. It's all yours."

"Cool." Rix stepped forward to inspect his new bike. It reminded him of a feline in motion, a blue jaguar. He trapped a brimming smile with pursed lips. Don't gush. Don't show any emotional weakness. "You could have shined it up a bit."

"It's not your birthday, is it? Just get on." Niko picked up his helmet from a shelf along the wall and tossed it to him. "Manual shift, one down, five up, just like mine."

"No electric start?"

Niko grinned. "Don't be a wuss."

Rix pulled on his helmet and strapped it under his chin. He unscrewed the gas cap and found a reflection close to the top. "Where to?"

"Tower Hill. It's a dirt trail out in the boonies. Just follow me."

"Am I street legal on this thing?"

"No. I didn't bother with the fine details. We'll head off-road if we spot a patrol."

Rix kicked his starter down, and the bike barked to life on the first try. He revved it up with just a touch of the throttle and felt a pulse of hot power between his legs. He tipped it side to side to check the balance and pressed down on the handlebars to gauge the resistance on the front shocks. He nodded his eager satisfaction to Niko with what he hoped might pass for boyish charm.

She strapped on her helmet and kicked her bike to life. She revved it twice and popped her clutch on the third count. Her bike lurched like a tiger out of the gate and made it halfway down the driveway before the front wheel touched ground again. She spun a sliding turn out into the road and booted it up the boulevard.

Rix eased his bike into gear and followed her with care. The last thing he needed was to wipe out at the end of the driveway like an idiot. If he was going to score with this chick, he had at least to look respectable on two wheels. No point in taking any chances until he got the feel of the new machine.

They headed out of the suburbs and past the perpetual construction zone of urban sprawl, out into the rural badlands of abandoned farms and tilted realtor signs. Soon they were off-road on a rutted dirt pathway heading north. Niko was showing no mercy and eating up the ground ahead, climbing rocks and jumping over decaying tree trunks. Rix could feel his bones beginning to ache with the pounding vibration of the landscape, but he dared not slacken his pace. His hair was plastered with sweat in the back of his helmet.

He caught up with her finally. She stood beside her dormant bike and tipped up a squeeze-bottle of nutrient water. Her helmet perched backward on the seat like a shiny black beetle. He idled up beside her and shut off the ignition.

"Hey, slacker," she said and tossed her hair with a quick shake.

Rix flipped up his visor. "Got tired of breathing your exhaust."

"Sure."

"We parking?"

"Yeah, let's grab a snack." She pulled an energy bar out of a side pocket and held it up in invitation.

Rix pulled off his helmet and took a deep breath through his nose. The country air smelled pungent. "It stinks."

"There's a swamp on the other side of this ridge. Come and take a look." Niko headed up a rocky slope.

Most of the trees were dead or dying, their denuded limbs grotesque against the bright blue sky. Rix suspected some new bug, some imported caterpillar with no natural predators. So much for global Earth. A few coniferous saplings were pushing up into the vacuum, sucking the sunshine like newborn babes. In a few more years the rocks would be green again, another cycle of life underway.

The air was hot and dry, and the lichen crunchy underfoot, like walking on stale toast. The sound of his boot heels seemed amplified by the stillness, a harsh grinding noise. A wafting breeze grew more fetid as they approached the summit.

"It smells horrid," Rix said as he caught up.

Niko laughed in response. "You are such a city slicker."

A narrow lake stretched out between two ribs of bedrock, with dead tree stumps sticking up above the surface. Rix felt his face wrinkle with displeasure. "What is that smell?"

"It's just bog. This is a beaver swamp. It's a secret lake. The beavers build dams to hold back the creek water. It's hardwired into their brains when they hear a trickling noise. Eventually the water backs up and makes a lake."

"It kills the trees."

"They eat the trees. That's what beavers do. Their front teeth keep growing, so they have to keep chewing to wear them down. Look, there's one over there." Niko pointed with delight in her eyes at a dark blob moving in the water. "Sit down," she directed. "If we're quiet, he might come in close."

They made themselves comfortable on the rock and peeled foil wrappers off nutrient bars. Niko offered a water bottle and Rix took a deep slug to wash the dust out of his throat. "So this is it?"

"Just a pit stop. You don't like the view?"

Rix shrugged. "I dunno. I thought maybe we were goin' on a mission. You know, smugglin' stuff."

"Not today. This is our down time. Just kick back, man. You're too tense. Want to smoke a joint?"

"No, I'm good."

"Phillip used to bring me here when I was a kid. I got attached to the place."

"My grandfather?"

"The same."

"I never met him."

"Maybe some day. He's a busy guy."

Rix scanned the horizon with more care. The exposed granite looked grey and barren but for a few tufts of brown grass and weeds. The dead deciduous trees stood like a regiment of scarecrows along the horizon. Only the lush green coniferous trees gave evidence of life, verdant spruce and long-needled pines, the next generation.

"Why here?"

"Why not?"

"Was he trying to teach you something?"

"I don't know. I guess so."

"Well, what do you like about this place?"

Niko turned her head to face him. She swallowed the last bite of her energy bar and folded the wrapper into a pocket in her leathers. "I feel connected to something out here. Something primeval. I feel part of some grand design, that I'm not just the product of a test tube, you know?"

"Our friend's coming in pretty close," Rix whispered, looking past her. The beaver seemed to be dragging something. A stick poked up out of the water at an odd angle and seemed to move along with him. "What's he carrying?"

"He's got a tree branch in his mouth. He's taking food home to the nest."

"You can see that?"

Niko tapped beside her right eye. "Digital zoom. It's new."

The beaver's bulky frame moved fast through the water, his head barely above the surface. He swam past them, close to shore, and continued on down the lake.

"People think they work all the time. You know . . ." Niko held her fingers up to indicate quotation marks. ". . . like busy beavers. But I've seen them play. I've seen them lock their snouts together and wrestle. Could be some sort of mating ritual."

"Have you ever seen them have sex? Do they do it like dogs, or what?"

A look of condescension flashed across Niko's face and was quickly disguised with a smile. "I'm sure I don't know. Is that all guys think about?"

Rix winced at the barb. If she knew how much he had secretly longed for her, she would probably slap his face and leave him in the dust. He could never confess his love for Niko. He could never reveal his midnight fantasies. "Yeah, whatever," he said.

Niko shrugged off any offense. "They look pretty comical up on dry land, waddling their fat asses around, or scratching themselves with their huge hind feet. Their front paws are small, with long, curving talons like fingers. They can rotate a branch while they chew the bark off. I think they're fascinating."

"Well, where are they? It must take an army to dam up this much water."

Niko glanced up, checking the position of the sun. "It's too early. They come out at dusk. But we've got to get a move on to make Tower Hill today."

Rix jumped up. "Bonus," he said, eager to get away before he said something really stupid. He could hardly keep himself from touching her when they sat in such proximity.

Niko seemed to have lost some of her energy as she rose. Her cheeky charisma had worn thin to betray a pensive frown. She dragged her shoulders back and stretched her arms.

"Hey, I totally grok the nature thing," Rix said. "Just so you know. Thanks for sharing this special place with me."

Niko's lips curled to one side as she quickly regained her natural insouciance with a tilt of her eyebrows. "Now don't get all geeky on me." She swung her helmet up and started back toward her bike.

Rix followed dutifully, watching her slim body in motion. Nice butt.

The blat of their bikes broke the tranquility like a bad dream. Their fumes fouled the air. They sped off down a narrow cross-country trail into a heavily forested area where tiny blue caricatures of a winter skier marked the direction. In the aftermath of momentary serenity, enclosed now in a canopy of leaves, the noise seemed to Rix like a hell of a racket. No wonder the wild animals waited until dusk to come out and play.

Tower Hill was a precipice. The path turned up on an exponential curve that seemed to approach infinity. The incline appeared to curl over at the summit, an impossible angle. They sat on their bikes at the base of the behemoth and looked up.

Rix took off his helmet. "No way," he yelled. "It's an overhang."

Niko flipped up her visor. "It's not an overhang. It's just an optical illusion."

"No skier ever went up there."

"We're not on skis."

"Have you ever seen anyone up there?"

"Not an actual person, but I've seen fresh motorcycle tracks, cigarette butts, condoms."

Rix squinted narrowly at her and pressed his lips. Was this some sort of macho test? Some weird mating ritual of an advanced species? He turned back to his bike and pulled on his helmet. He looked up Tower Hill. If he waited any longer, she would go first to show him off. Then she'd laugh at him from the top as he made his foolish efforts. No way. Far better to crash and burn early and be lavished with her sympathy. He kicked into gear and lurched ahead with a quick wheelie. He spun a turn in front of her and kicked up a spew of dirt and dust. She flipped down her visor.

Rix doubled back down the path to set up for his climb. He needed a good straight acceleration lane if he had any hope in heaven of getting to the top. The path was a bare crevice up the side of the mountain, with mature trees on either side. Any deviation would be painful.

He felt a strange erotic urge, a rush of testosterone in his blood. He could imagine the pinnacle of success. He could envision it in his mind's eye. The air would be clear up there, and pure, and a fresh breeze would tousle his hair.

He gunned it.

Metal screamed under him, an extension of his own mortal body. He gathered speed like a rocket. He caught a bit of air on a small bump in the path, but he held his trajectory firm and hit the base of the mountain right on target. The fight of gravity against him was like an extra g-force as he turned upward. He drove up over the handlebars, straining for balance, throwing the bike where he wanted it, but his back tire spun briefly on a rock and he knew he was doomed.

Momentum took him higher, but he had lost the critical edge of acceleration. His front tire was above his head and barely touching terra firma.

The world cartwheeled, and for a vulnerable moment he lost all reference to the skyline.

From that point on he could only hang on to the bike and hope it didn't land on top of him. The engine whined frictionless and went silent as his hand slipped off the dead-man throttle.

He landed on his visor, and grit pushed up into his mouth as he slid on his helmet. The bike crashed down beside him and slid on leaves and debris until the handlebars caught on a rock.

He lay immobile in the sudden silence, testing his bones one by one. Everything seemed intact, so he sat up and looked back down the hill.

Niko was already off her bike and climbing.

Rix smiled.

The Soul Savers complex stood on the highest hill in New Jerusalem, glistening like a silver jewel on the northern plateau. The grey quartz bricks in its construction had been imported from an airless asteroid, a regularly baked and frozen geological treasure-house that orbited on a long elliptic around Cromeus Signa. The building dominated the landscape like a crystal cathedral, a place of pride and worship and mystery revealed. Its regal spire towered grandiose and majestic like a lighthouse above the square cinder-block architecture of the city.

Over the glass entrance doors, supported by heavy metal brackets, two upright palms protected a white dove in flight. Helena stared up at the sculpture for a few moments, wondering if the dove was being released and flying away, or in the process of being corralled and coddled. She couldn't decide.

A young man at the reception desk kept his eyes downcast and murmured barely audible responses to Helena's questions. He found her scheduled appointment and opened the appropriate door with a finger touch, then swivelled his chair back to his computer terminal in dismissal. Helena dramatized her thanks to the point of parody, having grown weary of this quiet and chronically reticent culture, safe in their serfdom to an invisible master. Where was the natural ambition of the human species, the driving force of progress? She had expected a new breed of pioneers on the frontier of space and had found contented automatons instead. Was this the future?

Ian Miller met her in the appointed briefing room, having arrived discreetly by an underground entrance. He introduced two female technicians by their first names only, Kathrin and Louise, and ushered Helena into a private cubicle full of electronic imaging equipment. A reclining chair sat in the centre of the room underneath a large silver helmet that looked like a full-coverage hair dryer. A track on the floor trailed from the chair to the large black orifice of a body scanner.

"The neural helmet enables us to upload total brain activity in three dimensions," Ian Miller explained, "and to this we add complete biometric schemata to produce the complex physical and emotional responses of true life." He pointed to scanning equipment inside a coffin-like enclosure. "This holistic approach to humanity has been lacking in the common V-space environment, but our breakthroughs in technology enable us to capture the elemental human spirit—physical, mental, and emotional."

"Is that what you call a 'saved soul,' Ian?" Helena peered up inside the neural helmet at a mesh of wires and laser probes.

"It's a complete record of brain experience and bodily life. I would say that constitutes a soul."

"In the religious sense, the word denotes an entity distinct from the body."

"What? A ghost?" Ian Miller chuckled. "Come now, Helena.

All human experience resides in the brain; we both know that. Personal identity, memories, dreams, cognition—just look at the dysfunctional states caused by injury or disease, the personality changes due to strokes or drug use. Can you name one facet of experience not produced by the human brain?"

"Oh, I don't know. Intuition? Near-death experiences?"

"Both of these have been produced by artificial brain stimulation, as has the transcendent ecstasy associated with common faith systems. Nowadays, you can buy religious experience from a plug-and-play dispenser. A near-death experience is subjective science at best. Did you know that a severed head can see and hear for fifteen or twenty seconds? It doesn't mean anything."

Helena was unconvinced by the uber-technology around her. She had never been a student of religion or the occult; she fancied herself a scientist, a phenomenologist, a reasonable woman.

"I think a near-death experience and an after-death experience might be qualitatively different," she said as she watched the two technicians power up computer systems at two distinct control centres.

Machines began to hum and whine around them.

"When you unplug, Helena, your V-space experience dies. Likewise, when your brain stops, you stop—unless your soul has been saved. The Helena Sharp that we both know now is merely an electrochemical pattern of energy that is subject to deterioration and decay. A reborn Helena Sharp will be a superwoman, a hard-drive reality that will live forever. It's up to you, of course."

"I have an open mind, Ian. I'm just not convinced that life is as simple as you describe, that it can be reduced to source code and sent along a fiberoptic cable."

Ian Miller nodded and gestured toward the silver couch. "The proof, as they used to say back home on the isle, is in the pudding."

Helena set her lips with resolve and sat down. She buckled herself in with a wide belt across her waist and settled into a comfortable position. Ian Miller clasped her wrists and ankles to supporting arms with velcro straps.

"Are you coming along?" she asked.

Ian's face twinkled with amusement. "I'm already there. I'll meet you on the other side; don't worry."

The neural helmet slowly descended to fit snugly to her shoulders. Black foam pads pushed toward her eyes, forcing them closed. A hiss of regulated air whispered on her nostrils. She heard the click of needles and wires around her and felt lasers tickle her scalp. Her pulse quickened with anticipation. She thought about her father, whom she remembered only as a shadowy archetype, a baby's image of a loving giant, long dead now and far away. In heaven, she had been told as a child. In heaven far away.

Pleasure fell like rain around her. A heavy, palpable feeling of goodwill enveloped her like a blanket. Pure joy burst forth from her solar plexus, lifting her burdens far beyond her weary shoulders, taking her pain away, cleansing her mind of distrust and misery and all other fetters of humanity.

Ian Miller stood in front of her, as real as real could be.

"This is but a foretaste of a full upload," he said. "Follow me through the gate on your right into First Nirvana."

Obediently Helena stepped forward, marvelling at the brightness around her, the vivid colours and natural beauty. Trees grew alongside the walkway, real trees with real leaves that fluttered gently in the wind. Real butterflies floated above scented blossoms of pink and purple hue. The grey flagstones beneath her feet had been weathered by time and tinged with green mildew and white lichen. This new world seemed far superior to the V-net with its sterile props and caricature streetscapes. This world was complete, solid, and faithful like an old friend.

"The trees have long roots that reach down deep into the earth below," Ian said, noting her interest. "No programming expense has been spared."

His words broke her free from a spell of wonderment. This world was an artificial paradise, an illusion. She touched scaly tree bark with her fingertips. "Someone has made a huge investment."

Ian Miller waved backhand at the thought. "Money is nothing to Soul Savers. Our resources are limitless. We control the Macpherson Doorway, and we have what all Earth desires and will pay anything for—immortality. Those who upload early will have favoured positions in Heaven. We do not offer a simple life of ease to people like you, Helena. There are administrative responsibilities and much work to be done. You and I are not the type to lay on a beach and count grains of sand. The life we have created is the life we wish to preserve eternally, not someone's idea of false bliss from a vacation catalogue. Am I correct?"

"I suppose so," Helena said, musing.

Inside First Nirvana, her sense of joy became even more intense, like a numinous bubble threatening to burst inside her. She felt that she might break into song at any moment, into choruses of praise to the guardians of this magic place.

"We have a simplified menu for guests," Ian Miller said, pulling down a chart from the ether around him. "Horseback riding, ice skating, mountain climbing, or sky diving. Virtually every other facet of human existence is available to residents. Our programmers never rest. A Saved Soul never needs to sleep or be refreshed. A Saved Soul works and plays at the same time. We live and enjoy for all eternity. What's your pleasure today?"

Helena had raised a horse in her youth and was an accomplished equestrian, so she chose to visit the riding stables first. She found her long-dead steed, Night, standing sleek and black in his stall waiting for her, waiting all these years across the galaxy for her to brush him again and whisper gently in his ear.

At first, the shock of seeing him resurrected made her pause with clinical detachment. How could this be happening? What interactive mechanism had pulled this memory from her psyche and brought it to life before her eyes? But in time she gave up her feeble attempts at explanation and began to relax and enjoy the drama. The feel of Night between her legs again, his strong and stable body as he vaulted effortlessly over fences and fresh bales of sweet-smelling hay, obliterated all apprehension and fear, as though this world had been created for her unique pleasure, a composite of her own desires and recollections, a dream come true.

Ian followed beside on his own horse, a rare white Arabian that matched Night's every move with uncanny prescience. Together they raced across the landscape, challenging every hill and conquering every obstacle. They spoke only to the horses, encouraging them with love and wonder, as the four creatures danced in an intimate union that seemed almost telepathic. An hour later, sweaty and exultant, they rested the horses in a forest glade where a spring-fed stream bubbled down a rocky escarpment. They lay on a bed of thick moss watching a parade of clouds roll by above them. Their hands clasped together and their eyes met in earnest.

"Could it really be like this forever?" Helena asked. "It seems so lifelike—much better than life, every detail so intense and meaningful."

"Biology served merely to introduce us to reality," Ian Miller said. "Like the butterfly emerging from its chrysalis, we have been born again into transcendence."

"What of the Eternal virus, then? You've experienced both worlds."

Ian Miller sat up on one elbow to face her. "The virus prolongs life, it is true, but it also prolongs the agony of life, the heartbreak and tragedy of bodily existence. The struggle, the pain, the rampant imperfection. Helena, my darling, no matter how long the prelude lasts, and how wonderful the sound, when the true symphony begins all else is forgotten."

He smiled with confident ease, as though they had been lovers for years, and tilted toward her. She raised her chin to him and their lips met with bold certainty.

Zakariah awoke groggy with the lingering burden of drugs in his body. He recognized weightlessness in his abdomen. A series of straps confined him to an acceleration couch in the passenger section of a small shuttlecraft. In the dim light he saw that the other fifteen couches were empty.

He reached up to the control console above his head and tried a few buttons. A wave of fresh air spun down at him, a tiny spotlight illuminated his lap, and an amber light flashed on, signalling the cabin crew that he was awake.

A young man in a green flight uniform came through an aperture up front. The Soul Savers logo looked like two red snakes intertwined on his left breast. "We're just getting ready to land. Please remain buckled, sir."

"Where are we?" Zakariah mumbled, his saliva thick inside his rubbery mouth.

"Babylon. Fourth planet out from Cromeus Signa," the flight attendant said, businesslike. "Soul Savers has a research outpost here. Big stuff, expensive."

Zakariah prolonged eye contact with the man, his brows raised in query.

"The captain and I do a supply run out here every week. Lots of techno-wizards come and go. You're the first civilian passenger we've seen. You had a bit too much to drink last night, so the story goes." His expression said that he did not believe the story, that nothing would surprise him. "Just a couple of minutes and you'll be able to freshen up in the showers, sir. The cafeteria's one of the best outward from New Jerusalem. You'll not be disappointed."

At the green light Zakariah disembarked freely like a visiting tourist. He followed the crew to the showers and blasted drugs from his brain under a deluge of hot water. He traded in his hospital-issue clothes for a set of green coveralls from a wall dispenser and shaved a lost day's worth of stubble from his face. Clean and refreshed, he found his way to the cafeteria and got in line behind a milling crowd of workers. He loaded up a tray with pancakes and pastries and coffee and grapefruit juice and found himself at an automated check-out terminal with no ID badge to swipe. He tried typing Helena's name into the keypad. When that didn't work, he tried: Eternal Research Institute.

A cafeteria worker sidled over, a young woman with a finger on her earphone and pink on her cheeks. "Lost your card?" she asked.

"I just got off the shuttle and I'm a bit disoriented," Zakariah told her. "They told me I could eat." He shrugged and offered her a puppy-dog smile.

"Excuse me," the woman said and turned away mumbling into her shoulder mike.

Zakariah picked up a croissant and nibbled on it. There was no point in bolting for the door. He was trapped in a closed system and would have to live with it.

The woman turned back to face him. "Your code is ZEN101, sir," she whispered as she punched it in. "Unlimited credit," she hushed with a knowing smile.

"Those are my favourite two words," Zakariah said. "What is there to buy up here?"

The woman laughed and seemed genuinely intrigued. "Not much. We don't get a lot of visitors. You can sit over here." She shuffled him out of line to make way for other workers. "You don't look like a Babylonian. You from the inner colonies?"

Zakariah shook his head and sat down as directed. "Earth," he said. "Have a seat?"

She glanced quickly behind her and decided she could spare a few seconds. She appraised Zakariah from a safe distance across the table. Her eyes darted to his V-net plug and back to his face, enlightened. "Wow. Long way from home."

"Well, I hope it was worth the trip. Some pretty decent hardware upstairs, I hear."

"Incredible stuff." She bent forward with wide eyes. "I haven't actually seen the photonic accelerators, you know. But

I've heard some talk from the white-room boys." She nodded with pride. "State of the art and beyond. If something goes wrong, it could blow this whole planet out of orbit."

Zakariah smiled conversationally but felt his stomach twisting with discomfort again. "I wonder if they have a permit for that."

The woman laughed pleasantly. "I'd better get back. You have a nice day. I'm off at eighteen Signa, if you're not busy later."

Zakariah tilted his head, politely noncommittal. "I'll check my schedule."

After a good breakfast, he began to feel human again. He set off in search of some reasonable explanation for his presence in this outpost. Forcible detention was no laughing matter in any solar system. Surely there were legal statutes and greysuits to enforce them.

He walked through a maze of underground tunnels and chatted with anyone who seemed to have the time to notice him. He learned that the entire complex had been carved into the side of a mountain, the planet's surface harsh and forbidding, the temperature rarely above the freezing mark. Although it fell officially within habitable parameters, Babylon was home to only a few thousand families in three major outposts.

There appeared to be some good base metal deposits, according to airborne geophysical reports and preliminary drilling, and perhaps some traces of more strategic metals, but the Soul Savers complex was not concerned with mining or mapping or any traditional colony activity. They were building a gun, one janitor told Zakariah, that could punch a bullet through the fabric of space-time.

Zakariah began to get agitated. Had he been conscripted for

war? Hijacked for some military subterfuge? He continued his explorations and stumbled upon the company commissary, where he traded in his hospital slippers for a new pair of shiny black flight boots, top of the line and as comfortable as track shoes. He noticed a section of toques and other winterwear along the back wall. He picked out a red one with white trim and fingered it thoughtfully. The red leprechaun had been here.

He took off his sling and pulled a brown cardigan over his weak shoulder with little pain. He added black thermal gloves to his new wardrobe and a heavy black flight jacket with faux fur collar and foldaway hood. Then he pocketed an outdoor survival kit with matches and hardtack. At the automated cashier, he typed in ZEN101 and sauntered away like a department store supershopper.

Zakariah made his way upward, level by level, toward the pinnacle of the mountain, charting his pathway into memory, checking for air ducts, cargo elevators, any means of escape. At Restricted Access doors along the way he punched in ZEN101 to see what would happen. Some opened and some didn't, so he knew he didn't have carte blanche in this place. He was leaving a digital trail behind him like bread crumbs, but he didn't care. He needed hard information and was prepared to pay the price to get it.

At the top of the mountain he ran into heavy security—steel, bulletproof doors painted with yellow and green parallel lines and the red symbol of a hand signalling halt. He found three of these doors in three adjoining hallways and tried his ZEN101 code in each one to no avail. A fourth door hissed with pneumatic pressure and irised open. His breath caught in his throat. He felt like a crude beast being led gate by gate to the slaughterhouse.

His pulse hammered as he slid through the portal into a dark control room beyond. Banks of mainframe hardware lined three of the four walls, and two rows of computer monitors made semi-circles facing a fourth surface of black glass, possibly a window or digital monitor. He inspected some of the equipment and communication devices. It looked like a satellite launch system of some sort, certainly far more sophisticated than a simple spaceport tower. Was this the war room?

Zakariah sat down in one of the chairs, tipped it back comfortably, put his new boots up on the control console, and powered up one of the hard drives. A hum of life sounded through his board; a monitor turned phosphorescent and revealed a string of code as the mainframe booted up. He logged into the database and typed in his name. His picture appeared onscreen. He could not remember the last time he had posed for a photograph in realtime, but there it was. The caption underneath read: Zakariah Davis, Pilot, Alpha and Omega Project. A biography followed, somewhat terse but flattering. He exited back to the main menu and typed *Alpha and Omega*.

"I am so pleased to make your acquaintance finally" came a resounding male voice from every speaker in the room.

"Well, I just thought I'd drop in to see how you were making out," Zakariah responded drily.

"Yes, very good."

"Who are you?"

"I think you know."

"You're the Architect."

"As good a name as any."

"You're not—now how shall I put this delicately?—you're not currently inhabiting a human body."

"No, I've grown far beyond that now. The biological incubation period was very short in retrospect."

"Macpherson?"

"Excellent work! You have earned your reputation, sir." All the monitors in the control room suddenly blinked into action, and Macpherson's smiling face beamed from every one, a face Zakariah had seen in textbooks and holovids as a young student, a face dead and buried over a hundred years ago. His forehead stood bold and shiny above great mothlike tufts of eyebrows, his grey hair heavy at his temples but thin and sparse up top. His cheeks were hollow, his chin long and pointed, and his nose narrow and finely chiselled. His eyes were black beads, lifeless and artificial in a gaunt, cadaverous face.

"You don't need me," Zakariah said. "You've got everything sewn up here already."

The speakers emitted a harsh grating noise that might have passed for laughter in some circles. "I envy you humans, sometimes, the random causality, the flights of fantasy, the necessary friction that binds a personality together. Sometimes you say the darndest things."

"Okay, what's the run?"

"Just what you've always wanted, what you were destined for from before the creation of the world."

"Spare me the hyperbole."

"The Source, good buddy. Just you and me."

Zakariah shivered at the sound of it. He'd known it in his heart of hearts since he landed on Babylon. He'd known it all along. "I'm listening," he said.

"It's been a long time since I constructed the Macpherson Doorway, but my continued study of the wormhole phenomenon led to an interesting discovery. The Source uses tiny wormholes to transport the Eternal virus to mankind from outside our big-bang universe. This suggests the possibility of a multiverse or some alternate existence where our cosmic guidelines and constants may not have effect. And these are not naturally occurring quantum wrinkles like the Doorway itself, oh no. These are holes shot through a brick wall by sheer and incredible force. Each one of these wormholes requires more energy than has ever been produced by human effort. Utterly fantastic events that defy the imagination. Naturally I wanted to give it a try myself."

Zakariah chuckled in disbelief. "You're going to harness enough energy to blow up a planet in order to shoot me to a cinder on the other side of space and time."

"That sounds rather dramatic and is certainly not the case. At great personal and corporate expense, I have constructed a photonic phaser that will open up the merest pinpoint in the dimensional fabric for a scant forty-five seconds. A peephole, you might say. We're going to send in a digital stream of entangled quantum particles with a wide-spectrum communications protocol to record whatever visual, audio, or digital data may be available. It's pure scientific research, quite respectable in theory and practice, I assure you."

"Why?"

"Well, because it's there. Isn't that what science is all about? Isn't that what separates us from the monkeys, my friend? From the dinosaurs?"

Zakariah shook his head. "So snap a few pictures for the family album. You don't need me."

A coarse static of laughter grated in the room once again. "Ah, but there you are wrong. You are the kingpin in the whole plan. What can we really expect from the other side? A digital scream at best, a blast of raw data. No, we need an interpreter, an assimilator of meaning. You passed the test with flying colours when you plugged into my private V-net architecture. It took me years to code and encrypt that virtual world, but you sussed it out in a matter of seconds, without mechanical aid or conscious forethought. You have a feel for it."

"I almost died."

"Well, yes, that may be the logical outcome."

"You're crazy."

"You cut me to the quick, my friend. I know you've wondered where the Eternal virus originates. You've patterned your life on finding out. You're a victim of your own expectations, as we all are in the end. This is your chance to experience the truth, and the truth shall set you free from your own bondage. Remember, it's an *alien* virus, from an *alien* intelligence. There's a good chance these creatures may try to communicate with us. I'm sure you wouldn't want to miss that."

Zakariah deliberated for a moment, moist heat in his armpits, impossible odds stacking up against him. "When you get this close, it sounds pretty scary," he said.

"I knew you'd catch the vision. It's momentous really. Historic. I have great faith in a successful outcome. You've been roleplaying your meeting with the Source since your baby boy was born. You were created for it. I'm sure you'll come up with something."

"You're gambling everything on it."

"The search for knowledge is a risky game."

"You were human once. Do you still remember fear?"

The face on the monitors remained still for a few moments,

frozen in time like a photo in an ancient textbook. Colin Macpherson had cheated death. He had reanimated his corpse in a digital purgatory.

"No," he answered finally, "I've lost all fear."

Mia stared up at the giant display board at Richmond Station as she waited for her shuttle to commence boarding. Arrival and departure numbers blinked on and off as they were periodically updated, red, green, amber, and white status lights on a black background. Smaller screens detailed weather patterns, financial market data, and safety instructions on an endless loop. A news channel showed talking heads with strings of subtitles in three languages.

"Are you sure you want to go through with this, Mia?"

Jimmy offered a faxslip verification with a steady hand, though it was hardly necessary. Her palm print had already been recorded by the Richmond Station pre-launch scanners. Her return ticket through the Macpherson Doorway had been prepaid by corporate interests controlled by Phillip Davis.

"Is there a problem?"

"No. It's just a long journey from home." Jimmy looked straight into her eyes and held her gaze. He had a way about him, a gentleness of spirit in his face, a simple sincerity that Mia found comforting. No wonder he was such a successful con man. Everyone seemed to trust him. "It might not be easy," he said.

"Don't worry. I'll find him and bring him back."

"That's all we can ask."

"You're sure my luggage is free of drugs and contraband,

right?"

Jimmy smiled. "It does go against my better nature to pass up such an opportunity."

"You promised me."

"I give you my word as a crook and a scoundrel. You're clean, Mia. You wouldn't be much use to us in a colony prison."

"What about the trip back?"

"That I can't be sure about."

"Should I take precautions?"

"Yes."

A tingle of dread told Mia she was on the right track. "I know you're not helping me out of the goodness of your heart."

"You're an expensive insurance policy. That's all I can guess. We can't get any feedback through the Doorway. There's no reliable communications system in realtime, and there've been no messages. If anyone can find out what's going on, it's you."

"It was a smuggling operation all along, wasn't it?"

Jimmy pouted in thought for a few seconds, tipping his head side to side. "I guess there's no point in denying that."

"So dangerous people are all waiting for the payoff now."

"Not me. I'm a simple working man. I always get my cut up front."

"Phillip, then?"

"Just family and friends, as far as I know."

Mia nodded. She smoothed the sleeves of her flight suit, a drab green khaki that would attract little attention.

"Do you believe in luck, Mia?"

"I don't seem to be having much lately."

"What about providence, then? What about the spirit that's supposed to direct all Eternals?"

"Urban legend, I guess."

"That's it?"

"I've never felt any prophetic guidance, Jimmy. No great voice has ever helped me escape from a bad situation."

Jimmy seemed pensive, like a man on the verge of confession, and Mia prolonged eye contact to wring out his secrets. "I was a casino brat as a kid," he said. "My mother was a showgirl. I developed an understanding of fortune, a seventh sense, you know? I watch for luck, Mia. Patterns in V-space. We call it digital watermarking, in the biz, but it's more than that. Harmonics, you know, octave shifts. Sometimes the data speaks like music. That's what Zakariah sees."

"What do you see, Jimmy?" Mia watched his wizened face for any clue. His eyes darted down and away. He was hiding something.

"I see trouble ahead, and trouble behind. Nothin' but trouble everywhere I look."

"Sounds like a country song."

He grinned at that, and she wished she had not been so quick to make light of his burden of sin. By keeping him on edge she might coax more information.

"Just be careful. This whole thing came together too easily. I was warned to expect Zak before he arrived at my shop downtown, and then you showed up at my private lab right on schedule."

"Really?" Her pulse stepped up a notch. She became aware of her breasts rising and falling, of the air rushing through her nostrils. "By Phillip?"

"Yeah, the ultimate man of mystery. He has an eerie charisma. If you think I'm a heartless bastard, just wait till you meet Zak's father."

"How could he have guessed?"

Jimmy shrugged. "How should I know? You're the one who's immortal, you and your legion of superheroes. I'm just a stray dog picking up scraps under the table."

"You've been a good friend, Jimmy."

"Yeah. They'll put that on my tombstone. Everybody's best friend. I wish it was more. I never really learned about love. Never could bring myself to trust anyone." His roving eyes caught hers again and shone with natural empathy. "Neither should you, Mia."

"I'll keep that in mind."

"Go with the Eternal spirit, then, if you can find it. Maybe you'll finally catch a break." He winked at her playfully, and she felt a release in his benediction, a hallowed blessing from a common criminal.

Her launch status went green on the big board at Richmond Station, and she bent to pick up her pack as Jimmy turned away.

SEVEN

Zakariah paced back in forth in his assigned quarters, deep under the crust of the frozen planet Babylon, trying to decide if he was a prisoner or a volunteer. His door was unlocked but certainly monitored electronically by Colin Macpherson, the Architect of all. Everything around him was controlled, bent to a sure purpose, moving implacably forward. He hated the thought of it.

He lay down on his bunk and feigned sleep in the darkness, wondering about the gods of fortune and mechanical madmen. Life was a long list of insignificant details that added up to a mountain of evidence in the end. At every rung on the ladder, the choice to go up or back presented itself, at every crossroad, the choice of left or right, but reason alone often dictated the pathway, and the spirit of man prodded this way or that. Was free will just an illusion, a conjuring trick propped up by his puny rationalizations? Did his own father discover this truth years ago when he stole off in the night with Zakariah's baby sister? Was he merely following the path laid out for him, his own inexorable destiny?

"A pawn in someone else's game," he said aloud, finally, and rose to his feet. He donned his flight boots and shrugged his heavy coat over his cardigan. In the darkness he opened the air-duct grate over his bunk and climbed up into the tunnel. Down the hallway he kicked open another grate and dropped to the treadway. He jogged up the gentle slope to the elevator.

He arrived at the shuttle dock at shift change. A cargo shipment was half unloaded, the new crew yawning and sipping coffee, the shuttle pilot waving goodbye with a young partner on his arm. Zakariah exchanged pleasantries with a supervisor as he accepted hot chocolate from a free dispenser. The cup steamed pleasantly in the frigid air.

"Any traffic in the area?" Zakariah asked absently, looking away.

"Naw. We had a bogey earlier, but it turned out to be a corporate jet heading for the Silver Lake Minesite. The girls in Control are antsy as hens. We're expecting one more shuttle today with dignitaries from town. You in on the big event upstairs?"

Zakariah chanced quick eye contact and a plastic smile. "I have a small part to play."

"Good luck. Sounds like you might need it." The supervisor tipped his steaming cup at him.

"Thanks," Zakariah responded. He sipped hot chocolate and ambled away.

After circumventing the shuttle dock twice, he finally noticed a green light over one of the landing bays. He accessed through the launch gate and stepped into the shuttle. The passenger hold was empty, the lights all powered down. He crept through the galley and peeked in the door to the cockpit. A young man with a red toque sat at the controls.

"You're late, slumlord," the red leprechaun said, a young man with a wry smile.

Zakariah sat in the co-pilot couch and strapped himself in. "What's your name?" he asked.

"Colin7."

Zakariah peered at him closely, seeing a family resemblance, the narrow face and pointed chin. "You're a clone?"

"Yep."

Zakariah shook his head in wonder. "Macpherson has really got his bases covered."

Colin7 nodded. "That's the problem, slumlord. Our Father's a control freak—genius gone wild. He drove his wife to suicide long before the Doorway opened up—never gave her room to breathe or a voice to call her own. They never had any children. You ready to make your escape?"

"Blast 'em up, partner."

The shuttle leapt like a cat into the night.

"Will they follow us?" Zakariah asked after his stomach settled back down from his throat.

"The outpost is not equipped for search and rescue. Nor do they have conventional armaments. They don't even know I'm here." Colin7 made a gleeful sound of mischief. "I'm a genius, too, you know, a data chip off the old block."

"Why the mutiny?"

"Lots of reasons, internal and external."

"Name five."

Colin7 laughed happily. "Oh, very well. The Alpha and Omega Project is a wanton waste of resources that will seriously curtail corporate activity for years to come and could jeopardize hundreds of souls in storage. It has drastically upset the balance of power between the Overlords, the Municipalities, and Soul Savers Incorporated. How many is that?"

"Are you Eternal?"

"In a manner of speaking. A new clone is activated every sixteen years ad infinitum. We live, we die, we are custodians of our Father. We don't use the alien virus, nor do we need it. We live forever, and yet we are individually expendable. Meaning no personal disrespect, Soul Savers regards the virus as a mere biological anomaly."

"You mentioned external reasons."

"Ah, now we reach the crux of the conundrum. We believe our Father is tampering with reality as we know it by breaching the space-time fabric with such violence."

"But the Source does it all the time."

"Not by blasting holes with a subatomic cannon, I'm sure. What if the wall cracks? What if it tears or twists or falters or shifts one nanosecond out of alignment? And what do you think the aliens are going to say when we blow a hole in their living room?"

"I'm not convinced."

"You're here, aren't you? We both know why."

Zakariah reached up to rub the shadow of stubble on his cheek, wondering about life without skin, a mind without a body, a cybersoul lost in paradise. His hand swept up his face and across his furrowed brow. He rubbed a knot of tension between his eyes. His fingers circled there, pressing the skin up to his hairline. What a mess.

"I'm afraid he might succeed," he said finally.

"Exactly."

"There's no freedom in New Jerusalem."

Colin7 nodded unhappily. "The Architect controls everything and everyone utterly. With a track record like that, we can't just hand him the keys to the cosmic kingdom."

"I guess that's it," Zakariah said and smiled at last. It looked that simple, out in the open where he could see it. He felt that he had vaulted over a threshold in his mind. He had seen the devil and turned away.

"You're set up just fine back home, slumlord. You and Jimmy can kick back and talk about the good old days from a Prime level penthouse view. Helena's out of the picture now that she's been uploaded into Soul slavery. With her voodoo wetware in your brain, you'll be free to impersonate her to your heart's content. Money, power, prestige, Eternal life. I'm sure you can make it work."

Colin7 smiled with satisfaction. "We're six hours from your appointment with the Doorway. Get some rest." He reached over and patted Zakariah's knee. "You've done well, my friend."

Zakariah dreamed of dragons dancing too close to the sun. Their wings burned and they fell like arrows into a crimson, pulsating heart. Blood poured out like a river, and ships and rafts sailed by on the waves of ichor. They turned in all directions and beckoned to him to jump, to save himself. A waterfall lay ahead, and rainbows arched above it. Thunder rumbled in a cloudless sky. The earth shook and he jumped skyward. The wind whipped his cheeks as he gathered speed. His eyes watered and he blinked tears back to his temples. Too fast. Too fast. From this height he could see the rainbows were full circles, targets of light. They aligned into a cone, a tunnel, and he angled toward the centre, spinning like an arrow. Suddenly he was falling out of control, down, deeper, and in panic he turned to grasp a rainbow rung just out of reach. A dark, bubbling cauldron of smoke lay below, and he kicked and flailed as he plunged toward hell, his arms and legs outstretched, spinning in a kaleidoscope of colour. A moist heat rose to meet him, the fetid breath of devils. He bumped to a halt and opened his eyes with a start.

"New Freedom Transit Authority," the red leprechaun told him happily. "Here's your ticket verification." He handed over a faxslip, smiling. "Go home now, slumlord. No harm, no foul."

Zakariah stumbled onto the landing and looked around, recognizing nothing. He shuffled along with the staff and porters until he found a ticket gate and a barrage of security scanners.

Helena Sharp stepped up to block his way, her face wary with distrust.

Zakariah gaped at her. He sighed like a doomed man, feeling frayed around the edges and dreading another confrontation.

"You coming home?" he asked her.

"I am home, Zak. This is where I belong. We're building a new world, an infinite playground. There's a place for you, too. Lots of Eternals have signed on. Soul Savers offers true immortality, true paradise."

Zakariah shook his head and lowered his eyes briefly. "They could pull the plug on you any time."

Helena dismissed the idea with a quirk of a smile and a toss of her chin. "You could get shot in a terrorist attack," she countered.

"Forgive me, Helena. I made a mistake."

Her eyes widened. "Really?"

Zakariah matched her stare and held it. "I tried to manipulate you. I wanted to control everything. I'm sorry."

Helena's brows knit in confusion. "Very well, then. I forgive you. It doesn't matter now."

Zakariah held out his good right hand. She shook it firmly, sealing their mutual absolution.

"Are you here on official business?"

"I'm delivering a simple message for a friend."

"Are you required to detain me?"

"I have no power over you."

"Then I am free to enter the Doorway?"

Helena whistled a slow exhalation. "Your wife would like to speak to you first. She's in New Jerusalem at the Soul Savers headquarters." Helena offered forward a glowing handheld. "She came in last night."

Zakariah stared at her incredulous. Her bland face offered no clue, no explanation. He reached for the webphone with trembling fingers. A small vidscreen flickered to life. A snowy image of his wife appeared, surrounded by static discharge.

"Mia," he said, not daring yet to believe his eyes.

"Zak, I love you." Her voice was clear, unmistakable. How was this possible?

Zakariah felt a great vacuum in his chest, a breathless, painful void. His thoughts seemed removed from his body, distant and unconnected, his essence floating high above like a balloon on a string. He looked down on a foolish puppet, a man of wires and circuits. "How did you get here?"

"Your pal Jimmy helped me out. Some money came in from your father."

"My father?"

"I couldn't wait any longer, Zak. I couldn't live without you. I came to help you find the Source."

Zakariah remembered the hope that had once driven him, the hope now all but lost. The Source, his mission for Rix.

"They tell me you'll be arriving here today. I can't wait to see you, to touch your face. Zak, you're never leaving my side again, I swear."

Zakariah swallowed, it seemed, for the first time ever. "Tell me something no one else knows, Mia."

"What?"

"I need something to verify the communication."

Mia's image flickered, grim now and threatened. "Are we in trouble, Zak? Is something wrong?"

"Tell me something no one else knows!" he shouted.

Helena stepped back in alarm, and nearby eyes turned to note the disturbance.

Zakariah clenched his teeth in frustration. His fingers clamped on the handheld as though it were the rung of a ladder. His nightmare had come true, and he hung aloft above a boiling cauldron of deceit and guile, a soul-swallowing infernal pit of darkness.

"I fell asleep early on our wedding night," came the reply from across the starry night of space. "I had a glass of champagne at the reception and slept till morning. It's me, Zak. What's going on?"

All the fight drained out of Zakariah like water circling down a drain. He hung his head and felt his body contract in surrender as he hunched over the vidscreen sadly. "Nothing for you to worry about, honey. I was just heading home today, but I guess I have some unfinished business to attend to. I'll check in with you soon."

He signed off and turned to Helena with an icy glare. "She won't be harmed," he said.

"Of course not. She's an honoured guest."

"Don't try to hide behind semantics. This is extortion, pure and simple."

Helena shook her head. "Zak, I don't know what you're involved in, and, frankly, I don't want to hear the sordid details. You're a loose cannon, a cosmic cowboy. I wrote you off long ago. But know this: I did not betray you. If anything, you betrayed yourself. Whatever it is you must do, do it quickly and take your wife home."

"Fine," he said and cast his eyes down in defeat. "Take me back to Babylon."

Rix idled his motorcycle at the curb in front of the ERI office tower. He peered up into the darkness, trying to make out movement on the rooftop. Niko had been in the building for exactly one hour, certainly long enough for her simple checklist. He tapped his V-net plug for the correct time: 1:45 flashed against the black sky in his field of vision. He was right on schedule.

A bare sliver of moon lit the rooftop. A blanket of rural silence seemed to amplify the sound of his bike. The ERI complex was way out in the sticks, surrounded by farmland for miles around. He smelled dung and strange pollen and wrinkled his nose in disgust. He would never get used to this terrible smell. Rix had always envisioned country life in romantic terms, cows in fragrant pastures and native beasts in frolic, but the aroma outside the city seemed fetid to him, wild and repulsive. He had grown up with the smell of concrete and hot asphalt and had known only spiders and rats and horny tomcats prowling the fences.

A blinking light caught his attention. One-two-three. He focused his attention to the left edge of the precipice above him. A black furl appeared, barely a shadow, a black bat in the darkness. Niko.

He squinted at the night, imagining her pantherlike grace as she stepped near the edge. His pulse beat a quick tempo as his body froze with a rush of endorphins.

The light blinked again. One-two-three. Niko jumped.

A black wing caught his eye as she plummeted. No sound of alarm. No notice in the night. Damn, she was good.

Rix stepped the bike into gear and eased forward. He had practised the route and memorized priority targets. He smiled as his body relaxed into working mode, but kept his attention tightly narrowed. He followed her down.

"When do I get to fly?" he said as he pulled up beside her.

She tossed a package to him and continued bundling her wings into a tight roll.

"When you're old enough, cousin."

Rix looked down at the package—navy blue uniforms wrapped in clear plastic, name tags, security laminates. He hated it when she called him cousin. They weren't really cousins. They were related by test tube only, and his interest in her went far beyond family ties. He watched the curve of her hip as she worked, her muscles flexing under the skintight black fabric. She was a catwoman, a midnight fantasy.

She noted his attention and stopped moving. He darted his

eyes up to meet her gaze, feeling a flush of embarrassment, wondering if she might have guessed his thoughts.

Her shadowed face revealed no clue. She offered no comment,
and after a moment she bent to strap her bundled wings to an
aluminum frame.

"What did you find?" he asked, thankful for the sound of his
voice.

"T1 fiberoptic in the basement. Direct to the Beast. Couldn't
ask for better."

"No filters?"

She shook her head. "Not till the second floor hub. Any
techie could hack it." She slung her pack up over her shoulder
and snapped a clasp above her breasts. "Let's roll, cousin."

She jumped on the single seat behind him and pressed her
pelvis into his back. He edged up to make room for her, but she
curled both arms around his abdomen and held him close. He
stepped the bike into gear and eased the clutch gently into the
quiet night.

Zakariah walked of his own free will into the Alpha and Omega
complex on the planet Babylon, far from home and stripped of
all confidence. Below an immense umbrella of glass, the photonic phaser sat like a ponderous blue steel beast glinting with
promise. The whirling dust of stars twinkled unsuspectingly
beyond the canopy, and twin moons hovered above a craggy
horizon. The air was still and showed a mist of cloud from waste
heat vents around the perimeter. The concrete floor underneath
hummed with power, with a dissonant vibration, the cannon

itself a giant nozzle for vast forces below, a pistol atop a mountain of energy.

Zakariah stared up at the phaser like a man facing the ancient gallows of pre-civilization, numb with contrition yet dreading the end. The exchange tube on the snout of the weapon, where hyper-c photons of light would be split into both wave and particle in quantum paradox, looked like a bundle of fluorescent columns affixed to a slender silver core of metal, perhaps fifty feet long. The main trunnion was supported by huge metal stanchions that disappeared into the concrete without bolt or seam to unknowable anchors deep below. The ghost of Colin Macpherson looked on from every angle

A wire-cage elevator took Zakariah up several flights to a tiny cockpit that perched like a fruit basket on top of an elephant. He dismounted and climbed into the launch couch without protest. He touched his V-net plug and looked for an interface. He had been promised he would see Mia as soon as he completed his task.

Glass doors shuttered above him and sealed with a hiss of air as he pulled a V-net cable out of the console in front of him. He gave a thumbs-up signal to the technician outside, who replied in kind and rode the elevator back down to the ground.

"No delay to destiny," he said as he jacked in.

Zakariah Davis stood alone in a cold grey room wearing the well-preserved body of a female white Caucasian from Earth, his eighty-seven-year-old wetware twin.

Can you hear me, Helena?

Yes, came the faint reply in the back of his mind, filtered and protected by anti-surge hardware and anti-viral software.

So they've got you working now, too?

Apparently I've run up a large debt to Soul Savers Corporation. I'm

working it off in trade. Colin Macpherson owns the company.

They call him the Architect.

I can see why. He controls everything.

I tried to warn you.

Zak, if I had known it would lead to this . . ..

Never mind, Helena. It's the Source calling us. I see that now. You sure you don't want to come along? For old time's sake?

You hardly need me getting in your way again.

I could use the moral support.

I'll be right here, Zak. If anything goes wrong, I'll pull the plug.

A window of light opened up in the grey wall before Zakariah. A pattern of randomly shifting colours danced.

"Portal's up," he said, aloud for the record, and placed his hand against it. "No access."

We're at ninety percent, Helena told him, *cranking it up.*

Zakariah stalked his plain grey room, pushing on the walls around him, itching to run, to fulfill his final mission. He remembered his first play for access time up Prime, an unknown rookie taking fledgling steps with big corporate interests. He had hacked a Korean test-market version of a new database driver and sold it to a competitor days before the North American release date. Then, after the competitor responded by incorporating portions into their own development program, Zakariah had fast-tracked and sold the whole package back to the Koreans and the Japanese consortium that had licensed the original research, thereby giving everybody the standardized protocol they really wanted and earning a backdoor into three multinational corporations and a nasty pile of loot.

"You can't go up Prime without an angle," Jimmy had told him a hundred times in preparation. "The V-net eats hackers for breakfast and sends them back with their fingers cut off." The expression seemed archaic now that retinal print technology had replaced traditional fingerprint records, but the sentiment was timeless.

What would Jimmy say if he found Zakariah now, crashing Paradise without an invitation?

A deep explosion sounded as the subatomic phaser cannon reached sonic thresholds. The grey walls shimmered and swayed slightly. He reached for the window. His hand went inside. "I have access," he said.

Wait! Helena screamed above the chaos of background noise. *We're extending the particle stream . . . Slowly . . . Slowly . . . Okay, jump.*

Zakariah dove through the window into the blinding light of a burning sun. He shielded his eyes, but the light shone through his fingers, through his eyelids, into his brain, revealing all. He inched his way forward, sensing no landmarks, no distance, nothing but blinding, unyielding light in a shimmering torrent.

Can you hear me, Helena? he asked. *The light is overwhelming. I have no contact.*

He felt no oscillation, no source code at all. He sensed no deep harmonics, no pulse on which to build compatibility. There could be no communication here, no commerce with such pure and violent resplendence.

"Is anyone out there?" he asked. "I only have a few seconds."

As he said the words, time stopped. He recognized it instantly. His pulse stopped beating. His respiration quit. The light froze around him in a crystalline magnificence that was absolutely still and quiet. He stood inside a scintillant luminosity, a cut-crystal vase with a million gleaming facets. A peaceful tranquillity flooded through him, a feeling that he had always been in this place, that he was coming home after a long absence.

"I'm dead," he whispered, though he felt no ill effects.

As he studied the silent majesty before him, he began to notice subtle variations in the brilliance, a vague shift of intensity that might be the beginning of a shadow here or there. He narrowed his attention to this minutia of movement, zooming in on every fine detail. Finally, stooping down, he noticed a toe, a bit of skin and bone, a toenail.

"Contact," he said, and his voice sounded foreign, ridiculous, an impure dissonance in a symphony of excellence.

The toe became a foot after an age or longer, a burning appendage like molten metal on a background of white light, a human foot.

Zakariah felt peaceful, superconscious, with the quick mental agility of infinite access. His physical state transcended emotion with a serene knowledge of joy. This was the way things always were, the way they should always be.

"Who are you?" a Voice sounded from above.

Zakariah fell back in surprise, slowly, gently, and waited for his shoulders to hit the floor. They didn't, and he kept falling, somersaulting backwards, head over heels into the glorious light around him. Without a reference point, he couldn't stop moving. He twisted but found no horizon. He reached but found no handhold, no ladder, no signpost. Nothing but bright white perfection everywhere he looked.

A hand reached out and grabbed his shoulder, and he realized with a start that he hadn't been falling at all. He had been standing completely still in the blinding white stillness of time.

"Why have you come?" the Voice said, and Zakariah felt the meaning on his face like a physical vibration. The sound was light and the light was word, a modulated spectrum of varying intensities that expressed language. The strong hand that held him appeared translucent, shiny, like golden glass. It was as deep as space itself; it had constellations and supernovas glittering inside it like jewels.

An alien arm began to take shape as Zakariah's eyes continued to miraculously adapt. The arm was as long as creation, as long as time standing on end and suns burning to cinders. Zakariah followed the arm to the shoulder, past the life and death of a thousand worlds, and tried to imagine where the face should be. He peered intensely in that direction, looking for simple communication in the hush of heaven.

"Are you the Source?"

"Did you come to buy my blood?" the Voice replied. "What would you offer in return?"

Eyes of fire appeared suddenly, angry orange eyes, and Zakariah cried out in anguish and melted down, cringing, crumpling, to fall at burning feet. He disappeared into himself like a dustmote swirling into a grey funnel. His ego shattered and dispersed, leaving him naked and alone and insignificant on the edge of eternity.

"I'm sorry . . . sorry," he whimpered. He had to sound warning. He had to tell Macpherson, the Overlords, the World Council, old Jimmy. He wondered with panic what allegiance he might call his own.

"Peace," the Voice said, as once again the alien hand stretched out to rest on Zakariah.

Peace did come with the word, like a soft blanket of comfort, and Zakariah drifted, content at last.

"This kingdom is not compatible with your own," the alien said. "Look at your hands and see."

Zakariah opened his clenched palms and saw that his whole body had become a ghost, ethereal, invisible. He did not exist here; he had no substance, no shadow. Only his veins showed solid, gleaming with the quickened bloodlight of the virus.

A dimension faster than light, a world beyond space and time.

The fiery eyes were framed now with a face, a sad face that had seen a thousand hearts break and more, that had seen wise men die and martyred souls ground underfoot.

"You are a king among thieves," the Voice pronounced in final judgment, "and unworthy to enter."

The simple statement brought a curse upon humanity like a physical blow. Zakariah was the chosen representative, the first contact. What excuse could he offer for the sins of all mankind, what penalty could he pay for a race of criminals from the womb?

Overcome with a flood of conviction, Zakariah hunched his shoulders and cried. He sobbed without solace, across all time, across all space, for all humans. He wept for a people destined for extinction. In a world of light, there could be no darkness. Ever.

Helena watched the glass umbrella above the launch stadium melt and drop like rain, as the exchange tubes on the phaser burned cherry red with incandescence. A brilliant diamond of white fire glowed at the business tip, where a rip in the space-time fabric was held a few molecules apart, and light of all spectrums shot out like laser beams glinting off the facets of a revolving jewel. A halo of condensation formed around it like a smoky wreath. A high-pitched whine like an angel screaming cut through the air like a razor, vibrating her to the bone. The photonic cannon glowed with a backwash of heat from the wormhole, the equipment around it scorched and melting. Steam spiralled up from the floor like devils dancing in a burning house.

In the control booth beside her, behind bulletproof blastglass, Colin5 manned his recording apparatus and looked out over a smoking wasteland.

"Fifteen more seconds," he said evenly. "Pull him back now if you are able, Helena. Gamma rays are reaching a critical level."

"I've lost him in the brightness," she cried from under her neural helmet. "It's like the heart of a sun. I can't search for him. The alien will kill us all. His eyes are on fire!"

"Three . . . two . . . one . . . Power out," Colin5 intoned steadily. A sonic boom sounded that rattled the blastglass and shook them like rag dolls. The fiery diamond of light winked out and the phaser cannon stood silent, steaming hellishly in the frozen air. A soft snow began to fall as clouds of moisture began their slow return to the surface.

"Systems check," he directed. "All terminals lock down and report." A series of terse replies echoed among the small team of harried technicians. One by one, green lights flashed on their boards and backup disks slipped into shielded containers.

Colin5 smiled finally and typed in a security clearance. A team of firefighters stormed the stadium floor and began foaming every flame with white powder. He keyed an access code and thumbed on a microphone. "The wormhole is closed, Father. We may safely resume online activity."

"Excellent," Macpherson exclaimed above a steady din of warning alarms and sirens. "Do we have everything recorded?"

"A wealth of data. More than we could ever have imagined. A first communication with the aliens. Hard evidence from a new multiverse. The Alpha and Omega program has been a resounding success, a brilliant step forward." Colin5 raised both hands in the air, reaching for the stars. "Today we are giants of time!"

He dropped his arms and glanced toward Helena. "Any last words for the record?"

Helena sobbed, confined in her launch couch under the neural monitor, still hotwired to her twin avatar. She choked and gasped for air. "No, nothing else."

"Is the runner alive?" Macpherson asked.

"Yes, biometrics are stable," Colin5 said. "Can you find any consciousness, Helena?"

Helena probed the laboratory V-space in search of Zakariah. "He's back in the grey room, but I'm not getting a clear signal. His mind is curled up like a turtle shell. His heart is broken."

"Brainscan data?"

"Theta waves, possible dreamlike state," spoke a technician. "Feedback pattern in the amygdalic region consistent with emotional breakdown."

"Any permanent damage or disease in anyone's estimation?"

Silence stretched out in the negative.

"Very well," the Architect said. "Trigger his mindwipe circuit and upload the return package for our business associates. Prepare the runner for transport back through the Doorway."

Colin5 typed in appropriate computer codes.

"No," Helena whispered, too weak to intervene.

EIGHT

Silus Mundazo examined the small sheaf of documents carefully. He frowned and glanced up over his reading glasses at Zakariah in the seat opposite his desk. He threw the papers on his desk with disdain.

"What do they say?" Zakariah asked.

"You expect me to believe you haven't read them?"

"The diplomatic pouch was sealed."

"A minor detail to someone of your kin."

"Have we met before?"

"So that much is true. You've been mindwiped."

Zakariah nodded, juggling the weight of foreboding that he now took for granted. "That much is true."

Silus Mundazo grimaced and shook his head. "These papers reportedly come from Director Sharp, asking me to cooperate in a ludicrous scheme to allow you access to her launch couch so that you can impersonate her in V-space."

"I noticed the hybrid avatar. Is that your work?"

"Hardly. I was against the whole procedure. It was Helena's idea."

"She must have had good reason."

"You don't remember a thing?"

"Not much."

"You have a wife and son, did you know that?"

"Sounds complicated."

"You poor sap. You're in no position to take Helena's place. You don't even know who you are."

"I'm a quick study. All I need is Prime access and a few hours to run the numbers."

"What proof do I have that she's alive?"

"I've seen her in person. She's been unavoidably detained."

"So you say."

"I need your help, Doctor."

"Why should I trust you? On the basis of this flimsy evidence?" He pointed at the paperwork before him.

"I have one more bargaining chip." Zakariah reached in an inner pocket and brought out a black velvet jewellery case. He handed it forward.

Silus Mundazo took the case and lifted up the hinged lid. He winced as a flash of light bathed his face. "My God," he said. "An activated sample."

"Is that enough?"

"Where did you get it?"

"I can't remember. I found it in my personal effects."

"Do you know who it's for?"

"I'm offering it to you for your cooperation, Silus."

Dr. Mundazo closed the case with a snap. He offered an outstretched hand. "Deal," he said. "We'll kick-start the inoculation program immediately."

Zakariah reached forward and shook his hand in a traditional groundspace contract. He resumed his seat. "So what's the latest news?"

Silus opened the velvet case again, as though to test reality one more time. He peered closer into the light, tipping the case back and forth in study. "Madame Shakura has been making threats and noise again," he said. "Now that Chairman Tao has been hospitalized, she's vying for the Chair as an interim measure." He looked over with a scowl. "About as interim as taxes and crypto. World Council funding will quickly dry up unless you make an appearance as the Director. If you want to play Broadway, that will be your first step."

Mia tracked down Jimmy at his downtown office in the back of a defunct computer repair shop. She stood outside a plain wooden door, still dressed in her khaki flightsuit, and composed herself as best she could. She felt lost and out of place, an invisible ghost walking a strange planet she could no longer recognize. So much had changed in so little time. She pushed open the door and called his name to the glimmering shadows beyond.

"Mia. You made it." Jimmy stepped into view from a doorway near the back. He looked gaunt and worried, like a man who has gone too long without sleeping. He came to her and grasped her hand with genuine affection. He hugged her like a father.

"How did it go?" he asked, but his voice said he knew too much already.

"Terrible," she said.

Jimmy stepped back, holding her arms and peering into her face.

"You don't look so good. Come and sit down."

He led her behind a chipped and dented countertop to a black swivel chair with foam stuffing poking out at the seams. He set her into it carefully. "Can I get you a drink or a sublingual sedative?"

She waved him away. "No drugs. I've got to work this out." She rubbed her knees with both palms, pressing the fabric down, smoothing every wrinkle.

He nodded his bald head, his eyes squinting with shared pain. "What can you tell me?"

Obsolete computer parts lay on shelves under the counter, the carefully printed tags yellowing with age. Coils of wire hung on the austere wall behind her, dead and dormant. "I can't find Rix. Everything has fallen apart. Zakariah has been turned into a zombie."

Jimmy grimaced with new pain. "Mindwiped?"

"Or worse. Brainwashed. An armed security team was guarding him like visiting royalty while I was treated like a peasant." Mia held a palm to her throat to catch her breath. Her words were spilling too quickly from her lips, rushing out in raw catharsis. "I could not even get eye contact from my husband on the shuttle trip back. It was so frustrating. I can't believe it. He doesn't even recognize his own wife." She slumped into her chair.

Jimmy stared at her in puzzlement, his brow furrowed above bushy grey eyebrows.

"Zakariah came back?"

"Yes."

"With you?"

"Not with me, no. He was blanketed by security goons."

"You were on the transport with him, though?"

"Yes, of course." Mia stopped abruptly, frozen with alarm.

"What's wrong, Jimmy? What have you heard?"

Jimmy shifted his body weight uncomfortably, puzzling some new paradox. "Zakariah has been reported missing on the far side of the Macpherson Doorway—presumed dead."

"He's not dead. He's home."

"Official reports indicate the Director returned alone. Is it possible that you made some mistake? Perhaps from a distance someone looked a lot like Zakariah?"

Mia eyed Jimmy narrowly, wondering why on Earth he would not believe her. Could there be some other complication? Some reason why they could no longer speak heart to heart? She wondered why she had ever trusted him. "Is that what Rix has been told? That his father is dead?"

Jimmy sucked air through gritted teeth. "V-space has been buzzing with his obituary. Rix would be right on the bubble. He's being groomed as a runner."

"He must be devastated, poor kid. Do you know where I can find him?"

"I'll see what I can do."

"Did you set me up, Jimmy? Did you see this coming?"

"You can't really believe that, Mia."

"What *can* I believe, Jimmy? You tell me." She rose to confront him, wanting to clutch his shirt collar and wring his neck for information. She could torture the truth out of him with a few simple pressure points. What was he trying to hide? Who was he working for? Phillip?

Instead she stood impotent and defenceless before him. She could no longer muster her chi. "I've lost everything, Jimmy."

Again his face seemed to mirror her internal agony. "We'll figure this out, Mia. Everybody knows Zak was working closely with the ERI when he disappeared offplanet. He was seen arm in arm with the Director, Helena Sharp, strolling the grounds like a prince in waiting.".

"He would never sell out. Not Zakariah."

"He was using her, Mia. He was playing her like a friggin' piccolo. Maybe this is all an act, a complicated charade. Maybe Zak is pulling the strings at the ERI."

Mia squinted at this new possibility. She thought back to the shuttle trip home. She remembered the vacancy in her husband's eyes. "He's gone, Jimmy. He didn't recognize me."

"He could still be in play, though. Mindwiped or not. Rumour has it that an activated sample is up for bids on the white market."

For a moment Mia gaped at him, fighting back exhaustion, feeling dangerously close to a breaking point. An activated sample? Up for auction like a computer trinket? Finally she noticed her tongue drying out from the rush of her panted breath. She closed her mouth and swallowed.

"Stay here with me, Mia. Let me plug up and search for his shadow sublevel. There's a cot in the back." Jimmy thumbed over his shoulder. "Get some rest and shrug off the space lag while I find out what I can."

Mia noted the smell of stale cologne and perspiration in the air. She found the sensation vaguely comforting—a memory from a simpler time not long ago, a time when her soulmate risked his life regularly but at least remembered the sound of her voice. She had nowhere to go now. She had lost everything. "Don't try anything funny, old man. I'm still a married woman."

Jimmy's eyebrows popped with surprise, and his face took on new animation, new hope. He nodded with a hearty chuckle.

"No wonder Zak thinks you're the greatest."

Mia mumbled thanks and perfunctory blessings as Jimmy showed her to a supply room with a rumpled bed and a makeshift table fashioned from an old door laid over two metal filing cabinets. The grey walls were lined with shelves full of obsolete computer parts—boxlike disk drives, video cards, buckets of archaic memory chips with tiny copper contacts like piano keys. She smelled dust and inexorable decay.

She lay down fully clothed and pulled a blanket up onto her legs. She thought about Zakariah. Could he still be out there somewhere, hardcopied behind a veil? Was he impersonating the Director, pretending to the crown? Or was he a soulless automaton, programmed like a robot now that his memory had been wiped clean? She shivered at the thought. How could she blame her husband for seeking sanctuary with the ERI? She had suggested the same thing to him just weeks ago. Perhaps it was all her fault. She remembered their time together at the north sanctuary. She remembered the weight of his body. Oh God, she would give anything to have him back.

Rix slipped through Sublevel Zero like a needle through smoke, leaving barely a whisper behind. His lithe and muscular avatar was cloaked in pure silver like a molten mirror, an image he had produced himself with Niko's illicit upgrade access. He was recognizable to only a few chosen users and left behind an after-image that could not easily be recalled or measured. Posthuman and invincible, he slid past the token guardians in this unregistered area—no one could stop his smooth and effortless journey to his goal.

A band of pirates cornered him, crowing at their good fortune.

"Look what we got here," one said triumphantly, "some kid with illegal wetware."

"Chinese manufacture," said another, a grey giant with a barely discernable outline.

"Out wanderin' with more money than good sense."

Four pirates shifted positions warily, looking for access, hoping for a system lock. The echo of their mumbled voices sounded ghostlike, eerie.

The pirate leader, a stocky white avatar with a hideous grin, began to set up barriers of grey steel in the background, systematically closing down backdoors and access tunnels. The ether around them darkened perceptively.

"You cannot take me," Rix stated. He set a splay of rainbow encryption in front of him with a wave of his arm as a warning.

The pirate leader paused to study him momentarily, then quietly resumed his work.

Rix altered his programming so that suddenly his avatar appeared in spectral reverse to his original orientation—his pupils white, his face dark, all colours replaced by a haunting, solarized opposite like a photo negative. It was an old trick but usually enough to build incompatibility. Three henchmen followed his example, chuckling to themselves as they tugged impenetrable grey walls behind them, leaving one avenue open, back to the fourth pirate steadily programming below. He launched golden parameter lines from his abdomen like gossamer webs that clung to Rix on impact.

"Don't even think about it," Rix said and cut the wires loose with a short anti-viral knife. They flew away like kite wires.

The pirate leader frowned. He gesticulated an unspoken code to his compatriots. He snapped his fingers and a spider web of cable fell up from below Rix, tangling around his legs.

Rix stooped to slash the net free with his cyberknife, but as he did the three pirates facing him pushed forward and locked their grey walls together into a box. By nature the grey walls were mathematically infinite top and bottom, leaving one narrow doorway open.

Rix had seen this trap before, schematically, and recognized its efficiency. At the moment he had more to lose than the pirates imagined and therefore had a significant advantage in will, which, at this depth sublevel, put him in a supreme position. Time was not to his advantage, so he quickly activated his escape subprogram and launched into the thick grey walls, careening off them like a billiard ball, sucking energy and inertia from them and accelerating toward the fourth pirate, who had time merely to gape in alarm before imminent collision. At the last nanosecond, Rix shut his system to drone status with full and powerful shielding, collapsing into a silver projectile which pierced the pirate instantly and blew him into shards as his system crashed. A shock wave hit the other pirates like a concussion, a red flash of turbulence, and they cringed and scattered.

Rix stepped into a darkened antechamber precisely on schedule.

"You remembered our emergency cipher. I'm so glad." A woman stood before him with slender cheeks and crinkled eyes, old enough to be his grandmother but young enough to pass for his mother, a rejuve user or perhaps Eternal. Her sandy brown hair was parted at the side and swept across her brow, her nose

long and narrow. She carried the official harmonics of a regent—
an expensive avatar out slumming.

"Who are you?" he asked, keeping full defence systems up
and his presence ghostlike, uncommitted.

"You know better who I am than I do." The woman smiled
and tilted her face at him as though inviting recognition. Her
hand crept up to her chest as she waited for his response.

"You're not my dad," he said pleasantly.

"No?"

"I'm sure of it."

The woman sighed, visibly shaken. She appeared to be
making no attempt at artifice or logistic security. She was
imaging plain street clothes, a striped blouse covered with a zippered yellow cardigan, navy dress pants and matching loafers
with decorative white laces.

"I could take you down," Rix said. "Your codes are faulty."

"Yes, I know. It's a poor but necessary attempt at disguise."
She spread her hands helplessly. "A regent this deep, you know."

Rix nodded, sensing now the dark core code behind a filmy
drapery of weakness. He struggled to remain calm as he drowned
in psychological turmoil, considering terrible alternatives. The
rumours were true. His dad was dead. His wetware system had
been pirated, perhaps reanimated from his corpse, his private
access ciphers plundered, his passwords laid bare. The entire
Eternal community might be at risk, his family, his friends.

The powerful avatar before him was as clean as black ice and
had an aura that felt like teeth clenched on tinfoil—impossibly
expensive, otherworldy. His real dad had disappeared offplanet in
difficult circumstance, according to published reports. Who
knew what technological advantage might have come from

beyond the Macpherson Doorway? Who was this zombie woman?

"I have another message for your mother, Rix," the woman said finally, imaging an airplane ticket and hotel reservation.

Rix whistled. "Atlantis?"

"Just dinner and a movie. Nothing fancy."

"That's it? Right out in the open?"

"Something terrible has happened."

"How did you get this source code? Why are you trying to impersonate my father?"

"I lost some data in a mindwipe, Rix. I left backups in V-space. Treasure chests. Do I seem that much different to you?"

"You don't know me."

"I'm afraid it's even worse than that."

"How so?" he asked, feeling cold creeping in like a flood.

"I can't remember your mother either."

Rix allowed a shiver of interference to run through his mirror-like avatar from top to bottom, his nonverbal response as elegant as any expletive. They stared at each other, a father and son, an empty galaxy of V-space between them.

"A regent has very limited access sublevel," the woman said, attempting a businesslike decorum. "I could use your help with a few things."

In reply, Rix snatched the proffered tickets and backvaulted out of the room.

Madame Shakura made no attempt to conceal her impatience as the Director of the ERI, Helena Sharp, coalesced before her in an opulent Prime Level Three meeting room. The small Japanese woman looked white and vicious, her avatar as solid as marble, her face bloodless, her pressed lips a streak of scorn. The padded shoulders of her dark, tailored suit made her appear manlike and severe. She represented a consortium of immense wealth and political power that stretched far beyond state borders and continental boundaries.

"You ignored two official requests for a meeting, Director," she said with a voice dripping acid. "You returned from your mission three full days ago."

"What's our encryption status?" Zakariah asked as he checked his own avatar for stability by glancing through his palm, the opacity of which gave him a rough guideline. He stretched long feminine fingers and made a show of examining his perfect cuticles while he counted disciples from the corner of his eye. Ten members of the World Council sat in their appointed places. Chairman Tao's seat was empty.

"We have Triple-A encryption from the Beast," the Japanese woman uttered icily, still bristling for some apology.

"And the security problems we encountered prior to my departure have surely been rectified," the Director challenged instead.

Madame Shakura's eyes widened. In her culture such disrespect was akin to a declaration of war.

"I am the ranking spokeswoman while Chairman Tao remains hospitalized," she said with barely contained aggression, her face a stern mask of outrage. "World Council members are vowed to complete silence outside this meeting, on penalty of death. The Eternal Research Institute, on the other hand, is in complete disarray."

"I have been away. I have taken steps." Zakariah stepped

toward an empty chair and slowly took a seat. He reclined and folded his hands across his belly in a gesture of ease. "Eternal blood supply has increased by two percent in my absence. Have your quotas all been met?"

Nods and grunts arose in response. No one dared to challenge the spokeswoman's public authority. Madame Shakura had wasted no time cementing her position long before this meeting. Zakariah had dredged what information he could from Helena's personal files and private memoirs: Director William Ortega stood out as being the next obvious in line for the chairmanship, a corporate banking official who spent most of his time on Prime Level Five at the top of the V-net. Ortega sat to the right of Madame Shakura, a small, swarthy man with short hair and a moustache, Argentinean by heritage. Prime Three was far beneath his common station and must seem like a seedy, budget hotel in comparison. Unfortunately, the regulatory structures uplevel would not allow for such an informal collusion as the World Council.

Zakariah carefully tested the harmonics of each member one by one, looking for any subtle infiltration, any offkey coding or vacant parameter. Too much was at stake to let a whisper pass in the night. The council members, well aware of the Director's special gift, waited quietly for Helena Sharp to finish, as much for their own safety as for the security of their meeting.

Madame Shakura sat quietly fuming, her face greedy with the hope of glory. When Helena's eyes finally met her own, a smile of anticipation graced her face, a thin, ruby curve on a ghostlike face.

"The Source of the virus?" she asked, barely a hush.

"The Source lies outside of space and time as we know it," Zakariah said. "Completely inaccessible by current technology."

Madame Shakura's smile faded to a vicious red gash.

"Any idea of exerting influence or control is, frankly, a pipedream at this point. I am pleased to report, however, that a first contact has been made." Zakariah knew this much and no more and winced inwardly at what it had cost him.

The council members murmured like waters disturbed as anxiety became a palpable animal among them. The World Council had been the primary funding base for the Eternal Research Institute for more than a decade, the financial investment incalculable, the personal and professional sacrifices a matter of private despair.

The Director calmed the waves with a feminine palm upraised like a standard, a promise of important news. "An activated sample has been obtained."

At this announcement, the entire meeting degenerated into a babble of accents and accusations. Members stood and shouted in unison, protecting their political spheres with raw hostility. Apparently, this was to have been the last meeting of the World Council, the members having voted, at Madame Shakura's insistence, to pull the plug on the ERI, to cut the Director loose to the black-market bloodlords.

He turned to stare at her. Madame Shakura had lost face again, perhaps irreparably, but she smiled like a Cheshire cat in love. It had been a win-win situation for her personally, regardless of the outcome. She would live forever now.

For a moment the meeting resembled a group of schoolchildren whose teacher had left the room on a washroom break, giddy with emotion pent-up too long. But one by one the council members remembered their standing in life and sat down, guilty with responsibility, vulnerable now to a new authority.

"This is a great day for mankind," Madame Shakura pronounced in blessing, now openly grinning her joy. "How soon can we expect our allotments?"

"Let's not get ahead of ourselves," Zakariah insisted, his voice deliberately strong to reinforce his superiority. "There is still significant laboratory work to be done."

"You have our full resources at your command," Director Ortega spoke up.

The Director nodded, rehearsing Mundazo's notes in his mind and collecting his demeanour. "Since replicating the virus has not worked in the past, our initial strategy will be to dilute the activated sample by mixing it with blood that is already Eternal, but not from the Source. So far, our research team has diluted at a ratio of one hundred to one without any appreciable decline in the activation rate, which we are measuring by timing the release of photons from the mitochondria of individual cells. These measurements are for technicians, really, because an activated sample glows, my friends—the virus produces light from no known source!"

Zakariah paused for effect, letting the miraculous stand on its own. Light was the ultimate mystery, ubiquitous and yet unknown. A wave, a particle, a quantum packet of potentiality— who could fathom its true nature?

"We have fifty samples ready to test immediately, and fifty more to continue our experiments."

The Director smiled with sure triumph. Zakariah could imagine Helena's pride as though it were his own, as though they were still connected. She had fought a malicious war in political trenches and sacrificed a decade of her life to reach this pinnacle, to survey the future from such a high and lofty peak. And he alone had endured to reap the benefit of her work.

"I'm looking for volunteers," he announced grandly.

Niko arrived home grim with resolute purpose. Rix could tell from the moment he saw her that something was wrong, something had changed. She moved with the graceful agility that she normally used with her working persona, quick and efficient. She bent and rummaged in a closet by the door as he rose to greet her. She pulled out a bundle of grey cotton, his deflated duffel bag, and tossed it into his arms.

"Time to go," she said.

"You're kicking me out?" His voice had an edge to it that he didn't like, a keen tone of panic and disappointment that he wished he had better concealed.

"It's time to move on, that's all. Your father is back."

He stared at her, blinking, wondering if it could be true. "Where?"

"ERI headquarters."

"That building we scoped out?"

"Yeah."

"I don't want to go," he said, wondering how much he could tell her without risking his heart. "I want to stay with you."

Niko paused and looked at him with a puzzled frown. Had she seen something in his eyes, something he could not bring himself to confess?

"It's nothing personal, Rix," she told him with careful calm. "There's been a new development, something unexpected.

Zakariah has obtained an activated sample of the virus."

The news seemed to hit him like a dream, something insubstantial. He pondered her words as though they might be a foreign language, as though the meaning might be abstruse. Had he ever expected such a possibility? Had he ever allowed himself a glimmer of hope that his father might succeed in his quest. "For me?"

Niko pressed her lips with uncertainty, her shrug barely a twitch. "We can only assume, Rix. You've got to get on the ground. You've got to find out."

"Come with me," he blurted.

Again she paused to appraise him, to search his face with quiet intent. Her body language said that she could not possibly follow him, her muscles rigid and her neck upright. "I like you, Rix. You know that."

He hung his head, feeling a crash of doom around him. He recognized an ache in his abdomen that he supposed was love, some arcane emotion. He could not dare tell her. "When?" he said.

"Right now, Rix. It's the chance of a lifetime."

He felt robbed of elation. He felt like a sleepwalker, a powerless observer distanced from an inexorable drama. Could Zakariah really have brought him Eternal life? Would the virus separate him from mortal humans forever? Would he ever see Niko again?

He should have known his relationship with her would never last. He had been foolish to harbour thoughts of intimacy. It had all been a fantasy, some infantile infatuation. He stared at the duffel bag in his hands. He had to get packing, if only he could move a muscle.

"I'll gas up the bike," she said. "Bring your ID. You'll be going back on the grid."

He forced his eyes up to look at her again, to lock an image of her in his memory. She stood with her arms akimbo in a stance of delicate insouciance, her black knit tunic barely covering narrow hips, the faded blue denim on her legs like a second skin. Her low-cut neckline exposed the tendons and bones below her throat, a gentle hollow of shadow and ridges of rib under her tawny skin. Her breasts stood out bold and youthful, and he captured them with his eyes. He wanted to touch them just once.

"It's not the end, Rix. It's the beginning." She tipped her head up, her eyebrows perfect arches above dark lashes, her nose small and pert, her lips like pink pillows. She seemed to be daring him to say something, to admit the truth in his heart. Or did he just imagine it?

"Will you visit me, at least?" he asked. His voice sounded plaintive and weak, and he hated the sound of it. "I just can't say goodbye."

"I'll try to get a message to you. I can't say anything for sure."

He nodded, feeling numb. "I thought you cared about me."

"I do care about you. We're family."

"I don't want to be your cousin, Niko. I want more than that." He searched her face for rejection now that his declaration hung in the air around them. He had waited too long. He should have told her the day they first met, the day he had fallen in love.

Niko nodded with a crooked smile of resignation, her eyes wide with amusement. She unclasped a black leather belt at her waist and pulled it free. She gripped her tunic and pulled it up over her head. She dropped it to the floor.

Rix stared in amazement at her slender torso, stunned speech-less. She reached behind her back to unclasp her bra and shrugged her shoulders forward. It fell at her feet with barely a whisper. She hesitated for a moment and brushed at her hair.

Rix stepped forward and cupped her breasts with both hands. They felt softer than he had imagined and warm. His fingers moved with gentle rhythm, and he bent forward to kiss her.

She responded hungrily and clutched him with her arms. Her palm slid up the back of his neck, and her body pressed hot against him as their lips lingered. Rix heard a soft moan but couldn't tell if it was Niko's voice or his own. A rush of raw sensuality overwhelmed him. The world fell away, and his lust for her became the sole focus of his experience. His hand found the small of her back and rested there in the hollow above her naked tailbone. It seemed a focal point in her frame, the place where her tiny waist blossomed into mature hips and buttocks, where the slender girl became a woman.

Their lips parted, and Niko gazed into his eyes, her face flushed, her breath panting. She took his arm and led him back a few steps to a chair by the door. She sat and pulled him up close.

Rix reached for the single button at his waist and twisted it free. He paused, hardly daring to push his luck, but Niko reached for his zipper and tugged it down. Rix felt her roving fingers at the waistband of his shorts, a slow and sensuous tickle. He stared down at the top of her head and her naked shoulders. Nothing else seemed to matter.

STEVE STANTON

Mia woke to the sound of knocking at her door. She blinked her
eyes in a momentary panic of disassociation before recognizing
the grey walls of her current hovel.

"It's Jimmy, Mia. You have a visitor."

She sat up, brushing tangles from her hair with her fingers.
She unlocked the door and swung it inward.

Rix smiled at her from the threshold. "Mom," he said, and
her chi sang as she rushed into his embrace. His arms were
strong, his upper body bulky with muscle.

She pulled back to look at him, holding her hands on his
shoulders. He had shaved off his unruly shock of hair, his scalp
now a close-cropped brown shadow, his ears exposed, his V-net
plug blinking. He wore a tan suit jacket overtop of a white collared shirt unbuttoned at the neck and looked more like a young
businessman than the teenage urban hero she had left behind just
weeks ago.

"Where have you been?"

"I've been staying with a friend. Just chilling out. I hear
you've been roving the universe. Still squandering my inheri-
tance, huh?"

"You look good," she said. "I wasn't worried."

He smiled in recognition of the white lie, for he knew her too
well. "Not even a little?"

"Maybe a little."

"Well, you always look marvellous," he said, and she suspected a similar fabrication. She brushed tears of joy from her
cheek with the back of her wrist.

"I'll leave you two to get reacquainted," Jimmy said.

"Thanks for the scoop, man." Rix bowed with a genteel confidence that Mia had not seen before. Who was this young man?

How did he know Jimmy?

"Yeah, thanks, Jimmy," she echoed.

"No worries. We'll go out for a bite to celebrate. My treat."

Rix made himself comfortable beside his mother on her cot. His eyes appraised her closet boudoir, her backpack of dirty laundry strewn on a makeshift desk.

"So, we're in big trouble again."

"I'm afraid so."

Rix bobbed his head with recognition. So what else was new? "I'm heading for the ERI. They've got an activated sample and I'm going for it. I've pinged them already and demanded to be put in the program. They're doing some kind of experiment."

"That sounds great. Have you seen your father?"

"I can't be sure. Have you?"

"Yes."

"He's alive?"

She took a steady breath. Her hands fluttered on her legs like wounded birds. "He's been mindwiped, Rix. He doesn't remember us."

His face went stony, his eyes hard. A bristle of stubble stood out against his suddenly white skin. He showed no emotion, no teenage angst, no echo of childhood.

Mia ducked her chin, feeling lost and unbalanced. Her stomach felt like a vacant, gnawing hole. Just a few weeks ago she had kissed her boy goodbye. Now, suddenly, he stared at her with adult cynicism and pride. "He teamed up with the Director of the ERI. They went offplanet, through the Macpherson Doorway. I went after him . . ." Her breath caught in her throat at the memory. ". . . but I failed. Something went wrong."

Rix nodded. Old news. Somehow he knew already.

"Did they sleep together?" he asked.

Mia felt tears burn behind her eyes. "What?" she whispered.

"Are you guys divorced?"

"No! Certainly not! How can you ask that?"

"That woman has pirated his system. She's got all his crack-codes, all his secrets. They've joined together into some kind of cyber-freak."

"You've seen him in V-space?" Mia's heart jumped like a wild bird. "The real Zak?"

Rix reached into his suit jacket and pulled out a faxslip, an official document with registered barcode. He held it up—an airline ticket and hotel reservation. "I didn't think it was him at first, but I guess maybe it was in a way." He offered the voucher to her trembling hand. "You'd better be careful, Mom. He's pretty spooky."

NINE

Mia made the short hop to Atlantis through the lower stratosphere aboard a standard commercial jet. The Atlantis spaceport sprawled over an archipelago in the lower Caribbean Sea, controlled at a distance by the Republic of Colombia. The mean temperature hovered close to thirty degrees Celsius most of the year, and Mia perspired freely as she made her way slowly through immigration where her passport and papers were checked by young Spanish-speaking boys who relished their authority without ever appearing impolite. Her attempts at filling out a Spanish customs form on the plane were corrected fastidiously before she cleared the gauntlet.

A young and beautiful black man approached her out of a crowd of sweaty tourists.

"Mia Davis, my name is Umberto," he said in greeting, and he bent to take her one small suitcase. He wore black pants and a black-and-white polyester shirt with a blue name tag. He checked her hotel reservation and led her to the appropriate taxi, a silver-grey minivan with signs of rust on the wheel wells. She climbed into the front passenger seat and glanced behind her at two young lovebirds holding hands and smiling, still fiddling with their wedding rings. An older couple, sixtyish, sat in the row behind, and they all exchanged pleasantries in English as the driver sped off with both side doors wide open. Instinctively, Mia felt for a seatbelt and buckled up, glad for the confines of her front seat compartment. The gusting air refreshed her clammy skin and quickly dried her clothes as she scanned the tropical scenery on either side of the highway—untrimmed palm trees and thick forests of wild sugar cane. She smelled manure and sun-ripened pollen.

The passengers disembarked minutes later at the Paradise Island Hotel, a small but clean establishment decorated with pink stucco and natural stone, across a narrow road from a vast, white beach. A salty breeze swept shoreward and tousled her hair as young Colombians vied for luggage from the back of the van. Two security guards stood at the door with creased, brown uniforms, peaked hats, and holstered pistols. They inspected her with a cursory nod, and she felt rumpled and haggard under their quick appraisal. She rubbed awkwardly at the tangled thatch on her head, feeling shaggy and unkempt as she made her way to the reception desk. All the tourists seemed to be paired up around her, and Mia felt a pang of loneliness. Why had Zak chosen this exotic venue for a meeting? Why the elaborate courtship ritual?

A young Latina woman with black hair drawn starkly back to a bun took a cursory look at her papers, handed her a keycard, and barked a quick and fluid command in Spanish to the young black man holding her solitary suitcase. He ushered Mia up one flight of stairs and down an open-air hallway where spicy green iguanas scurried along the walls and jewelled hibiscus reached just beyond the railing. In her room, he showed her simple furnishings and a lovely ceramic bathroom and shower and waited long enough for a single American dollar, the currency equivalent of several thousand local pesos. A fruit basket sat on a wooden dresser. The note attached read, "Dinner at eight on the Terrace Restaurant," in Zak's meticulous handwritten script.

Mia opened a sliding glass door to a small balcony facing the ocean. Two white plastic lawn chairs sat waiting for her under the business end of a humming air conditioner. Only then did Mia smile. The sun was drifting to the horizon behind a forest of palm trees, their long feathered branches dancing in the breeze. Small electric cars and motor scooters drove quietly by, and tourists in colourful garb ambled on the sidewalks or reclined in lounge chairs on the beach. A few congregated around a green-roofed gazebo where drinks were doled out in plastic cups.

A space shuttle launched in the distance off to the left, turning the air to a rough rumble that was palpable on her skin. All eyes on the beach turned in unison to look. Conversations stopped in mid-sentence. Mia imagined worshippers in reverence, new believers in the techno-gods of man. Seconds later the flares disappeared through the clouds as the thunder faded, and husbands turned back to their wives, and children to their fathers.

Mia sat and stretched aching legs. She wondered how safe it might be for an Eternal in Atlantis, feeling vague unease in this strange environment. Mainland Colombia had never signed a treaty with the Eternal Research Institute, and kidnappings were common, but an island spaceport city like this would certainly be well guarded and protected. Zak would never knowingly lead her into danger. Not the old Zak. Not the man she loved.

She checked her wristband, which she had already advanced to local time on the airplane, and rose to shower and dress for dinner. As she passed the fruit basket, she chose a green banana, unpeeled it quickly while she kicked off her shoes and wolfed it down to tide her over. The banana tasted exotic and alarmingly sensual, freshly ripened in the tropics instead of in transit to a northern supermarket. The taste made her feel earthy and alive, vulnerable again to sensation after a long absence. She peeled off her clothes and stepped under steamy hot saltwater.

She arrived for dinner freshened and anxious, feeling like a teenager on a first date. She scanned the crowd for her husband, her lost lover, the missing segment of her broken heart. The stakes were high, but she planned a temperate performance, a modest opening gambit. She would not gush and smother him. Nor could she feign disinterest. She would play the coquette to win him anew.

Her first sight of Zak filled her with growing apprehension. He seemed a stranger, his posture subtly altered, his expression unrecognizable. He wore a black tuxedo with a white ribbed shirt front and black bow tie—an affectation she had never seen in their long years together, and he did not smile the familiar and playful smile that he always used in her presence, even in bad and dangerous situations. Instead, he sat like an undertaker with a sombre pallor as she approached his candlelit table at the end of a long balcony terrace overlooking the ocean. The wind from the beach whistled her scanty dress against her thighs like a clinging wrapper.

She balanced her chi against a blooming fit of nervous agony. Her chest heaved with an uncomfortable rhythm. Her once graceful legs felt uncooperatively rigid, her steps stilted and tentative on heels tall enough for a streetwalker. Her future was on the line.

She posed like a fashion model in front of him, smoothing the wrinkles on her filmy blue dress. She had never imagined flirting with her own husband like a stranger, nor was she sure what rules might apply, but she wanted to press every advantage. She hoped to arouse something more than memories, something primal and basic, something predictably male.

It didn't work. His eyes never left her face as he rose to greet her. He offered his hand like a distant cousin or uncle might, took hers, and shook it with a firm squeeze. All business.

Mia forced a smile nonetheless. "It's so good to see you again," she said. "I've missed you terribly." Her breath caught in her throat.

Zak smiled a bland caricature. "Please sit." He gestured with an open palm. "I'm sorry for everything."

Mia perched gingerly on her chair, her nervous system still priming for fight or flight. She took a cleansing breath. "I understand how difficult it must seem."

"I've had a bit of a setback." Zak pointed to his right temple and twirled his index finger.

"I know."

"I didn't recognize you on the shuttle, I'm sorry. I didn't know I was . . . that we were . . . uh, connected." He arched his eyebrows and shrugged his shoulders in an attempt at levity, a peace offering.

Mia smiled. "You've scanned the public data, of course."

"Yes, I know we're married."

"Seventeen years."

He nodded. "That's a long time."

"You don't remember any of it?"

"I'm sorry."

Mia felt a fresh wave of panic. Her life had been wiped out, her glory days sucked into a black hole. All that was left was a few shards of evidence, a birth date and marriage certificate, a few blood tests and a DNA signature. Is that all life comes down to in the end? She did not trust herself to speak.

Thankfully a waiter approached to interrupt her turmoil. He set a wine glass in front of her and added a splash of clear liquid from a carafe.

"I took the liberty of ordering white wine," Zak said, and when she made no response he nodded almost imperceptibly to her glass. "Is white okay with you?"

Mia tore her eyes from him and took her glass in hand, tasted it quickly, and set it back down. "Very nice," she said to the short Latino man beside her, who smiled graciously and filled both goblets. He then spewed a lightning quick rendition of the menu in English that seemed baroque with Spanish accent and impossible for her to follow. She fingered the slender gold chain she wore at her neck, a honeymoon present that her husband would never remember.

Zakariah noted her anxiety and ordered a seafood casserole for both of them. He sipped his wine. "It's from Chile," he said. "Very dry."

Mia took a mouthful absently and looked out at the ocean, now dark and silent. A steady breeze rustled the palms, and their branches waved in slow dance like hula girls. As their waiter rushed to the kitchen, a young girl approached with a small basket of bread and two plates of mixed-green salad, her face beaming.

"Thank you," Mia said. "*Gracias.*"

The girl bowed with pleasure, vibrant and innocent, so obviously free of tragedy.

"Were we happily married?" Zak asked when they were alone again.

Mia winced. She forced a swallow of wine down her aching throat. Happily married? It sounded so bland and banal.

"I mean, you know, was it a marriage of convenience, as they say, or politically motivated in some way?"

"My God, no," she blurted. She covered her lips with her fingers and sat back in her chair, surprised by the harshness in her voice. She composed herself and tried again. "I mean, really, we were as happily married as anyone I have ever known."

"I see." Zak nodded, looking somewhat relieved. "That must have been wonderful."

Past tense, Mia noted grimly. She gulped more wine. "You don't seem like a robot. You're not brain dead."

He cast his eyes down as though embarrassed at his vulnerability. "I remember how to speak, how to dress myself, and act in public; I remember school lessons from decades ago, lots of vivid details from my youth—just nothing recent. I'm sorry. This is very awkward."

"I'm not letting you off the hook, Zak."

"What?"

"You're mine. You belong to me."

Zak shook his head. "I don't think so."

"We could start over. You owe me that much. Let's pretend we just met. What do you think of me so far?"

He blinked with surprise. A quick grin played on his face. His eyes moved slowly, lingering on her body. "You're gorgeous," he said.

Mia recognized that smile, finally, a smile without artifice,

STEVE STANTON

and with it she found a promise of hope. "Well, you're pretty cute yourself."

He blushed and raised his wine glass in salute. "A toast to new beginnings, then."

"To new beginnings," she replied.

Their glasses met with a clear clarion ring.

Their server brought two shallow bowls full of stew in a thin tomato sauce and placed them grandly with a bow of courtesy to the lady. He refilled their wine.

Zak looked askance at his food. "How is this a casserole? It looks like soup."

Mia spooned through her own bowl looking for anything recognizable. "It's supposed to be seafood?"

Zak held up a bit of white meat on a fork. "This is a piece of tentacle. I recognize the ring shape."

"Calamari," she said. "So it's just people and places that you can't remember, or what?"

"Well, it's hard to tell what's missing exactly."

"It must be different kinds of local fish," Mia offered and tasted a sample. "Not bad."

Zak took a few hesitant bites and gagged with disgust at a piece of gristle on his tongue. He spit out a white lump into his napkin and placed it on the edge of his salad plate.

"I don't know what that might be," he offered in apology. "Octopus perhaps?"

Mia shrugged. "It must be a catch-and-release casserole."

Zak burst out with a laugh, and Mia joined him in a mutual release of tension. The sound of his gaiety lulled her into the past. She felt a camaraderie, a connection, and she clung to it like a talisman in her mind as the first blush of alcohol swam through her blood like an elixir.

"Catch and release. That's good," he said.

They giggled like school chums and began to chronicle exotic seafood specimens like amateur biologists. They drained a carafe of Chilean wine. Disaster had been averted, and Mia allowed herself the luxury of peaceful imagination well into dessert, when the tone of conversation turned businesslike once more.

"We really should discuss living arrangements," Zak told her abruptly.

"Well, I don't usually invite men back to my hotel room on a first date," Mia replied coyly, feeling a pleasant flush of romance in her wine-tingled cheeks.

"My plane leaves in three hours," Zak admitted and looked at his wrist monitor for punctuation.

"You're leaving already? Just like that!"

Zak held his palms upward with innocence. "I'm in the midst of difficult negotiations," he said. "I just wanted to get you settled."

Mia's situation suddenly came into clear focus—a tropical paradise, no return ticket. "So this was merely an exercise in containment," she stated with flat precision.

"Certainly not."

"You must have been curious at least."

"Mia, please. I'm acting in your best interest."

"You're just as headstrong and callous as you ever were. You're reckless on your own. I'm not letting you out of my sight."

"It's hardly your decision."

"I'm making it my decision. Don't make me resort to violence."

"You've got to be kidding."

"I'll hogtie your ass if I have to."

"Are you drunk?"

"You'd better hope so, because you'd never beat me in a fair fight."

"Okay, settle down. Let's be reasonable."

"You need me, Zak. I know you better than you know yourself."

Zak eyed her carefully, but his expression was softening around the edges.

"I could be your helpmate," Mia continued. "I'm a good worker. Above all else, I'm the only person you can trust now."

A shuttle lifted off from the spaceport in the distance, the sound overpowering, rumbling in waves over them, the rocket flares illuminating the sky, revealing all from the darkness.

Zak reached for his wineglass and stared into the last dregs, balancing it in his fingers and tilting it gently back and forth. He looked like a handsome baron in his tuxedo, a prince of industry. He was Eternal and had once loved her with all his heart. Mia knew she could win his trust again. All she needed was a chance to prove herself.

When silence settled again a number of seconds later, Zak's face remained stolid.

"I know too much already," Mia said, desperate now and ready to gamble.

Zakariah smiled his doubt and spread his fingers with invitation.

"I know that you're impersonating the Director of the ERI, Helena Sharp. That alone is enough to land you in prison. I know that you've installed some voodoo wetware to operate her avatar in V-space. I know that you are playing another big, fast, crazy game like you always do."

His eyes glazed with ice, and Mia knew she had scored a direct hit. His smile didn't falter. "That's pretty good. For the record, I have her official approval and full cooperation."

"I know you have an ampoule of activated virus and have initiated laboratory trials. You'll be the target of every bloodlord on the planet once word gets out. I'm the only person you can trust."

Zakariah began to rub his sternum with his fingers, lost in thought, his facade cracking around him. Mia had seen it before and took comfort in the recognition. He hated being a pawn in someone else's game.

"It was supposed to be for Rix," Mia whispered. "That's why you went offplanet in the first place."

Zakariah nodded, breathing deep through his nose.

"I love you, Zak."

He stiffened against her declaration. "I can't drag up the past with you, Mia. I just can't do it. The past is gone."

"Fine. I understand that." She held her palms up as though to ward off the sentiment, her fingers spread as wide as she could stretch. "I fully understand. But you can't treat me like a child after seventeen years of marriage."

"What will it take to secure your silence?"

"I'm not trying to blackmail you, for God's sake. I just want to be your partner. You're still my husband."

Zak squinted past her shoulder. His probing eyes had locked onto something behind her. His body slumped with some new realization, his face blank with concentration.

Mia twisted to look, sensing alarm. She could see nothing

amiss. Just tourists and hotel workers. She turned back. "What is it? Are we in danger?"

"Probably. Have you met my father, Mia?"

"Not in person."

"More importantly, have *we* met my father? Am I supposed to know him?"

"No," she stated. "Not to my knowledge."

"I had a sister once, too. Her name was Niko."

"You're starting to remember?"

"No. These memories go back so far they were never erased. Tell me anything you know."

"Your father left when you were quite young. He had financial difficulty and lost everything to loan sharks. He was . . . mutilated . . . his left arm."

"Yes?"

"As far as I know there has never been any personal contact. Jimmy told me that one of Phillip's companies funded my jump through the Doorway. They have corporate interests in common."

"Jimmy?"

"You former partner. A man you used to trust." Mia looked back over her shoulder, searching for dragons. "He's a smuggler, primarily. A field technician."

"You're looking well, my son." Phillip approached with the quick efficiency of a businessman, a no-nonsense attitude that seemed a stark contrast to the pervading *manyana* sentiment on the island. He wore a tailored grey suit with a light blue collared shirt. He deliberately held his right palm open at his side to indicate that he was unarmed, a gesture that seemed both natural and eloquent. He carried a small briefcase in his left hand.

Zak and Mia stood in unison to meet him. "Dad." Zak held

his arm forward.

"Zak, my boy." They shook hands. Phillip's dark eyes were hooded by bushy eyebrows, his curly hair trimmed above his ears, grey at the temples.

"Have you met my wife, Mia?"

"I've not had the pleasure, but I see you've done well for yourself." He shook her hand delicately, evincing great respect in a lingering touch. "I'm honoured to meet you at last."

Mia saw now that Phillip was not carrying a briefcase in his left hand. His arm itself ended in a briefcase, or some sort of computer terminal. He had no thumb or fingers.

"I'll get you a chair," Zak said.

"No, I believe I'll just take young Mia's place, if you don't mind." He smiled and sat down. "I'm sure she has some packing to do."

Zak turned to her with nothing but questions in his eyes.

Mia grabbed a chair from a nearby table and scraped it across the floor. She positioned herself between the two men. "I'm managing Zak's affairs now," she said.

Phillip grinned. "Is that so?"

She nodded. "I'm in charge."

"I didn't expect a social call after this many years," Zak said.

"You don't even know how many years it has been. We could be best of friends."

"I doubt it."

A commercial aircraft took off from the spaceport runway and blanketed the room with noise. Zak gestured with the wine carafe, but Phillip waved away the invitation with an upright palm. Phillip's face was tanned and boyish, his nose as perfect as modern surgery would allow. His grey suit had a lustre of silk or

some expensive synthetic, and he smelled exotic, lightly aro-
matic. He was clearly rich enough to afford chronic rejuve but
didn't look Eternal in Mia's estimation. The wrinkled skin on his
biologic hand showed his true mortal age.

"Why did you stay away so long?"

Phillip shrugged. "Honestly?"

"I don't see any need for deception at this point." Zak folded
his fingers in front of him and waited, his eyes cold.

"I've watched you from afar. You haven't needed more than a
nudge from me along the way. Up until recently, you haven't had
anything I needed."

"And now I do?"

"Yup."

"And that would be . . ." Zakariah trailed off, leaning forward
over the table with wide eyes.

"A direct and unfiltered fiberoptic link to Seventh Heaven.
Two plugs. You and me. It'll be a blast, I promise."

"Prime Level Seven, unfiltered. That's impossible."

"To all appearances." Phillip smiled amiably, showing perfect
white teeth. "No one will suspect a thing."

"You're a gamer?"

"Corporate intelligence."

"A spy?"

Phillip chuckled and shook his head. "I'm a broker, officially.
I have an office on Prime Five. I'm making a special jump for a
client—nothing elaborate."

"You're crazy."

"Perhaps."

"Why risk it? What could possibly be worth such a reckless
stunt? Money? You're obviously rich already."

"Money doesn't interest me. It comes in and out like the tide, and there are no trustworthy receptacles in which to contain it."

"Are you Eternal?"

"The virus doesn't interest me either. I get daily rejuve and all the Eternal blood I can transfuse. It's just like taking vitamins to me."

"It comes from people, you know."

"Cattle, most of them."

Mia shook her head. This man was psychotic. "Why should we trust you for an instant?" she interjected.

Phillip swivelled his eyes to her and back to his son. "You can't trust me. That's patently obvious."

Zak turned his palms up with a shrug. "Okay, then, why should we do anything you say?"

Phillip grinned. "Simple extortion, my boy. It's the oldest edge in town. That's what I do. Specifically . . ." He flipped open the computer terminal at the end of his left arm to reveal a miniature touchscreen and buttons. He stroked it with his right-hand fingers like a virtuoso on a harp. ". . . I have here an active satellite link to the mainland media. I have all the data I need to shut down this spaceport and cause a riot at the Eternal Research Institute."

"I'm not your boy."

"You're vulnerable, Ms. Helena. Frankly I don't think you're going to pull off this silly masquerade anyway, but you can buy a little time by helping me. I can't control every variable in play, of course. Just a prod here and there. Information is like lubricating oil; eventually it finds its own level despite our best efforts. I've invested considerable time and effort, so there's no point in trying to talk me down."

Mia felt foundations crumbling beneath them. Zak seemed

astonished. "Where in the world would I find a direct and unfiltered fiberoptic link to Seventh Heaven?" he asked.

"The ERI has a main shunt in the basement. It branches from there into the Operations Room and elsewhere throughout the compound."

Zakariah's eyes narrowed as he considered specifics. "Who could rig it?"

"Jimmy can do it."

"Jimmy?" He stole a sideward glance at Mia. The tip of his tongue tapped on his upper lip.

"You don't remember old Jimmy? He was your main man on cheap street. Mia can vouch for him. He taught you everything he knew and watched you zoom away up Prime without him, but he came into a stockpile of cash in the end."

"You blackmailed him, too?"

"Nope. Got nothing on him. But Jimmy and I speak the same language. The money was channelled through a casino he did some work for years ago. Jimmy puts in backdoors everywhere he goes—that's his signature. On the record he simply had a lucky night at the roulette table. We came to a business arrangement that was mutually advantageous.

"Don't worry, son. I've looked after everything. I've booked the seat beside you on the plane, and Jimmy's already flying in from his ranch house in Vegas. You just tell your security goons at the Institute that your wife and father are visiting for a few days. Anyone who checks will see it's all legit. I've already got access laminates for the whole complex."

Zak slumped like a broken man resigned to his fate, a hunted pawn trapped in a corner. "I don't know my way around Prime Seven," he said absently.

"I'll show you the ropes, kid. We're just going to slide a bit of data. That's always been your specialty. But this time we'll be right under the nose of the Beast."

Jimmy arrived at the Eternal Research Institute at the same time as two black stretch limousines with mirror-tinted windows. A tangle of cars were parked out front, and servants in uniform were trundling carts of luggage in the main double doors. He surveyed the scene with dismay. It looked like he had stumbled into prime time at the MGM Grand.

He eyed a phalanx of security guards with distrust as his taxi driver slid a window down to await clearance. The guards wore token firearms in button-down holsters. They were not looking for trouble—merely hirelings on parade. The meter clicked steadily as a green-suited traffic cop approached the vehicle.

Jimmy studied the schematics carefully. The roadway approaching the Institute was cordoned off into three lanes with bright orange pylons. The complex was divided into four sections: a six-storey central headquarters of concrete and glass with three wings attached by narrow corridors equidistant from the hub.

The stretch limos moved forward into the lane furthest right, closest to the main driveway. Jimmy's taxi was directed to the lane furthest left, the low-priority route for service vehicles. Their slow progress came to a halt almost a quarter mile from the front doors at a small guard station where an unarmed patrolman stood sweating in his navy-blue ERI uniform.

"No vehicles past this point today," he said apologetically to Jimmy past the taxi driver's shoulder. "What's your business?"

"Computer tech," said Jimmy, measuring the distance he would have to travel with his heavy toolkit. He held up his stolen ID card, which matched the smart fibre in his company-issue uniform, courtesy of Rix and the catgirl.

The guard scanned the proffered barcode, checked his clipboard monitor, and looked up. "I've got you as a priority. Give me a minute to expedite you through this mess."

"Can I get a cart for my toolbox?" Jimmy asked. He rested his hand on the large black box on the seat beside him.

"We'll get something," the guard said as he handed a plastic debit voucher to the taxi driver.

The driver swiped the card and handed it back. The meter stopped its onerous momentum and chirped happily as currency changed hands instantaneously via satellite link.

Jimmy exited the cab and delicately hauled his black box out onto the sidewalk, hoping his care and precision would go unnoticed. On his closely shaved head he wore a black baseball cap that dropped down artfully over his brow. He was a burly man but would leave a bland description of a tradesman behind. He had spoken fewer than a dozen words to the cabbie and hoped to do the same with anyone else. No strings, no dancing.

The security guard ambled back from his booth as the cab drove away. "This orange badge will get you in the central complex but nothing above the second floor. It will expire at five o'clock and must be returned to this station before you leave," the guard droned. "Any deviation from your assigned schedule will get you in a load of crap, especially today. The place is crawling with VIPs."

Jimmy shook his head knowingly with conspiratorial chagrin. He scanned several squads of greensuits in front of him and stroked his thick moustache and goatee.

"We don't need all these hired guns," the guard continued as he pulled a small cart from a broom closet. "Our people are equipped for anything. We've had full-scale riots right here at my station," he added with pride, trying for eye contact.

Jimmy arched his eyebrows briefly with requisite respect. "Thanks for the cart," he said and turned away quickly. He placed his black box with precise ease and pretended to kick it to the centre of the dolly. He manoeuvred it gently up the long sidewalk, navigating to avoid as many tremors as possible. As he approached the glass doors up front he studiously avoided the greensuits and headed toward a single navy blue patrolman on duty.

"Computer tech," he said, tapping the laminate he now wore around his neck. "Where's the service door?"

The patrolman glanced toward the menagerie at the main gate and grimaced with empathy. "Okay, follow me," he said and strode away fumbling with a large ring of keys clipped to his belt. He unlocked a painted grey door thirty metres to the right and held it open.

"Thanks," Jimmy grunted as he tipped his cart gently over the threshold onto shiny tile floor beyond. He kept to the right as he had been instructed, avoiding the noisy crowd milling in the main foyer, keeping his head down but recording the layout with roving eyes. He took a service elevator to the basement without incident and met Phillip Davis precisely on schedule.

Mia bustled her way past the mercenary squad at the ERI with less than feminine finesse. Her husband had security clearance as a field operative, and her son was inside. She demanded to see the Director, and Silus Mundazo was summoned to the gate to sign her pass. He took them up to his office on the third floor and briefed them on the day's events. He looked harried and over-whelmed, but Mia could tell he was a man of great strength. He was a co-founder of the Institute and had worked with Helena in the heady days when their dreams were little more than scientific speculation. He had medical credentials unrelated to the field of hematology, but he carried the Eternal virus and had sold his own blood on the black market to fund early research.

"It is of critical importance that all fifty dosages be adminis-tered under strictly uniform and repeatable conditions. Without a clinical control group we are already operating on the fringe of science."

"I'm sure history will afford us this privilege," Zak said.

"Nevertheless, I really must see to it myself."

"Of course."

"Chairman Tao will be arriving by air ambulance from Singapore in twelve minutes. His condition is critical but stable. I think you should intercept him personally, Zak."

"I agree."

"I have taken the liberty of creating an ID badge for you . . ." He handed over a laminated badge, dark green—full access. ". . . Operations Director Davis."

Zak hung the laminate around his neck.

"Madame Shakura and her entourage are in the lobby demanding a face-to-face meeting with Helena Sharp, of course—eight authorized subjects in total."

Silus turned to face Mia, his face blandly suggestive.

She rolled her eyes and shook her head in resignation. "Fine.

Who am I?"

He smiled at her theatrics. "We'll use your own name. We're not secret agents. You're one of Helena's executive secretaries." Silus offered another green ID pass.

"And how do I explain her absence?" she asked as she draped it over her head. She brushed at her dishevelled hair with her fingers. In her estimation, this whole situation was moving wildly out of control. She did not have enough backstory to make any plausible representation.

"Well, Helena is not Eternal, so naturally she is on the official list of fifty subjects. Your story is that she has already gone to prep under strictly sterile conditions. Any meeting is out of the question. Afterwards we will feign complications and play it by ear. Who knows, perhaps Madame Shakura will take a liking to you." He handed her a wristband monitor. "I'm locked on this speed dial. I'll walk you through the rough spots."

Mia peered at him, appraising him anew, gaining confidence from his quick mind. "You are very good at what you do."

"Helena left me in charge, so I'm making the best of a bad situation. Let's move now, folks. Zak, you have eleven minutes to get to the rooftop helipad."

Zakariah tapped his V-net plug to confirm the time. He bent close to Mia. "Thanks for helping out," he whispered. "I'd like to spend some time together, when we get through this. You know, to give it a chance."

"That would be great." She followed him with her eyes as he stepped through the door. Was this the new beginning she had prayed for? A blossom of love?

"You okay?"

"What?"

Silus pursed his lips at her.

"Sorry." She met his gaze. "The fiftieth subject, using Helena's name?"

"You guessed it, Mia. I snuck Rix in under the radar."

"He's fine?"

"Safe and secure. He's in final prep now. Rix is a capable and confident young man. You must be very proud. Get the Shakura entourage settled in the East wing as quickly as you can. I'd like to get all eight subjects in prep within the hour. We're making headlines today." He reached for her and smoothed the fabric on her upper arm, barely a caress. "Don't worry," he said and showed her his matching wristband. "I'm right beside you." He whisked out of the room.

Mia stood in a daze, tying to summon enough energy to pull off this charade. She felt as though she stood on a great precipice, surrounded by infinite potential. In a few hours, her son might be Eternal. In a few hours she might win back her husband from a pit of despair. One last run. One last pay-off. Her dreams were almost close enough to touch. She could almost get her fingers around them.

Could it really be true? For once in her life, could circumstance finally work in her favour? A week ago she had been without hope, a bare grit of coral on the seashore, tossed by tides and scorched by the sun. Now, another blessing. She'd had more than her fair share of happiness in the early years with Zak, when they had both believed in providence. Was there indeed a god directing the Eternal virus? Had this entire situation been choreographed so that her own clumsy prayers might be answered?

Mia bent to her knees in meditation and took the time to close her eyes and drift with deity. Precious moments stretched out as she stilled her voice within. The way of the warrior was a path of humility, a reconciliation of fire and holy water. She mustered her chi for one final battle.

Mia arose empowered to find a woman standing in the doorway watching her—a blond dignitary wearing an ebony business jacket over a yellow v-neck sweater with black skirt and stockings. She looked severe.

"Can I help you?" Mia asked, fingering her laminate for legitimacy.

"I think you can, yes. My name is Helena. This is my office. One of them, anyway."

"The real Director?"

Helena smiled at the notion of a false Director. "You must have met Zakariah."

"I'm his wife, Mia." She stepped forward to offer a handshake.

New warmth spread in Helena's face, and Mia wondered for a moment about her offplanet relationship with Zak. She looked a bit mature for his taste but showed the timeless health of a disciplined regimen. Perhaps a rejuve user or chronic vampire.

"Has he recovered any memory?"

"No."

"I'm sorry."

Was that an admission of culpability? Mia could see no guilt in her placid brown eyes.

"I have an appointment," Mia said. "Madame Shakura and her entourage are waiting for me downstairs."

"Goodness! Well, that would drive anyone to their knees." Helena offered a conspiratorial grin. "I'd offer to help, but I find I'm lagging the pace a bit here. I've been away, as you probably know. I'll have to plug up and run the numbers for a few minutes." She nodded toward an open doorway where her launch couch sat waiting.

"Of course."

"How many vials do they have?"

"Just the one, but it's been diluted two decimals. Fifty subjects in the first trial."

"Doctor Mundazo is on the ground on this?"

Mia chopped her hands out firmly. "Silus has everything under control."

Helena dropped her gaze as though peering doubtfully over imaginary sunglasses. "It looks like a zoo downstairs."

"Nobody said it would be easy."

She smiled. "I like you, Mia. You've got some spunk under that pretty face. Zak is a lucky man to have you."

The thought of her husband seemed to tighten Mia's throat. He was probably in the basement by now, a master criminal preparing to hack the Beast in Seventh Heaven. She became aware of a simple swallow, a forced breath.

Helena winced with empathy. "Perhaps he'll come around in time," she said. "A stroke victim recovers new brain function daily. And Eternals are steadily regenerating."

Mia ducked her head, trying to compose herself. It bothered her that she was so transparent. She would never make a good field agent. "There's certainly hope for him."

"Well, I won't keep you from your work," Helena said to defuse any further discomfort.

Mia held up her wristband. "Can I tell anyone you're here? Is there anything you need right away?"

"Tell Silus I'm just checking my email. Business as usual."

The boy is late," Phillip Davis said as he tapped spectral colours on the computer touchscreen at the end of his arm.

Jimmy returned delicate tools into foam compartments in his black box and locked them down with velcro tape and heavy-metal shielding. Satisfied at last, he looked up. "What is that gadget anyway? Some early form of biosystem interconnect?"

Phillip nodded. "The landmark advances in neural interface were made by the prosthetic industry, long before wetware surgery became commonplace. I have upgraded, of course, to stay ahead of the trend." He held up his cybernetic arm for inspection. "I have exponentially more storage area here than any temporal implant, and, of course, I have fiberoptics bundled into my spine now, direct to the cerebral cortex."

Jimmy whistled, looking at Phillip with new wonder. "Why are you out slummin' with an old fart like me? What's the game here? Money?"

Phillip chuckled and shook his head. "I'm adjusting reality. Bartering influence, you might say."

"Influence?"

"Money is for scorekeepers and bureaucrats."

"Well, I don't mind checking the score now and again."
Jimmy snapped his tool box shut and placed it on his transport
dolly.

Phillip smiled. "I know you're a hardware guy, and I respect
that."

Jimmy checked his wristband. It was not like Zak to be
late—not when realtime was chiselled out in nanoseconds. "So
you're just doing a favour for a friend. Is that right?"

"Friendship has nothing to do with it, but, yes, we all play
by the same rules."

Jimmy nodded. He really did like this guy—he was pretty
suave for an evil genius. Phillip had quick wit and a foxy
charisma, but his heart was made of superconductors way down
the Kelvin scale.

Two black office chairs with padded armrests had been positioned side by side in the centre of the room. Two V-net plugs
lay coiled on the floor, spliced into the main cable and secured
with black electrical tape. No single component could be traced
to Jimmy or his allies, and he had long ago had his fingerprints
surgically removed. He had fulfilled his contract and could walk
away squeaky clean any time. But he waited. He still had a soft
spot for all the young sliders from back in the day.

"How long before we abort?" he asked.

"My working parameters are not for you to know." Phillip
glanced toward the door, a sheen of perspiration beginning to
glisten on his brow.

Jimmy snuffed at him and began to whistle a tune from a
breakfast-cereal pop-up. No sweat off his bum. These days, it
seemed like everybody was a prima donna up past Prime Four.

A knock sounded like a judge's gavel in their sterile closet.

Neither man flinched.

"Get the door," Phillip said as he moved to sit in one of the chairs. He picked up a coil of wire and eyed the network receptacle as though checking for dirt or disease. He slipped it into a slot just below the crook of his elbow. His eyelids fluttered and closed as he slipped quietly into V-space.

"Zakariah," Jimmy said and reached a warm hand for his long-lost friend. "I hear you've had quite a trip to the top."

"Jimmy?"

"You don't remember?"

Zak's mouth worked into a tight line. "Not exactly."

Jimmy grinned. "Probably just as well. Have a seat." He gestured with a strong arm toward the unoccupied chair.

"And listen carefully," he began as they approached the jury-rigged launch couch. "You are working from extreme disadvantage. This guy is hardware heavy and a psycho to boot. I know you've been supercharged, but this guy is state of the art, Prime Level Six. You with me?"

Zak nodded.

"I don't trust him and neither should you. Just get in, get the goods, and get out. Any backlash from the Beast will do more than burn you—it will kill you outright on an unfiltered line. Abort at the first sign of trouble. The very first inkling. You got it?"

"Mia says I can trust you. Is that right?"

Jimmy grimaced and shook his head. "All those long years—wiped out like a faulty hard drive." He placed a hand on Zak's shoulder. "Listen, kid, you were like a son to me in the early days, but don't take my word for it. You've never trusted anyone, and this is no time to start."

"I had a son once myself."

"Don't worry about Rix. He's got the Davis gift. I'll be watching out for him." He offered a nod as a token of his sincerity. He wanted to say more but had neither the time nor the eloquence. "He reminds me of you, back when cybersaurs roamed the Earth."

"What's the run this time?" Zak picked up a length of V-net cable and coiled it in his lap.

"Total hush-up. Phillip's doing a favour for a friend."

"What's in it for you?"

Jimmy shrugged with casual ease. "A backdoor into Prime Seven could come in handy some day. Rumour says the Beast may be vulnerable. The old bugaboo, you know. Control the AI, control the world." He offered a mischievous leer that he hoped Zak might recognize and respond to.

Zakariah made no show of camaraderie. He looked grim and professional. In the old days, Jimmy had seen him banter with the best of them right up to ground zero. This time he seemed distant and thoughtful, letting anxiety take him down like a victim. The kid was getting old. He was losing his edge.

Zakariah looked back only once, barely a recognition of presence, and plugged into V-space.

Niko crept stealthily into the sterile lab where Rix sat in a white gown wired with biometric relays. She wore a dark flightsuit with a medical company monogram on the breast pocket.

"What the hell are you doing here?"

She smiled. "I wanted to see you. You asked me to visit, remember?" She pulled up a chair. "So how are you?"

"Fine. Everything's going great." He grinned. "Thanks for coming."

"Did they give you the virus?"

"No. Another fifteen minutes or so."

"How do they do it?" She pantomimed a needle pointed to the crook of her arm with her eyes wide in query.

"No, it's sublingual."

"Ahh." She nodded. "Kinda takes the fun out of it."

"You have a weird sense of humour."

"I know. That's why you like me."

Rix was content just to watch her again. Her simple movements seemed to fascinate him. He was way beyond puppy love now. He was seriously falling deep and wide for this chick.

"So, I've got to get back to work soon. Duty calls." She gave a wan smile.

"I'd invite you to stay, but it's supposed to be a sterile room."

"I just wanted you to know . . . I mean if things work out for you . . . that you're welcome home any time. I miss you." She took his hand between her palms. "And to wish you luck, cousin. The best luck."

"Thanks." Oh, man, she was beautiful.

"And, well, to give you this." She fumbled in the pocket of her flightsuit and handed him a picture. "As a keepsake, you know. Just in case."

It was an old photograph, an antique chemical reproduction now fading slightly pinkish. Two young children stared out from a distant age with big smiles and innocent eyes. The boy was dressed in a collared shirt with all the buttons done up to the neck. He draped a brotherly arm around a girl in a fluffy lavender dress, barely a toddler. They looked like they might be on their way to a festive family event, puffed up proud for the camera.

"It's your dad and . . ."

"A distant cousin?"

"Yeah." She looked impish. "Very distant."

Rix peered closer at the photo, looking back through a window in time. Roots. He had lineage in history. He was not just dust on the wind. "Are you sure you want to part with this?"

Niko tapped her forehead with a finger. "I've got a copy. Not to worry."

"Well, thanks. I appreciate it."

Her eyes roamed away, and she seemed momentarily pensive, as though considering an awkward thought. "Anyway, it was a pleasure getting to know you. I mean, working together."

"Niko, is anyone supposed to know you're here?"

She pinched her V-net plug and shook her head. "Not for nine more minutes." She stood up and held her hands aloft, grinning. "Okay, okay. I can take a hint."

She bent down to kiss him. Her lips tasted of strawberries.

"I'll see you," she whispered.

The tall cityscape of Prime Level Seven sheltered a narrow avenue of entry, a constricted vestibule for corporate authentication. Structural edges appeared hard and sharp, defined with mathematical precision. The lighting was subdued, pinkish, reminding Zakariah of an inner-city twilight in realtime. The avenue was criss-crossed with pencil beams of red laser light that moved slowly, sweeping the entire area from roadway to ceiling.

Phillip stood like a statue immediately to his left, his online presence looking perfectly human, his business suit lustrous and impeccable. "Helena, you're looking well," he said.

"Sorry I'm late."

"This backdoor is protected by defence-in-depth and hybrid firewalls," Phillip whispered as he stroked his wrist controls. "Hold out your hand."

Phillip reached over to touch Zakariah's open palm. A red glow sprang up around them like an aura, matching exactly in hue the laser beams monitoring the hallway.

"This subprogram replicates the signal exchanged by the beams when they cross each other, making our movements indistinguishable. The white searchlights above we will have to manually avoid." Phillip pointed up the roadway with a nod.

Zakariah noted the ghost lights, wider and more faint than the red lasers, and blinked his understanding.

Phillip stepped forward into the red lasers, which diffused into his force-field surface without giving an alarm.

"We could still be subject to surveillance," Zakariah warned as he followed. "Any program tracing the number and position of random intersections will see our shadow."

"Not if we dance," Phillip offered and began a slow ballet that zigzagged down the avenue like a martial arts exercise.

Zakariah followed, contorting in a comfortable rhythm, avoiding red beams where convenient and white beams on pain of death, spiralling through the entry gauntlet to where Phillip waited and watched in appraisal.

"That's quite the body for an old spinster," he said.

"Don't get cheeky, Dad. She's not your type."

"You're not still mad about your mother, are you?"

"Why shouldn't I be? You left her to die."

"Don't be silly. She stayed behind of her own accord. We grew apart. It happens."

"You took my sister."

"We divided up the assets."

Phillip entered an alleyway to the left and palmed access into a cathedral of cut glass filled with white security beams that broke into prisms on the multi-faceted walls. "This encryption algorithm would take hours to decipher but can be easily circumvented. To the ceiling, my boy." He jumped with Zakariah right on his heels. He reoriented and stood on a rough granular surface, then raised an arm to indicate the scene before them. "Because of the angle of this architecture, the white beams are sparse here, geometrically. We go one at a time to allow for complete freedom of movement." He dove, ducked, rolled, jumped, and swam his way through a maze of light, and splayed himself like a salamander on the far wall.

Zakariah eyed the beams. One touch and it would be over. One mistake. Hard data was a merciless foe. He launched his avatar and let his inner senses loose to guide him. Mia liked to call it her chi, her body energy, but Zakariah imagined something greater, some unconscious power, an invisible spirit guiding him. He twisted and contorted around pencil flashes of light without thinking, without waiting for his brain to define his movements. He lived the path. He knew it in his heart, and he arrived safely to meet his father on the other side.

"This is as far as I have been," Phillip said as they stood side by side on a thin ledge. A christmas tree of portals lay on the wall beside them. "The second green door over is the one we want. I have all the entry codes, which rotate on a timed schedule every five minutes. What we do not have is the background retinal key, but I know it can be bypassed by system security in case of emergency. I can get you to the appropriate terminal for three minutes."

"You want me to hack it with no prep?"

"It's downlevel gear, practically archaic. Easy access for a man of your talents. This is a low-priority area for bureaucrats and bean counters, the weakest link in the chain. I doubt a human has ever walked this path."

"What are we doing here?"

"We're sliding a few beans. It's a proxy vote."

"That's it?"

"Almost too easy, isn't it?"

Zakariah glanced around with nervous anxiety. He had to admit that things looked pretty clean at the moment. "Whatever reason drove you away from my mother was no excuse to abandon me as well."

Phillip glared back at him. "Would you really want a small child to be caught in a tug-of-war between hateful parents? To be ammunition in a vindictive struggle? I think not."

"You never gave me the choice."

"The codes will rotate in fifteen seconds. We can go now or take five minutes for you to collect your wits and settle long-standing grudges."

Zakariah set his teeth with an incoming hiss of air. "No delay to destiny," he murmured.

"That's my boy."

"I'm not your boy." Together they dove for the conduit.

Phillip worked some white magic for several seconds at the portal, then entered and activated a standard flatscreen subterminal. He keyed in some code, reading from his palm panel, then stepped back to allow Zakariah access. "Two minutes and forty-five seconds," he said.

The algorithms looked harmless, the system stable if not dusty from disuse. Zakariah tried some background harmonics and slipped easily to the core program. The coding was ancient, old corporate American stuff. He recognized the language and began looking for classic patterns he had learned as a child. An alert flashed briefly on the periphery of his field of vision. "We've been tagged by a sniffer," he said.

"Keep working. It could be a random sweep."

Zakariah had not stopped, of course, not with a countdown in progress. Seconds later, he successfully bypassed the retinal-scan subprogram and keyed a manual access. A door irised open in front of them.

"I don't know," he warned Phillip as he followed him inside. "That sniffer has definitely locked onto something." Was this the first inkling of trouble Jimmy had warned about?

A vast datafield floated in front of them, columns of numbers in linear streams like spaghetti. Money, financial reports, years of accumulated corporate evidence. They could rewrite history from here with a single nudge of an upraised middle finger. Or get lost for hours looking for trees in the forest. Without a map their alterations might be little more than graffiti.

Phillip zeroed in on his target without hesitation. He reached into a tangle of cyber-spaghetti and tweaked a relatively inci-dental bit of data.

A warning note hit Zakariah palpably like a pneumatic wave. "We are definitely on a hit list. One of us must be carrying some-thing foreign."

Phillip smiled with satisfaction and nodded. "Macpherson

promised as much."

"What are you talking about?"

Phillip gazed into unfocused distance, momentarily enraptured by his imagination. "The holy grail. The leash on the Beast."

"You're crazy. That sniffer is going to hit any second and lock down this whole area."

"We're done," Phillip said, backing up quickly as though coming to his common senses. "Leave no trace of entry."

"Are you kidding? We don't have that much time. There are too many parameters."

"If you can't delete, then redirect. Any script kiddie could pull it off."

Zakariah ground his teeth as he wiped out critical evidence. V-space did not give up her secrets easily. Every movement left a permanent record, every vibration a telltale sign. Even with his best efforts, he knew forensic testing would reveal blank spots, areas of programmed vacuum, missing clocktime. Nothing traceable, nothing noticeable. He stepped out and closed the portal behind them.

"Clear," he said as a purple net of phosphorescence began to fall from the sky.

Phillip brandished his cybernetic arm like a medieval weapon and sprayed a rainbow of anti-scan encryption in a wide arc above them. Zakariah ducked instinctively, wondering if there might be a public zoomtube within a million miles. Not in Seventh Heaven.

A full alert sounded with a noisy barrage of digital sirens. Purple dust began to fall like snow from the ceiling of the crystal cathedral, sticking to their avatars like glue. Phillip brushed in vain at his shoulders, cursing.

"We're open targets now," Zakariah told him. "Just dive for the portal." He nodded upward with his chin to their entry point on the far side of the room, past cobwebs of red and white lasers. Distance in V-space could be deceptive, but it didn't look like more than a few hundred metres.

"Death to the Beast!" Phillip shouted. And they both dove for the opening with arms outstretched over their heads like superheroes. They sliced through laser tracking beams both red and white, setting off bursts of sparkling fireworks. They had but seconds now. Zakariah glanced at his father one last time.

Phillip grinned at him with manic pleasure, wide-eyed with adrenaline and a wild lust for danger. "I told you it would be fun," he said.

The crystal cathedral telescoped around them as an egress filter kicked in. The exit portal shrank in the distance as prismatic walls stretched like elastic into oblivion. They were trapped on an exponential curve, always approaching their target but never quite able to reach it.

They stopped at the realization, hovering in a tangled web of light, and Zakariah searched desperately for any escape. An alternate route? A portable conduit? Could he program a temporary zoomtube up this high in Prime? He wished he knew his way around this strange uplevel architecture. Only the eminent worked here, the new royalty of V-space—billionaires, brokers, and financial figureheads. Is this where his illustrious career would end? Caught hacking joe-data with his pants down?

Phillip lifted his arms in exultation, or challenge perhaps, and yelled something unintelligible in a strange machine language, a talisman of raw code.

The Beast appeared above them in the form of a giant bear-like creature with the face of a dragon. Two long horns curled back from the top of its head and made a full circle of ribbed ivory bone. A snarling mouth gaped open with fangs exposed.

Phillip wielded his gauntlet of light like a small sword and shouted again. Zakariah backed away from his futile display, still hoping for a means of escape, a flaw in the source code around him, anything. He longed for the jumbled datastream of Sublevel Zero, the crowds of vulnerable users around him, the black patches of trapdoor access in which to hide. Prime Level Seven was firewalled shut at every avenue, sealed up like a coffin, the programming clean and sparse and sterile.

Zakariah looked up as the Beast approached. Every system had some inherent weakness, some governance that could be bent or broken. Data coming in always let data out somehow. Even a black hole spewed streams of antiparticles into space. Self-conscious or not, the Beast was a man-made program, a glorified cybertracker, a half-blind servant to all. Zakariah searched for deep harmonics and found a steady hum of infinite power, a cold and clinical perfection. No cracks, no crevices.

The Beast swooped down on them with cavernous jaws agape. Phillip stabbed with a weapon now puny in comparison, and Zakariah jumped to avoid gleaming teeth like javelins.

The Beast swallowed them whole and darkness enveloped them. The silence of negative data stretched infinite in all directions, an inky, eerie black. No sound, no smell, no programming on which to hang a frame of reference—the quarantine total and absolute.

Deep within the Beast a fire glowed bright orange in the distance and grew closer as the two hackers fell down the dark tunnel toward hell. Zakariah's panic settled into a calm and vacant dread. The fire burned cold, an all-consuming data incinerator. He knew the psychic backwash would fry them on an unfiltered cable.

Phillip screamed his resistance and turned back to Zakariah. "Macpherson!" he yelled. "Activate System Intelligence!"

Macpherson? What the hell?

"Ground zero!" Phillip shouted.

"What are you talking about?"

"Zak, I couldn't put you in play before your time! Only you can understand that. Activate System Intelligence!"

The rushing wind began to calm, and Zakariah felt his movement slow to a halt as he watched Phillip windmill toward a burning abyss below him. He felt a hand on his shoulder and turned to see Helena Sharp staring at him with bright brown eyes.

"Where are we, Zak?"

He wondered if he was already dead, if he had slipped into psychosis. Helena was wearing a skirt suit similar to when they first met, expensive black jacket, black stockings, high heels. He wondered if the memory was being dredged up by the last spasm of dying neurons in his brain.

"What are you doing here? You're supposed to be on the other side of the Doorway." She looked younger than he remembered, more vibrant. Her avatar was as detailed as real flesh, every hair, every mole, the slight flush on her high cheekbones, the subtle tilt of her nose.

"I'm back on Earth. I just got in. I was working on Prime Three when I heard you calling." She gaped at the raging hellfire below them. "Where are we, Zak?" she asked again, her voice now quavery with fear.

"Prime Seven. We're inside the Beast."

Helena blanched with alarm. "Impossible," she whispered. "I don't have access."

"I think someone in the Cromeus colonies must have been tinkering with our circuits. Some quantum connection. Either that or you're a complete delusion from my fragmenting consciousness, a digital deconstruction."

"Are you screwing with me? Is this some sort of game?"

"Helena, we're about to be incinerated like bad data in a cybertracker unless we can find a way out of here."

"We could crash the hardware. You said yourself we couldn't operate twin avatars in the same spot without crashing a system."

Zakariah blinked with surprise. He stared at his hands, long feminine fingers that mirrored her own. Twin avatars in close proximity. "I love you, Helena."

He reached to hug her with both arms. He melded with her and shared her essence. Their lips met and passed through each other as four arms entwined around a single frame. A feedback loop coiled like a venomous serpent within them and unleashed.

V-space exploded.

A bright white blast was followed by an angry red pulse of pain that left behind darkness in its wake. Silence seemed to tickle in the aftermath like a dream lost and forgotten.

Zakariah's forehead stabbed him as he squinted at his old friend Jimmy. He noted the acrid smell of a smoking V-net cable. "Can you hear me, Zak?"

"Yes." His voice sounded foreign and distant.

"Can you move?"

"No."

"You should be dead," Jimmy said as he clipped away smoking remnants of cable from behind Zakariah's left ear. "Burned on an unfiltered plug from Prime Seven." Jimmy shook his head. "You should be dead."

"My father?" Zakariah asked, remembering now, slowly putting reality back together piece by broken piece.

"Burned. Totally fried. He's comatose, but he's breathing and his left pupil is responsive. We've got to get out of here."

Zakariah nodded and tried to rise from his chair. A wave of nausea rushed through him and he retched a dry heave from his empty stomach. He tasted bile in the back of his throat.

"Easy, cowboy." Jimmy grabbed under his shoulders and hoisted him up.

Zakariah wavered and found hesitant balance.

Together they wheeled Phillip to the service elevator. Zakariah held the door open while Jimmy went back for his black toolbox. He pushed a heavy dolly across the room and over the threshold. The only evidence left behind was an illegal shunt, one black office chair, and two twisted stumps of charred V-net cable. Nothing could be traced back downtown.

Zakariah braced himself against the wall of the elevator as Jimmy vibrated with nervous anxiety.

"Can all three of us fit in the air ambulance upstairs?" Jimmy asked.

"No, not with your toolkit also. I'll stay behind. Helena's back."

"The real Director? Oh, that's just peachy. The jig is up, man. Time to clear out."

"She was down there, in the belly of the Beast. I've got to

make sure she's okay."

Jimmy stared, his lips working around bitter questions on his tongue. He swallowed them down and looked away. The less he knew, the better. He fished around in an upper pocket of his coveralls and pulled up a dummy network plug. He offered it forward. "At least put this on your ear. You look like an escaped lab rat."

"What do you know about System Intelligence, Jimmy?"

"System Intelligence, huh?" Jimmy squinted at Phillip's lolling head and turned back to Zakariah. "The soul in the machine. It's a technical concept. If you can upload consciousness into an AI, you can control it, reason with it, blackmail it, whatever."

Zakariah nodded. "A new vulnerability."

"Every system is weaker than the sum of its parts."

"Phillip mentioned it. He called out to Colin Macpherson, the dead physicist."

"Phillip's a psycho."

"Could the program be carried in a wetware installation? By a human, I mean? Running unnoticed in the background?"

Jimmy winced. "I doubt it. The parameters would be fearsome. Think about it. The soul of a machine? How big is that? How would we measure it? I'm sure any workable configuration will require a hardware component. It's still just street chatter, as far as I know."

The elevator opened onto a rooftop helipad where the air ambulance sat waiting. Zakariah stepped out and signalled to the pilot with a circular finger motion. Huge blades began to turn as they trundled Phillip across the tarmac in his black office chair. His head lolled and spittle dribbled from his chin.

A female pilot jumped out, young and slight in a neatly pressed flightsuit. "What happened?" she demanded.

"Ah, office accident," Jimmy said. He looked at Zakariah and popped his eyebrows in signal.

"Right, office accident. Bad fumes. He'll be okay. Just needs some fresh air."

The young pilot bent to examine Phillip. She rolled up his sleeve and fingered the burnt cable in the crook of his elbow. She swore under her breath and stood up. "This man needs medical care. Get him in the back. Who are you guys?"

"Zakariah Davis, Operations Director." He flashed his laminate like a sheriff's badge. "Everything is under control."

The girl stepped forward to challenge him. Her brow was furrowed above silver-rimmed, aviator sunglasses. Her thin hair tangled in limp curls to her shoulders. She was skinny as a rail but carried herself like a commando.

"How far in was he when the blast hit?"

"Are you a medic?"

"He's a close business associate."

The girl's expression was intense, her lips grim, and Zakariah could think of no reason to shield her from the truth. "Unfiltered Seventh Heaven."

"But you're still standing?"

Zakariah paused for a quick self-assessment, checking his physical and mental health, testing for surety. He could hear his neck creaking as he moved his head. He smelled a resin of asphalt from the tarmac. He stared at his open palms. "I think I may have deflected the damage. I think I may have hurt a good friend."

The pilot's stance softened, and she looked back to Phillip.

"Help me," she said.

Together they lifted Phillip onto a backseat stretcher and strapped him into the harness. They stood outside while the pilot climbed aboard and grimly went through her checklist, sounding the ritual to herself as though addressing an imaginary copilot.

Zakariah took a deep breath to calm himself. "Thanks for hanging around. I know it wasn't in your contract."

"Hey, I was never here." Jimmy winked playfully. "I'll just park your dad in a hospital waiting room and disappear into the woodwork. I imagine his colleagues will find him soon enough."

Zakariah nodded and took one last look at his drooling father. He tossed a two-finger salute to the pilot and ducked away under whirling blades.

"And good luck with the girl," Jimmy shouted after him.

Zakariah turned. "Which one?" he yelled into the gusting air.

Jimmy laughed and cupped his hands around his mouth. "You young sliders are all the same!"

ELEVEN

Zakariah arrived at the Director's office to find Silus Mundazo wringing his hands in front of his holodesk, a grimace of disbelief carving deep worry lines on his face.

"Silus. Have you seen Helena?"

Mundazo looked up. "Where the hell have you been?"

"I've been handling crowd control. There's been a security breach. Where's Helena?"

"She's on emergency intravenous up in her penthouse suite. Some kind of V-net power surge fried her wetware. We're running diagnostics."

"Brain-dead?"

"No, not brain-dead. She's comatose, but her prognosis is good. Never mind her right now. Look at these test results." He wheeled his chair back and gestured with his palm to the charts on display.

Zakariah stepped close and bent forward. The data seemed incomprehensible, but the red lights were plain.

"The activated virus is not taking hold," Silus said. "Thirty-seven reports so far have all come back negative."

A shiver of dread gripped Zakariah. "No way. How can you

be certain so quickly?"

"I think I know the signature of an active viral culture by
now. We're getting good cellular rejuve but no regeneration.
None at all." Silus Mundazo held his hands up and quickly
rubbed his forehead back and forth across his fingertips as
though shaking off grim notions of truth. "The entire experiment is a failure. The years of planning. The investment.
Madame Shakura has already dissolved the World Council. She
wants Helena's head on a silver platter. Chairman Tao went into
cardiac arrhythmia and is now on life-support."

He glared at Zakariah. "Did I mention that a government
team just drove an army truck up to our front door and comman-
deered our police force? A brigadier-general, no less, yelled in
my ear about Prime Level Seven security protocols. I can't
believe Helena could be involved in some arcane conspiracy. She
mentioned your name just before her V-net plug exploded in my
face!"

"She was under the wire?"

He pointed to her empty launch couch. "She was sitting right
there when it happened. To my knowledge she was no deeper
than Prime Three. She was checking messages and catching up
on correspondence, not hacking the Antichrist."

Zakariah spread his arms in surrender. "Silus, I honestly don't
know what happened. I thought she was in the Cromeus
colonies. All reports said she'd been permanently uploaded into
Soul Savers Incorporated and her body sent into stasis. I never
thought I would see her again."

Dr. Mundazo slapped his palms down on the armrests of his
chair and leaned forward. "She said she loved you. That hardly
sounds like a long-distance relationship."

"She said that?"

"Loud and clear. Her eyes popped open out of a V-net trance and she yelled, 'I love you, Zak' just as the power surge hit. She went into convulsions. I clipped her cable as soon as I could, but it was too late." He collapsed back into his chair, overcome by the memory.

Zakariah sucked a cleansing breath down deep into his solar plexus. "This is a filtered conduit," he said, more to himself than to the doctor. "Helena would have been spared the brunt of trauma from the Beast. She'll probably be fine in a few days. We'll pop in new wetware and she'll be as good as new."

Silus Mundazo looked up at him, aghast. "You were there," he said. "I knew you were behind this whole mess. You're a criminal. You delivered a fake virus so you could use our V-net access for some foul treachery! You could have killed her. You've ruined a lifetime of work. You've sold out your blood brothers for a bowl of pottage!"

"Settle down, Silus. You're raving. Get a grip."

"I'll do no such thing. You're a menace. I'll have you arrested." He reached for his wristband, but Zakariah stilled his hand.

"Don't put yourself in danger. Let's just try to figure this out."

"You can't be trusted."

"Helena trusted me. She brought me into this, remember?"

"Well, she paid a high price for that."

"I'll check on her. I'll make sure she's okay. Don't worry."

Silus Mundazo glared at him, paralyzed by indecision.

"The activated virus was not a fake. You checked it out yourself."

"I don't know. It appeared genuine to our limited measurements."

Zakariah touched the flatscreen to scroll down the subject list. "Has Rix reported yet?"

"No. He's been moved to a dormitory in the East wing. Mia's at his bedside waiting for the data."

"Rix was the only reason I went offplanet in the first place. Mia told me all about it. The virus was for him, Silus. I brought it back for him and couldn't remember who it was for. I know this sounds crazy, but what if each ampoule has only one target? What if the virus is DNA specific?"

Silus licked dry lips. "There has never been a mass contagion."

"Exactly. Not even two at a time. Always just one person, one ampoule broken on the tongue."

Silus shook his head. "It doesn't make scientific sense, and it doesn't bring us any closer to commercial production. How could a virus be so selective? How could it be manufactured to finite schematics at such a distance? You'd have to postulate grand designs and cosmic conspiracies. No way."

He stood and stalked away in disgust. He wheeled and turned, his shoes stomping the ground. "It hardly matters what happens now. Our funding has dried up like ashes in an urn. We'll be selling blood on the black market by morning."

Zakariah found Rix sequestered in what was once a supply closet in the East wing, sleeping on a portable hospital gurney. He felt no sense of recognition at the sight of him, no emotional attachment. The boy was a complete stranger, his own son, and the realization hit him like a blow. Rix was dressed in street clothes, a black sweater with ornate silver embroidery at the shoulders, and blue denim pants. Mia hovered on a chair at his bedside and jumped up to meet Zakariah as he entered the room.

"Zak, you did it. The virus has taken hold." She hugged him fiercely, forcing the air from his lungs in a huff.

"You sure? There's been no report to Mundazo."

"I've got the test results locked down for now. It's not safe. This place is a madhouse of frustration and bitter rivalry." She clung to him like a strong vise, her muscles like iron. "None of the other subjects have reported positive," she whispered. "Not a single one. Madame Shakura is intense with anger. Chairman Tao died just minutes ago. I'm afraid someone might try to kidnap Rix or worse. We've got to get him out of here."

Zakariah stared over her shoulder at his son's sleeping form, feeling a cold vacancy, feeling robbed of any joy by the foul circumstance around him. "Mundazo's freaking out," he declared to her neck.

Mia sniffed behind his ear at a charred stump of cable sticking out of his head. "You've been burned again."

Zakariah pulled back and held her at arm's length. "The Beast took us out. Phillip's in a bad way. Somehow Helena got tangled up with us in V-space and got fried also. Something crazy happened. Something impossible. She came out of nowhere. She rescued me."

Mia clutched him close again. "I'm so glad you're okay. Let's disappear, Zak. Back to Atlantis. Let's get free of all this."

"We can't get out, Mia. We can't get away. This is bigger than both of us. There's no place to run from this kind of power, no place to hide. Someone's got a quantum connection in my head. I could be wired across time and space for all I know, straight back to Babylon."

"You're being paranoid."

"With good reason!"

"Whatever was in your brain has been cauterized now. You're tabula rasa again."

"How do I know that?"

"We could take Rix to the north sanctuary. Just for a few weeks. Let the contagion get a good hold on him."

Zakariah rubbed her back absently, revelling in the warmth from her body, the pressure of her heaving chest against him. He had been alone too long. His body ached for intimacy.

"You guys should get a room," Rix said. "You're so obvious."

His parents whirled apart to face him. Rix laughed at them.

"How do you feel?" Zakariah stepped close and put a hand on his son's forehead.

"I feel great. I'm not sick." He brushed him away.

"Just a touch feverish."

"That's good, right?"

Zakariah smiled. "It's a sign of contagion. Your metabolism is accelerating, starting to rebuild itself. Every flaw will be healed."

Rix sat up and swivelled his shoulders back and forth, working stiffness from his muscles. "I used to wonder why no one could describe the experience. Now I know. The virus is like liquid joy. It emanates from inside like a river, a flood."

Mia approached and took his hand. "The first few weeks are an amazing miracle. I'm so thankful." Her lips began to tremble as though she might cry.

"It's a virus, Mom. It's just biology." He pulled away from her show of affection.

Mia sniffed and dabbed tears from her eyes with her wrist, the warrior mother.

Rix looked at his father. "Is she always this emotional?"

Zakariah shrugged, wishing he could remember. "Pretty much, lately."

"Does Mundazo have my test results yet?"

"He'll find out soon enough. We were thinking about getting you out of here for awhile. There's a place up north, a sanctuary your mother and I prepared for emergencies."

"You guys go ahead. Mom needs a break. I've got a lot of work to do."

"Where will you go?"

"I'll stay here for now. Silus needs all the help he can get. This place is falling apart around him." He stood up. "The guy's a genius. I could learn a lot from him." He tapped the side of his skull with a forefinger.

Zakariah winced his indecision. "The ERI is a sinking ship."

"The ERI is all that's holding us back from anarchy, Dad. We've got to put our resources where they can make a difference."

His burst of exuberance made Zak feel old and weary. He remembered the passion of his youth, his grandiose expectations. Somewhere along the journey, his courage had drained out of him, his faith had withered. He had nothing left to offer the world. He stared at his son and wondered for the future. Perhaps Rix was a new breed of Eternal, not just a survivor, but a soldier of fortune. Perhaps he would not cower from injustice, perhaps he would not cringe from the challenge of evil.

"Go, then," he said. "Tell Silus to his face. He could use some good news right about now."

Rix hesitated, sensing now that this might be goodbye again,

STEVE STANTON

that their paths had diverged.

"You'll head up north?"

"I don't know. A friend is in trouble."

Rix patted the pockets of his jacket. "I have something for you," he said and handed forward his photograph. "A keepsake, just in case."

Zak recognized the image. He had seen it before, locked deep in his memory where mindwipe could never reach. He nodded at his son, feeling a maudlin weight in his lungs.

"Niko was cloned before she died," Rix told him. "We've been working together. She uses the same name. It's kinda creepy, when you think about it."

"Thanks." Zak held the photo up. "Give her my love."

Rix smiled. "Sure."

"Phillip's been burned. He tried to hack the Beast and failed."

A white horror ghosted Rix's face. So he knew about Phillip. He knew too much.

"This young girl," Zak said, "she wouldn't happen to be a helicopter pilot, would she?"

Rix shrugged. "I dunno. She rides a mean motorbike and kites like a bat-woman."

"I think I may have met her."

"Nice, eh?"

Zak grinned. He glanced at his wife. "Well, she's not my type."

"Of course." Rix ducked his head and nodded. "Thanks, Dad. For everything, I mean."

"It wasn't my doing. The virus is a free gift."

"Yeah, I get it." Rix turned to Mia and gave her a quick hug.

"Thanks, Mom. Come back and see me when things quiet down. And have some fun for once, will ya?"

Rix moved to the door and peered cautiously into the hall. He glanced back briefly, working his mouth as though perhaps he had left something unsaid. He decided not and stepped through the doorway.

"Let me see that," Mia said and took the photo from Zak's unresisting hand. "That's your sister when she was a baby?"

"Yep."

"And that's you. How old? Six or seven?"

"I guess."

"Oh, you were so cute." She put her arm around his waist. "You're still cute."

They left the East wing and took the main elevator up to Helena's penthouse suite in the ERI tower. The security guard recognized Zakariah, but checked Mia's laminate with a hand-held scanner. She didn't have clearance on his clipboard monitor, so he called down for authorization. He nodded at first, but his brow furrowed over as he listened.

He offered his phone to Zakariah. "Doctor Mundazo," he said. Zakariah put it to his ear. "Hello?"

"Zak, there's been a new development. We ran some standard tests on Helena, and the results have come in. She's Eternal. No question about it."

"Was she one of the subjects?"

"No. Her contagion is in full bloom. Three or four days at least. She must have got the virus offplanet, perhaps directly from the Source. We'll have to put her in testing."

"That's great, Silus. She should regenerate quickly from the brain burn."

"We can only hope. Look, Zak, do I owe you an apology?"

"Don't worry about it. The heat of the battle. Rix has tested positive. He's on his way to see you."

"Rix is sitting right here already. It's great news, but there's a lot we don't know. Tell Helena I'm looking forward to handing her back the reigns of power."

Zakariah returned the phone, and the guard nodded his clearance to Mia. They dashed forward to Helena's suite and knocked on the door. A young man ushered them in, a frail man with a pointed chin and wispy goatee. He led them quietly to Helena's bedside, where a clear plastic bag hung on a metal pole beside her bed, dripping life through a needle into her arm. The sun coming through a nearby window lit her face with a glow of health. Her gentle smile promised peace.

Zakariah felt tension slip away like a scarf from his neck. Helena would recover. He hadn't killed her.

"Are you a doctor?" he asked the young man.

"No, I was travelling with Helena. We are but friends of circumstance."

"How is she doing?"

"She'll be fine, slumlord. She's dreaming now. I've been watching her rapid eye movement. The eyes are conjugate even in dreams, you know. Fascinating."

"Do I know you?"

"Oh, we've met a few times offplanet. I wouldn't say we're intimate by any means. My name is Colin7." He offered a handshake and a mischievous grin. "I knew you before the mindwipe."

Zakariah studied him carefully but couldn't find any memory reference. "This is my wife, Mia."

"Enchanting." Colin7 took a bowing step toward her with

240

arm outstretched.

Mia shook his hand with reticence, her expression dour.

Helena groaned. "Zak, is that you?"

Zakariah bent to one knee at her bedside. "It's me. You're going to be okay."

"What happened?"

"Electrochemical backlash. Your circuits have been over-clocked. Your wetware will have to be replaced."

She opened her eyes and squinted through pain. "I don't understand."

"I'm sorry, Helena, I don't have any answers. It's probably all my fault."

Helena groaned again and shook her head weakly. "You cowboy," she murmured.

"Why did you come back? I thought you were happy in paradise."

"I don't know. For you, I guess."

"For me?"

"I was touched by your plight. And poor Mia." She tried to rise, and Zakariah gently lifted her shoulders and propped her upright with a pillow. Colin7 offered a cool glass of nutrient water over his shoulder and stepped back respectfully.

"Thank you," she whispered and took a few sips.

"What about your expensive upload? You gave up nirvana for me?"

"It was boring." She waved a hand dismissively. "Infinite experience grows quickly tiring."

"You're just saying that to make me feel better."

"It was too easy, Zak. It wasn't life. Not real life. Oh, it was satisfying, I'll admit. Too satisfying by far." She exhaled wistfully past quavering lips. She took a long drink of water and handed the cup back. "I missed the conflict of experience. I missed the pain. When I saw Mia's heart break before my eyes, I knew I could never go back to Soul Savers. I pulled the plug." She offered a weak smile. "You were right all along, in your own mixed-up way."

"I completed our mission, Helena. I brought an activated sample back. We ran it through the lab. We inoculated fifty human subjects but only one tested positive. My son, Rix."

Helena nodded. "The ampoule was for him alone. Silus must have been devastated at the outcome."

"He's coming around. He sends his regards."

"He's a good man."

Zakariah glanced over at Colin7 and bent forward to Helena's ear. "What about you, Helena? Where did you get your own vial? Are you free to tell me?"

She sighed, barely a whisper. "I didn't get a vial, Zak. I didn't contract the virus through blood transmission."

Zakariah stared at her in confusion. The virus was in the blood. It could not be transmitted by any other means. "But how?"

She turned her face close to him, her breath gentle on his cheek. "I saw it in a vision, Zak. I knew in my heart that the virus was inside me. Do you remember anything about the phaser cannon, the unapproachable light?"

"No, I lost some data."

She winced at his understatement. "I was offered a choice. I don't know how it works. Consider the metaphor of light itself. A photon is both a particle and a wave until we take a measurement, and then it decides to be one or the other. It's quantum potential is collapsed by observation. In a similar way, the mito-chondria of every living cell can be programmed to decay or regenerate. Does that make any sense?"

"Not really."

"I thought not."

"So by believing the truth, the virus springs up sponta-neously?"

"Perhaps the carrier is merely a catalyst, a ceremonial tech-nique."

"And the only reason the virus took hold in Rix is because he truly believed it was for him and him alone?"

"He knew what you sacrificed to get the activated sample. Somehow his expectation, his faith, if you will, made a difference to the outcome at a basic cellular level."

"Everyone could have the virus?"

"Everyone."

"Without cost?"

Helena tried to smile, but her effort made barely a slant in her pretty face. "The cost, Zak? We both know the responsibility is all-consuming."

Zakariah nodded. "It costs everything to live forever."

"Our old life passes away like a distant memory, a dream upon waking."

"We die and are born at the same time."

"I know it sounds crazy, Zak. Don't think I haven't wrestled with my own sanity."

"Can we use this in the lab, Helena? Can we simulate it somehow?"

"I don't know. But we have to try. It's all that really matters to me now."

"Perhaps there is hope, after all."

Her eyes fluttered with frailty, and she turned her face away.

"Hope," she repeated, lazy with weakness. "Hope and pain, they go together hand in hand." She drifted asleep, her breathing deep and regular.

Zakariah stood. "She's strong," Colin7 said. "She's a powerful woman."

Zakariah turned to face him as Mia took his place in vigil at the bedside. She warmed Helena's hand between her palms. Colin7 motioned with his head, and Zakariah followed him into an adjoining sitting room with a picture window looking down on vast parkland below.

"You make no secret of being a clone of Colin Macpherson, which you must know is illegal on this planet. Why have you come to Earth?"

Colin7 spread his hands. "I have nothing to hide. We have a history, you and I, and my Father, a delicate relationship. You have forgotten many things."

"Are you in contact with your Father?"

Colin7 grinned. "Now that *would* be a trick." He tapped his forehead. "I've been fitted with digital mnemonics for the trip. A complete transcript will be available to him upon my return."

"Why are you here?"

"I brought you a gift." He gestured to a humming boxlike appliance that Zakariah had taken to be air purification equipment. "It doesn't look like much, but I can assure you the contents are most enlightening."

"What is it?"

"Why it's you, Mr. Davis. A full backup." He held his fingers up to his big ears to dramatize quotation marks. "A saved soul."

"Really?"

"Absolutely. We uploaded a copy as part of our experiments, just before you talked with the aliens face to face."

"All my memories are in there?"

"Everything."

"And you're offering me back my old life?"

Colin7 frowned. "What is a man but the sum of his memories? The love and heartbreak, the passion and sorrow, the small victories shrouded in ultimate defeat. It's all here for the taking."

"Do you know anything about System Intelligence?"

"The ghost in the machine? A watchword, surely. An urban legend."

"I've heard that it requires a hardware component." Zakariah nodded to the humming black box.

Colin7's face contorted into a devilish grin. "Perhaps so, slumlord. In any case, you'll need everything here to proceed on your path of destiny."

"Why should I trust you?"

Colin7 held his arms up in a blessing of innocence. "This is a great opportunity for the right man, for that special person most gifted. Of course we'll get you rewired for V-space and upgraded beyond current standards. I think you'll find our resources most adequate, most adequate indeed. I'm sure you know the black labs have already pioneered Prime Level Eight. The time has come to rise above the rabble, my friend. Your time has come."

The mighty Beast fell from an infinite height in Zakariah's imagination, talons splayed into a grey void of negative data, spinning and gnashing white teeth like daggers in a vortex of oblivion. And Zakariah stood alone on a high hill with the key of System Intelligence, sheltering V-space in his wing like a concubine, and she would serve him utterly. Complete freedom. Complete free will. His own father had planned this crown for him, working in secret across time and space with the ghost of a dead physicist. This was his heritage. Control the AI, control the world.

Zakariah reached for the black box and hefted its great weight. He ran and hurled it at the sunny window with all his human strength. The window cracked and the box bounced back at his feet.

"What are you doing?" Colin7 screamed. He jumped on the spot in amazement, his hands clutching at his hair.

"What the hell is going on in here?" Mia demanded as she peered in the door.

Zakariah picked up the box and threw it again at the window. Safety glass shattered into a pebbly honeycomb as it crashed back to the floor. Components fell out and rolled away. The gentle hum degraded to a dissonant, coarse vibration. In a blind fury Zakariah picked up the box and launched it again with a grunt of exclamation, and his soul finally disappeared through the broken window into the clutches of gravity. An explosion sounded on the grounds below.

Helena cried out in the next room and Mia rushed back to her side.

Colin7 gaped in wonder.

Zakariah sucked exuberance like medicine from the air. "Tell your Father . . ." he wheezed. "Tell your Father that I decline his offer. I have a new life now, a better life, a woman who needs me and a son who loves me. I was not born for slavery in a gilded palace."

Zakariah stared in defiance at the young clone, his body

trembling with spent energy. In a panic of self-realization and doubt, he wondered what he had just done in such mad passion, what secrets he had thrown carelessly away. Was he strong enough to stand and fight on his own?

In surprise he watched a smile of respect curl on the clone's young lips, a smile of satisfaction, a glimpse of long-held plans coming to final fruition. The gesture would not be recorded on Colin7's digital transcript. This secret defiance might never reach his Father's ear.

"The vital decisions are yours to make, of course," Colin7 said evenly.

The sun was hot up north, the sky patchy with playful tufts of white cloud, the breeze unfettered. The air smelled sweet with wildflowers and pollen, and birds sang in a wild cacophony. Zakariah sat on a squat stump outside their cabin and watched his wife climb up a jumble of boulders at the lakeshore. She wore ragged cut-off shorts and a string bikini top, her exposed skin bronzed and beautiful. They had run out of sunscreen weeks ago, along with deodorant and toothpaste and all the modern trappings of ease.

Mia carried a coil of rope over her shoulder and dragged a trailing length behind her. The end was tied to a tall oak tree beside Zakariah, already notched and ready to fell. The tree was dead and standing dry, hard packed with BTUs and easy splitting, but it hung over the cabin like a grand dame with wide arms raised. Zakariah had roped the old lady near the top and had nipped a few branches with a handsaw, but it would still be a dangerous drop. She might have stood another winter, but if they left her to gravity she might flatten their tiny cabin.

Zakariah looked down at his bare hands, sun-browned and calloused from hard work, from chopping firewood and hauling water, from scrubbing clothes and building cookfires in a makeshift barbecue made of gathered rocks and a rusty metal grate. His knuckles were bleeding where he had scraped them against the bark, but the wounds were congealing nicely and beginning to darken. They had used up their cache of food long ago and were now reduced to foraging for wild raspberries and black brambleberries that grew in clumps along the shore. They carried water daily to a thicket of wild leeks in a clearing nearby and knew where to gather morels in the early morning dew.

Zakariah watched as Mia climbed up a rocky tangle where the cliff face had fallen away in broken shards. He marvelled at the strength in her body as her long legs propelled her higher, her supple arms reaching for crag and crevice. He longed to touch her, to caress her fine skin again. He wanted to make love to her in the middle of the afternoon, in the wilds of nature outside on the rocks, or perhaps nestled in a shady bed of moss.

"You're hung up," he yelled to her and pointed to where her rope had tangled on a stump.

Mia stopped and doubled back, tossing her line like a skipping rope to free it. The rope came loose finally, and she raised her chin with triumph. Zakariah gave her a thumbs-up signal and a wide grin that she probably would not see from such distance.

She continued climbing. What a beautiful woman she was, sure-footed and strong like a mountain llama on the rock face. The ancient granite was striated with jagged pink quartz like veins and arteries, as though the blood of Gaia might once have flowed therein. The land had been carved by glaciers long ago, the igneous bedrock crushed and crumbled and piled like forgotten toys beside deep gouges of lake and river. Zakariah wondered what it must be like here in the dead of winter, the surface covered with ice and frozen solid. Where did the animals find refuge from the wind and snow, the raccoons and the beaver, the deer and moose and giant black bears? How did life survive to bloom with such promise every summer? How could he and Mia survive a winter this far north?

His wife reached the pinnacle and looped her rope around a tree. She stood with her arms above her head, her palms to the sun, her face upraised in bold worship. She looked glorious.

She was probably praying again. She seemed to have fallen into the habit. He had seen her throw down her tools without provocation and shout her praise to the heavens with a voice like an angel. Other times she became sullen and meek and dropped her forehead with barely a sound. But he knew she was praying, her consciousness focused inward to infinity. She was convinced there was a Spirit guiding the Eternal virus, and perhaps there was. Zakariah had witnessed too many mysteries to argue against the possibility, but he was not inclined to rest on heavenly laurels. He would not give up his fate to unseen hands, to cosmic strategies. He would fight like a pirate till death.

Mia roused herself and bent back to her task. She pulled her rope taut and wound it around a sturdy pine stump. She tied a firm knot and stretched it tight. She waved an arm in the air and yelled.

Zakariah picked up his rusty crosscut saw and peered up the tree trunk one last time. The old dame was leaning badly but should swing with the gentle nudge of a rope when she began to waver. They were cheating gravity, but not by much, and a gentle wind off the lake worked in their favour. A couple of young birches would be crushed like kindling in the path of this hardwood monster, but the landing ground was otherwise clear. If all went well, she should miss the cabin by at least five metres.

He set his saw and pushed, and the bark gave way easily as he worked. The core of the trunk was dense and firm, and sawdust piled at his feet as he began to cut through rings of age. Decades stood here, perhaps a hundred years of growth, but even the old oaks must someday give up their ghost to Gaia. He paused for breath after a few minutes, wishing he had a chainsaw and a piece of protein in his belly. Sweat trickled down his naked ribs in hot rivulets. He rubbed his forehead with his arm and felt a coarse grit like sandpaper.

The rope was singing tight above him, and he could see his saw cut starting to gape open. If that rope ever snapped, he would lose her. His pulse began to race with panic as a cocktail of chemicals released into his bloodstream. He thought that he could taste each one. This was the heritage of man, a simple danger unadorned with digital bandwidth. This was life in the raw.

He smiled and bent to his work. He ripped his saw back and forth into the meat of years, and the tree cracked like a gunshot.

Zakariah froze. He checked for movement. Too late to quit now. Just do it. He set his saw gingerly and resumed his cut. He panted for breath as he worked. The tree cracked again, but he didn't stop. He could feel fibres snapping against metal teeth, his tool now an extension of his body, a living thing.

The gap widened and the trunk began to twist. The old oak howled with complaint as her back broke, and Zakariah jumped away in fear. A split in the trunk or a kickback could kill him at this point, but she toppled clean and fell with the sound of thunder. Baby birches bent and snapped like twigs and the ground shook like an earthquake. In a moment the crash was over, and the forest was silent. Even the birds ceased to sing.

Mia hooted exultant from her rocky pinnacle, her arms raised again with joy.

Zakariah pulled himself to his feet and brushed dirt from his pants. His stomach ached with hunger and spent adrenaline, but he felt a primeval satisfaction, a driving lust that must have guided his forefathers—the urge to build and destroy, to conquer and subdue, a hardwired destiny.

He cast down his crosscut saw and turned away. He walked toward the lake and stripped off his sweaty clothes. He jumped into the water and ducked his head under.

Mia joined him a few minutes later. She sat on a rock ledge and watched him as he swam and dove like a duck.

"Nice butt," she said, and he pushed a stream of water at her with the heel of his hand.

"Coming in?"

"Maybe later." She braced her arms beside her and reclined against a boulder.

He drifted close and stared up at her. A gust of wind wafted the curls on her forehead. Her hair had grown long and full to her shoulders, a soft tangle of gold.

"You look younger every year," he said.

"I am younger every year, silly."

He gazed past her at distant rolling mountains, an ancient backbone of land. The open landscape made him feel small and inconsequential, a bug on a vast surface. "We've got to get into town," Mia said, "or find a supply depot somewhere. We're low on everything."

"It's a long walk through the bush, but I guess we could use the exercise."

"I'd like to pick up a pregnancy test while we're there." She eyed him deliberately.

He paused for a moment and began to sink, but quickly splashed back above the surface. "You're pregnant?" he sputtered.

She smiled at his discomfit. "I guess that's what happens when you live for weeks on nuts and berries. It's not like there's a pharmacy within fifty miles."

"I . . . I just never thought."

"You don't expect me to apologize, do you?"

"No, of course not. It's great."

"It's a new beginning, Zak. We'll have to go back to civilization. We can't hide forever."

Zakariah kicked his feet and took a stroke backward, reluctant to hear his own secret thoughts given voice. He fingered the charred stump of cable behind his ear. He could get back to work.

"I noticed colour in the trees from the cliff top." Mia pointed to scant patches of orange and red among distant maples. "In a few weeks the leaves will start falling. We might even get a dusting of snow."

The thought made him shiver. The water felt chilly now that he had refreshed himself. "Where to this time? Back to the ERI?"

"It's up to you, Zak. I'll follow you back through the Doorway if I have to."

"With a baby?"

"I know you don't remember, but we had a child once before. It's perfectly natural."

Zakariah swam to shore and pulled himself up. The rocks

near the edge were slippery with algae, and he stepped out of the water with care. He picked up his sweaty pants and began to knead them under the surface. A swirl of sawdust floated away.

"Do you think I gave up too much, throwing my backup disk out the window that day?"

"You had your reasons."

"I couldn't risk contamination. I couldn't trust that little clone."

"I know, Zak. Look, whatever happened in the past is far behind us now, the good and the bad. Memory is a two-sided sword. I made a lot of mistakes along the way that I'm glad you don't remember. We can start again. We can start fresh. These could be the good old days all over again."

Zakariah laid his clothes out on the rock ledge to dry in the sun. He sat down naked beside his wife and draped his arm around her back. She rested her head on his shoulder and reached a hand to his abdomen. A family of mergansers swam in close to the shore, pecking at the weeds and diving in the shallows for food. The mother and father hung back at a distance, watching their brood protectively, ready to give alarm at any provocation. The young ducks seemed almost fully grown, wings strong and ready to soar, feathers tufted at the back of their heads like caps. They clucked happily as they zigged and zagged among the reeds and dove for minnows. A turtle climbed up on the shore and parked lazily on a driftwood log.

Steve Stanton's short fiction has been published in twelve countries, including translations into Hebrew, Greek, Italian, Spanish, Portuguese, Czech, and Romanian. In North America, his work frequently appears in *Rampike*, *On Spec*, *Neo-opsis*, *Tesseracts*, *Zymergy*, *Divine Realms*, *The Standing Stone*, *Prairie Journal of Canadian Literature*, *Poet's Gallery*, *BrightRedLife*, *ChristianWeek*, *Green's Magazine*, *Adventure Magazine*, *Canadian Writer's Journal*, *Mindflights*, *Pandora*, *Gateway SF*, *The Sword Review*, *Churchyard*, *Searching Souls*, *The Obligatory Sin*, *Christian Communicator*, *Dragons*, *Knights and Angels*, and *Chaos Theory*. He currently serves as the vice-president of SF Canada, the bilingual organization of science fiction, fantasy, and horror writers. Stanton lives in Washago, Ontario.